Adobe Moon

WYATT EARP: AN AMERICAN ODYSSEY, BOOK ONE

ADOBE MOON

MARK WARREN

FIVE STAR
A part of Gale, a Cengage Company

Farmington Hills, Mich • San Francisco • New York • Waterville, Maine
Meriden, Conn • Mason, Ohio • Chicago

LIBRARY OF CONGRESS CATALOGING-IN-PUBLICATION DATA

Names: Warren, Mark, 1947– author.
Title: Adobe moon : Wyatt Earp, an American odyssey / Adobe Moon / Mark Warren.
Other titles: Wyatt Earp, an American odyssey
Description: First edition. | Waterville, Maine : Five Star Publishing, a part of Cengage Learning, Inc., 2017. | Includes bibliographical references. | Description based on print version record and CIP data provided by publisher; resource not viewed.
Identifiers: LCCN 2017022895 (print) | LCCN 2017031951 (ebook) | ISBN 9781432838027 (ebook) | ISBN 1432838024 (ebook) | ISBN 9781432838010 (ebook) | ISBN 1432838016 (ebook) | ISBN 9781432838164 (hardcover) | ISBN 1432838164 (hardcover)
Subjects: LCSH: Earp, Wyatt, 1848–1929—Fiction. | Frontier and pioneer life—West (U.S.)—Fiction. | Outlaws—West (U.S.) v Fiction. | Peace officers—West (U.S.)—Fiction. | Self-realization—Fiction. | GSAFD: Biographical fiction. | Western stories.
Classification: LCC PS3623.A86465 (ebook) | LCC PS3623.A86465 A33 2018 (print) | DDC 813/.6—dc23
LC record available at https://lccn.loc.gov/2017022895

First Edition. First Printing: November 2017
Find us on Facebook–https://www.facebook.com/FiveStarCengage
Visit our website–http://www.gale.cengage.com/fivestar/
Contact Five Star™ Publishing at FiveStar@cengage.com

Printed in Mexico
8 9 10 11 12 13 23 22 21 20 19

For Susan
There is an alchemy that burnishes the moon to gold.

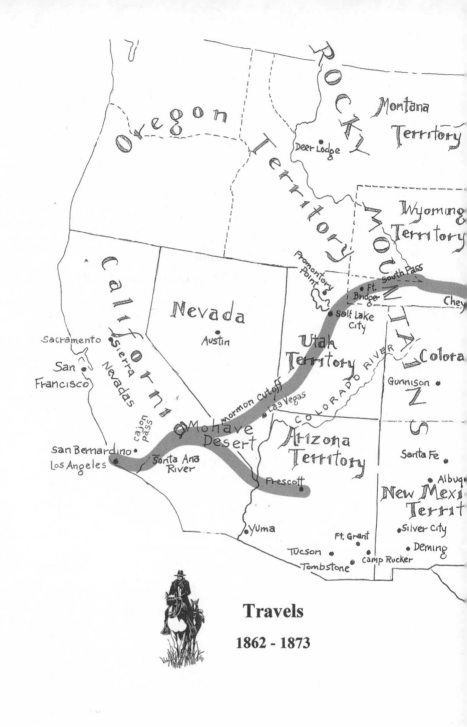

Travels

1862 - 1873

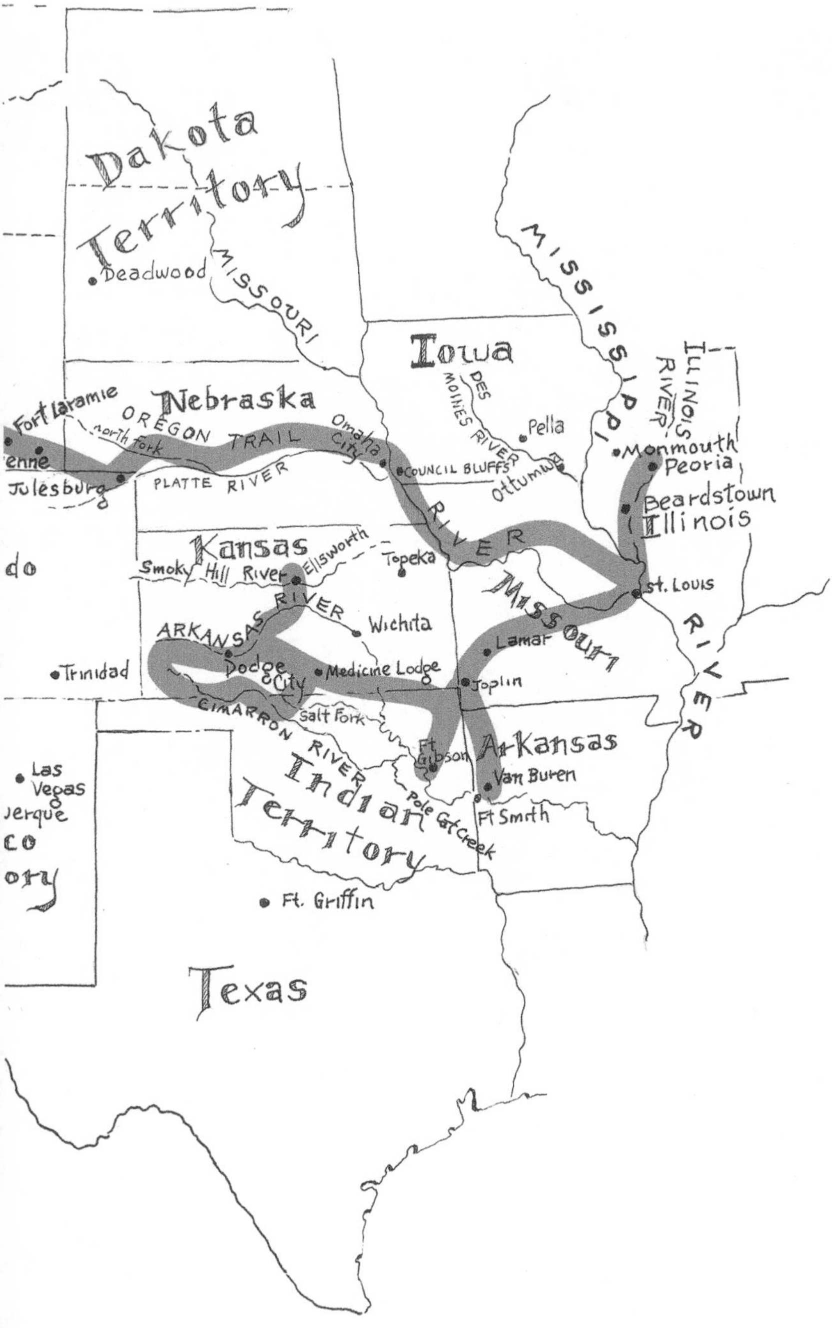

Dakota Territory
Deadwood
MISSOURI
MISSISSIPPI
Iowa
DES MOINES RIVER
Pella
Ottumwa
ILLINOIS RIVER
Monmouth
Peoria
Beardstown
Illinois
Nebraska
Fort Laramie
OREGON TRAIL
North Fork
PLATTE RIVER
Julesburg
Omaha City
COUNCIL BLUFFS
RIVER
Kansas
Smoky Hill River
Ellsworth
Topeka
St. Louis
Missouri
RIVER
ARKANSAS RIVER
Wichita
Lamar
Dodge City
Medicine Lodge
Joplin
Trinidad
CIMARRON RIVER
Salt Fork
Ft Gibson
Arkansas
Van Buren
Ft Smith
Indian Territory
Pole Cat Creek
Las Vegas
Ft. Griffin
Texas

"In those days a man could pick up, head out West, and start a new life . . . choose any name he wanted. But the man who made his mark in the history books is probably one who stayed true to who he was . . . no matter what he called himself."

~Harte Canaday, from *Last of the Pistoleers*

CHAPTER 1

Summer, 1862: Earp farm, Pella Township, Iowa

In the dark pre-dawn quiet he lay facing the window by his bed and stared at the stars hanging in the western sky. They floated over the land like the dust of jewels strewn across black water. These stars had become the milestones that marked his coming passage, and he gazed at them this one last time for the sake of preserving a memory, he supposed. One last view through the windowglass of his youth. Today he would be gone, to become a part of the larger world that waited for him. First the war in the East. Then, surviving that, he would journey west toward the promise of opportunity. It was all out there, he knew. Whatever enterprise a man was bold enough to reach for, the West would afford him a place to try.

Were anyone to ask him why he must fight, he might only say something about duty—a topic he deemed too personal to reduce to words. Once that duty was met, he would have earned his right on the frontier. He knew that the ragged boundary of the country was creeping steadily westward, like a charred line of black smoldering across a sheet of paper, and he needed to stay ahead of that flame.

It could not be said that he dreamed of places, for he was not the type to dream. But he planned his course with a deliberation uncommon to one his age. If one of those bright points of light out in the night sky was his lodestar, pulling him, he had not singled it out. He needed no such talisman. It was the pull

11

that mattered.

Carrying the bundle of clothes he had rolled inside the wool blanket, Wyatt, in his stockinged feet, picked his way across the groaning floorboards through the dark house. His boots stood just inside the kitchen door, and he sat to tug them on. Through the east windows the stars were thinning. Now they burned like the campfires of a vast and distant army fallen into deep slumber before the coming battle. Already he felt closer to the war.

He listened to the night sounds of the house—his father's rough snore coming from the back room, the hollow tick of the cherrywood clock in the hallway, the faint seep of air sucking through the vents of the woodstove. Outside, somewhere to the east, a coyote called a single sliding note, and it was that sound to which he connected, if only for its claim on autonomy.

Stepping outside onto the stoop he inhaled the coolness of late summer. It was too dark to see the cornfield—eighty acres he had been working since he had been old enough to sink a hoe into this Iowa dirt—but he could smell it. The stalks were heavy with the coming harvest, and already he felt lighter for being done with it all.

Inside the tack room he lighted a lantern and stuffed the blanket-bundle behind the heavy sacks of grain, and then he spread loose hay at the edges. Standing back to appraise his work, he imagined his father in the barn later—old Nicholas gathering up his blanket, saddle, and bridle for the ride into town. Satisfied with his cache, Wyatt stepped out to the stalls, hung the lantern, and doled out grain to each of the feed troughs. The horses nickered and nodded their big heads, some blowing air on his hands as he worked. He spoke to them quietly, letting the tone of parting soften his voice.

If only he could have saddled the Thoroughbred without delay, headed south to Ottumwa, and be shed of this morning of tiptoes and secrets. But that was not his plan. He might be a wayward son, but he was no thief.

When he walked back to the house, the oil lamp glowed inside the kitchen window. He kicked his boots together and pulled them off before opening the door. The sizzle of bacon had salted the air in the room, and his mother bustled about the kitchen as if she had never slept.

"Well, you're up early," she said, glancing up from her busy hands.

"Fed the horses."

He watched her sprinkle flour on the kneading board. She had never failed to provide a savory meal—whether sick or nursing an ailing neighbor or broken from the loss of a child. Wyatt had never seen defeat show in her face.

"Makin' biscuits, Ma?"

She looked at him as she leaned her weight onto stiffened arms and worked the dough in a rolling motion with the heels of her hands. Her lips parted, but she made no sound, as though she could not speak and labor at the same time.

"I could eat a coupl'a extras if you don't care," he added.

Her gaze ran the length of him, from wheat-straw hair to the recently darned socks. "You are gettin' to be tall as your father." She turned her back to him, and her shoulders hunched as she leaned into the dough. He watched her until she straightened from her work.

"We're all beholden to you, Ma."

Now she turned to face him squarely, her pasty hands splayed across the sides of her apron. "Well, aren't you full of surprises this mornin'," she said, wearing her crooked half smile. She lowered her eyebrows and canted her head as though trying to look at him from a new angle. "You want to eat something? I'll have the biscuits ready soon."

He ate at the sideboard, taking the servings as she prepared them. Outside the formality of the dining room and his father's presence, they talked comfortably, Wyatt following any subject she was inclined to broach. He could see she was starved for conversation, the kind he supposed a woman needed on a daily basis. When she turned her back to him as she prattled, he wrapped two biscuits in a cloth napkin and stuffed the package inside his shirt.

First light was blooming in the eastern sky when Wyatt stepped up on the old gnarled root at the blackjack oak. He took a final look at the field of corn spread before him. How often had he perched like this, balanced by the hoe—a tripod of man and tool set up at a distance to take a bearing? He had always wondered why the vast Iowa sky could not dwarf the field of green, reduce it to a size that seemed manageable. From the oak he could see the work's beginning but never the end. Once inside the interminable rows of stalks there would be a sense of neither. Only a blistered present, hard on a calloused past: chop, sweat, itch, breathe the dust, and swat the flies. And keep on.

The sun floated up through the trees now, breaking into a mosaic of burning red shards and then washing out the sky from its initial burnished gold to a dingy blue-gray. Morgan came from the barn, dragging a hoe that was half again his height. His sleepy eyes were half-hidden under the shock of hair fallen over his forehead, hair the same summer-gold tint as Wyatt's. He stopped next to the oak, shaded his eyes with his slender hand, and searched the fields alongside his older brother.

"What're you lookin' at?" he said, now squinting up at the side of Wyatt's face.

Wyatt shook his head and stared at the broad expanse of green. It wasn't just the size of the job . . . but keeping a rein on his two younger brothers. Their part was to lighten his load, but a day had seldom passed that they weren't fighting or wandering off. He looked at Morgan now, trying to see in the boy the man who would have to take over the farm work after this day.

He had told Morgan that he was joining the army, and Morg had held the secret close, as a brother should. Wyatt almost told him now that this was the day. All summer the secret had whispered inside him like a wind whistling through the cracks of a hastily built house. Yesterday it had been a gale in his ear. But now, on the day of his departure, a calm settled over him, and he decided to take no chances. He could wait.

"You need your hat," Wyatt said. "Where's Warren?"

"He's coming. Can't find one of his boots. Pa's lecturin' him."

Wyatt remembered when his father had toiled in a field, before the old man had refused to soil his hands with such work. Old Nick had conceived other ways of turning a dollar—a convenient credo of politics that milked a town of its coffers through the sleight of hand of the law and city governance. Mulling over his father's methods of subsistence, Wyatt felt all the more certain about leaving. He was finished soiling his hands, too.

"Go on back to the barn, Morg, and let the horses out." He pointed to the southwest corner of the cornfield. "I'll meet you yonder where we let off yesterday."

"Can I ride Salem back to the house to get my hat?"

"Just don't run 'im. It's too early. Here . . . give me that hoe, so you don't poke his eye."

Watching his little brother—wide awake now—dash off through the dew-wet grass, Wyatt wondered if he himself had ever displayed such fervor for manual labor. He remembered wanting to prove himself to his father, that was for certain, just as he remembered the futility of the effort.

"An' get Warren movin'!" he called out to Morg's back.

Wyatt returned his gaze to the drooping green blades of corn clicking against one another in the constant boil of the prairie wind. From where he stood, the corn appeared immaculate, reflecting the early morning light in metallic glints—a mirage that would flatten under the arching path of the sun.

Some men could see glory in farming. His father always claimed to be one. Wyatt could not. He doubled his leathered hands over the pair of rounded hickory handles, trying to take some measure of his own worth as weighed against Virgil, James, and Newton. For months now, his older brothers had been at the war, and every morning when he walked toward the suffocating green of the cornfield, he imagined what they awoke to: the smell of gun oil; chicory coffee brewing over a campfire; the throat-bite taste of cannon smoke drifting through the trees; maybe some blood dried into a cloth scab on their blue uniforms. And yet here he was, the corn crop stretched out before him thicker than any army ever force-marched across a battlefield. Straight and green and wax-bright, the field rippled in the wind like a prostrate flag. He was certain there was no glory in it.

With the country at war with itself, Wyatt's elevated status to oldest brother had covered more than dominion over the fields and his younger brothers; it included stewardship of the horses, which was no small part of the bargain. Whenever he could, Wyatt put himself in the company of these animals, assigning the more menial tasks to Morgan and Warren. He gave the most attention to the Thoroughbred, which was, aside from the land, the Earps' most valuable asset. Twice he had entered the stud in the town races and earned winnings. He patted the wad of bills in his pocket now, confident that it would sustain him until he could draw a soldier's pay.

Buoyed by the secret that had pulled him so early from sleep, he shouldered the tools and walked toward the field this one last time. When he stepped into the road that separated the house from the field, he turned to the steady cadence of a horse at a trot. A high-wheeled buggy with a flat, black canopy rattled along the road, approaching from the north. Wyatt leveled the hoes across both shoulders behind his neck, draped outstretched arms over the helves, and waited.

"Wyatt," the driver called as he reined up, stopping the buggy right in his path. Doc Howell nodded at the pair of tools on Wyatt's back. "Old Nick got you working twice the load today?" He had eyes that quickly engaged whomever he greeted, the wire-rimmed spectacles seeming to magnify his friendliness.

"Mornin', sir."

"I've not seen you since your little sister came down with the thrush." The doctor tilted his head and squinted. "You'd be about what now . . . fifteen?"

"Just about," Wyatt said.

The doctor lost his smile, but a curious probing fire held in his eye. "Well, I guess you grow up fast when you start running things." He nodded to the long wall of corn flanked to his right and turned back to Wyatt, studying the length of him, hat to boots. "Son, you look hard as a bundle of axe handles bound up with baling wire. How tall are you getting to be?"

Wyatt looked at the field, uncomfortable with the idea of describing himself. "Most of six feet, I reckon."

Wyatt tolerated the man's pointless questions, knowing it to be the doctor's habit for putting young patients at ease. The horse settled into its respite with a blow from its nostrils, and Doc Howell slackened the reins and propped his forearms on his knees.

"I sewed up that big Van den Newell boy last week," he said, dropping his voice to a low, confiding tone. "Seems I've got you to thank for some business. Any more patients coming my way I might need to know about?" The doc's eyebrows lifted high in pretended curiosity.

Wyatt's expression did not change. "Reckon he'll need to lay

17

off my brothers."

He felt an unexpected pang of guilt about abandoning his brothers today, but the feeling slipped away as quickly as it had come. They would have to learn how to deal with the Dutch bucks in the township. There would always be troublemakers to handle. Best learn it sooner than later.

The doctor straightened and smiled down the road. "Oh, I doubt that one'll be bothering anyone for a while." He gave Wyatt a look. "He knows who the scrapper in this town is."

Wyatt looked off toward the trees where the road curved. "Be best if you don't let on about that to my pa. He's trying to earn some votes outta the Dutch farmers."

Doc Howell's laugh cut off Wyatt's entreaty. "No need to worry about that, son." He arched his eyebrows again, and this time his smile curled with a hint of mischief. "You should have heard Old Man Van den Newell light into his boy. He knows all about it . . . how you licked the tar out of his oldest . . . and how he needed the lickin'." He saw the question in Wyatt's eyes and laughed the kind of laugh meant to put a man at ease. "Van den Newell's neighbor told him all about it . . . said you were not vicious . . . but businesslike . . . got the job done . . . quick." He gestured with the knuckle of a bent finger, like he was knocking quietly on a door between them. "That's good, Wyatt. You got none of that red blur that sucks so many young men into a blind rage. That kind of anger feeds off its own tissue and generally is of no use to a man."

Doc waited, his face open with anticipation, as if expecting some comment on this report. Looking off to the trees again Wyatt pulled in his lips, pressed his mouth into a tight line, and nodded.

"Still," Wyatt said, then met the doctor's eyes again, "it'll go better if my pa don't know."

Nicholas, Wyatt knew, might punish Morgan and Warren for

not fighting their own fight. He took in a deep breath through his nose and quietly purged it. Doc Howell frowned at his hands holding the reins. He shuffled the leather ribbons like he was rearranging a hand of playing cards. Two vertical lines creased into his skin above the spectacles.

"Old Nick can be a tough piece of meat in the stew, Wyatt, but you should know he's proud of you. Said you were methodical and straight-ahead. Said he'd never seen you make the same mistake twice. Said you would never stand for being the fool."

Wyatt considered the appraisal. "I don't reckon any man wants that."

Doc removed his spectacles and cleaned them with a white handkerchief. His face looked raw and naked without the lenses, like he had just awakened from a deep sleep.

"Couldn't prove it by me, Wyatt. Not with what I've seen." He hooked the spectacles around his ears again and lifted the reins.

The horse raised its head and perked up its ears. "Got to go see about a baby," the doctor said, squinting. He pointed with the knuckle again. "You might think on being a doctor, Wyatt. There're always going to be babies." His eyebrows bobbed. "Busted lips, too, for that matter." When he snapped the reins, horse and buggy picked up right away into the rhythm by which they had arrived.

Inside the rows of cornstalks Wyatt stationed his brothers on either side of him and began the steady litany of slicing steel into earth, heaping mounds of dirt over the corn roots—a rhythm redundant even before he began it. This had been his war. Two hours before school and three after. Sometimes all day, if the weather dictated it. Wyatt had always gone about it resigned and quiet, never speaking of it in any way. That was his father's rule. Complaint was a weakness, Nicholas always said, and no Earp displayed weakness.

As he worked Wyatt kept watch on the road. Morgan asked twice what he was looking at, but each time Wyatt only prodded him back to the hoeing. The three brothers hacked at the soil in silence as the trees across the road filled with a chorus of morning birdsong.

Finally, when his father took the chestnut mare at a walk past the open row where they worked, Wyatt stopped, feeling the onset of his emancipation as keenly as if a heavy chain had dropped from around his neck into the soft earth. He watched for a time as Morgan and Warren flailed at the dirt like young soldiers issued weapons beyond their size or mastery. Warren looked up, his dark hair framing his face like a warning of his brooding nature. It was Warren, Wyatt knew, who could be the problem.

"Morg," Wyatt said, "you're in charge now."

Morgan stopped working and straightened. "What do you mean?"

Warren stabbed his hoe into the dirt and stood in the pose of a challenge. Wyatt, setting his face like stone, held his eyes on Morgan.

"I'm goin' today."

Morgan swallowed hard. He drew the haft of the tool closer and pressed it to his chest, one fist stacked above the other, elbows splayed outward like folded wings.

Warren's eyes jumped from Morgan to Wyatt. "Goin' where?" he demanded. When he got no answer, his face flushed with anger.

Wyatt knelt and kept his voice both firm and gentle. "I ain't no farmer, Warren."

For once the youngest of the Earp brothers had nothing to say. He breathed through his teeth as he took in Wyatt's meaning.

"Wyatt's joinin' up with the army," Morgan announced. "Goin' off to the war."

Warren's face creased like a twisted rag. "Well, I ain't no damned farmer neither."

Wyatt took a grip on the boy's arm, but the shake he gave him was less a reprimand than a way to smooth out the boy's quick temper. "It ain't your time yet, so git that outta your head, you hear me?" Wyatt looked to Morg for help. "Keep on puttin' in your day's work, and when you're asked about it, just say I took off for town. You ain't gotta know why."

Morgan nodded, but tears had begun to well in Warren's eyes. Wyatt squeezed Warren's arm again and stood. He offered his hand to Morgan. As they shook, it occurred to Wyatt this was their first handshake that had not involved a wager.

"How're you gonna sign up in town with Pa working at the recruitin' office?" Morg asked.

"I ain't going into Pella," Wyatt said. "I'm headed to Ottumwa."

Morg frowned. "How'll you get there?"

"I'll get there."

"Well, when are you comin' back?"

Wyatt looked off toward the east as though an answer waited for him there. "Once the war's done, I reckon." He stepped back from his brothers, and they watched him from a combined stillness he had never before witnessed. "I'll try and write if I can get a hold o' some paper."

There was nothing more to be said. He turned and jogged for the barn for his bundle of clothes. The wind picked up and molded his shirt to his back, making him feel light, while all around him the downy seeds of prairie weeds lifted on the currents and trailed off ahead of him toward some untold destination to find their place of beginning.

CHAPTER 2

Summer, 1862: River road to Ottumwa, Iowa

Through the morning he followed the Des Moines River, until sometime after midday he jumped a freight wagon that carried him to Mahaska County. There he bedded down under the awning of a coach's way station. On the second day, an old Dutchman with a square-cut beard pulled Wyatt up behind his saddle. The old man started up asking questions in that chopping, rise-and-fall accent that Wyatt had been taught to despise through his father's constant mimicry.

"I'm goin' into Ottumwa," Wyatt explained. "Bound for the recruitin' station."

The old man turned partway and lifted an eyebrow. "Oh? And how old do you be?"

"Sixteen," Wyatt said, the lie slipping off his tongue so effortlessly, he fairly believed it himself. In that easy fabrication he felt the world open before him like the river off to his right, numinous and prophetic, ready to take him on the grand ride for which he yearned.

It was late afternoon when they rode in tandem into the township of Ottumwa, and Wyatt had barely begun searching the storefront signs for a soldiers' station when he saw his father step into the road and grab the Dutchman's horse by the cheek strap of the bridle.

Nicholas glared at Wyatt. "What's wrong?" he demanded, ignoring the Dutchman's protestations. The horse nickered and went wall-eyed, jerking its head as it began to circle.

"Let go uff my horse!" the Dutchman ordered.

"Has something happened at home?" Nicholas demanded. When the Dutchman kicked out at his intruder, Nicholas heaved down on the bridle with his weight. His boots skidded across the dirt as the horse backed away. Wyatt was almost unseated when the horse crouched. Then the material at the back of his shirt knotted, and he was jerked from the haunches of the horse. Squirming in his father's grip, he barely got his feet beneath him before hitting the street.

The rider regained control of his mount and circled to face Nicholas. "Take your hands off dat boy!" The Dutchman's jaw was locked with indignation, though it was no match for the storm brewing in Nicholas's dark eyes.

Nicholas's hands clamped down on Wyatt's shoulders and shook him. "All right, you found me! Now tell me what's happened!"

"Why are you in Ottumwa?" Wyatt said.

Old Nick frowned. "I come down yesterday," he barked.

When Wyatt said nothing more, the Dutchman lost all that remained of his patience. "He comes to join up fer da war!" he yelled. "Now let him be!"

The fire in Nicholas's eyes gathered into a baleful smolder. Then a growl rumbled up from deep in his chest as he threw Wyatt back onto the seat of his pants. The Dutchman started to dismount, but Nicholas swatted at the horse, forcing the man to regain his seat.

"This is my son, goddamnit! Now go about your business!" He glowered at the incensed old man, who turned his horse and whipped the tails of the reins sharply across its rear flanks. The animal crow-hopped and then moved with a stutter-step down the street.

One hand shielding his eyes, Wyatt squinted up at the

silhouette of his father, who appeared taller than he was by virtue of the black suit and hat he wore like a vestment of ordained power. On the lapel of his coat shone the provost marshal badge he polished once a week with ritualistic devotion. A great woolly beard wrapped around his broad jaw, giving him the appearance of something wild and untamable. Beneath his bushy eyebrows his glare was fierce as it fixed upon the roll of clothes now lying in the street.

Nicholas picked up Wyatt's travel bundle. "Your mother know you've run off?"

Wyatt pushed up from the street and stood, the clench of his teeth his only answer.

"You must've left yesterday," Nicholas growled. "Don't you think she'll be sick with worry, son?" The two Earps stared at one another with a willfulness differentiated only by age. "And what about the corn about to come in?"

Wyatt swiped at the dust clinging to one arm. "I thought you were in Pella."

"Well, I ain't," Nicholas barked. "What the hell's got into you, boy?"

"I ain't a boy no more."

Nicholas's jaw knotted, and he exhaled heavily through his nostrils. "You are, by God, long as I say you are." He scowled at the bundle. "So you think you're ready for a war."

Wyatt tried to push a rough edge into his voice. "I ain't cut out for farmin'."

Nicholas's face darkened, and Wyatt thought for a moment that his father might lose whatever restraint he had manufactured for the sake of the people who had gathered to watch them. But the old man's eyes closed, and he breathed in deeply, then out, the air wheezing from his nose, stirring the wiry strands of his moustaches. When he opened his eyes, his disappointment stung Wyatt more than a slap in the face. Then the stiffness in Nicholas's posture wilted, and the taut skin around his eyes relaxed, like a man forced into an admission against his will. His somber gaze fixed on Wyatt.

"You don't always get a say in that, son. You do what you have to do."

Wyatt had never heard this sound of compromise in his father's voice.

Nicholas snapped out of his reverie and began herding the onlookers away. Still carrying the bundle of clothes, he stepped closer to Wyatt. When he spoke, his voice carried the low rumble that he sometimes used in church when he dared to add his rough voice to a hymn.

"You ain't never quit on nothin' before, Wyatt." And with those words, Wyatt felt the seed of guilt take root in his gut. "I ain't hardly got what all *I've* aimed for myself," Nicholas continued. They were the most unguarded words he had ever shared with his son. "I know you're 'bout growed . . . but I need you to stick for a while more. Can you do that?"

Wyatt lowered his eyes to the street. "Yes, sir. I reckon I can."

Nicholas stepped forward and cupped his hand over the sloping muscle at the base of Wyatt's neck. "Hold up your head, son." Wyatt looked up to see his father's face spent but composed. The old man's eyes seemed to be gathering in the whole of him. "I want you to git yourself home now, and git back to your work." He leaned to position his face before Wyatt's wayward stare. "Will you do that for me?"

Wyatt looked down the street in the direction from which he had come. Beyond the cottonwoods, the river shone in patches of reflected light. His plan of leaving was like the river's current, already sliding downstream to a place too distant to retrieve.

"Yes, sir."

Nicholas handed the packet of clothes to Wyatt, and then he turned and marched across the street to the covered boardwalk.

There his dark visage was swallowed by the shade of the awning as he pushed through a canvas curtain that served as a door. A hand-painted sign next to the doorway read: US Government Recruiting Station.

With the sun falling off to his left, Wyatt started the long walk back to Pella, his only company the scuff of his boots on the rutted road. He traveled through the night and all the next day, seeing no one, his mood gone sour over the long journey ahead of him, but more so at having to move back into a tedious life he had not expected to face again.

CHAPTER 3

Spring, 1863: Earp farm, Pella, Iowa

On a cool day in April, after starting his brothers on the whitewashing of the barn, Wyatt tended to the horses and hammered new rivets into the worn leather harnessing. Like Morgan and Warren, he felt the loss of the barren season and its reprieve from the field work, but the feeling of life returning to the surrounding woods stirred him to be a part of it. With the desiccated stalks of corn long since slashed and plowed under, the crop land would lie still as a graveyard for another week to ensure the end of freezes before the planting would begin.

In late afternoon, while spreading hay in the paddock, he looked up to see two dun deer browsing on the bark of saplings beyond the curve in the road. No more than shadows moving against the gray scrim of barren trees, they foraged with an indifference to proximity to the farm.

When the deer dissolved into the shadows of the forest, a distant thunder rumbled in the west. Wyatt checked the angle of the sun, latched the barn doors, and walked to the scaffold where Morgan and Warren slapped paint onto the weathered boards. He stood for a time and watched them work, their weary strokes silently condemning the rote nature of the work.

"You boys paintin' the barn or yourselves?" he called out.

They turned in unison, each with a brush suspended in one hand. A streak of whitewash ran across Warren's forehead into his hair.

"Might be some rain comin' in," Wyatt said. "Why'n't you climb down off there and clean up. We're headin' across the road."

They watched him walk up the rise to the house and disappear through the kitchen door. When he returned from the house, he was packing the over-and-under that his father had entrusted to him—a combination shotgun and forty-four caliber rifle. The two boys scrambled down the rungs of the ladder, put away their buckets and brushes, and hurried to join him, walking with a quickened pace to match the stride of his longer legs.

Forming a flank, they crossed the lane and stepped into the twilight under the trees where they inspected the fresh stripping on a stand of young plum trees on which the deer had fed. Wyatt laid the weapon in the crook of his arm and instructed both boys to sniff at the mangled bark, but the scent held their interest for only a moment before their eyes settled on the gun. The old shoulder-buster was like a fourth member of the party, one to which the younger brothers showed uncommon deference. Each, Wyatt knew, hoped for a chance to use it.

"What're we doin'?" Morg asked.

"We ain't got to slave all the time," Wyatt said quietly.

Morgan allowed the little laugh that made his eyes crinkle. "Reckon when Pa sees the barn ain't finished he'll beat all of us? Or just me and Warren?"

"You got to learn about huntin' some time," Wyatt said. "I figure we can use the venison."

"Well," Morg said, adopting the devil-may-care tone he had been perfecting over the last months, "since I'm bound for a lickin', I reckon you're just about as bound to let me shoot."

"Do like I say and you might," Wyatt said.

Warren's eyes burned as they fixed on the gun. "Do I git to shoot?"

Kneeling to the forest floor, Wyatt clutched a fistful of dead leaves and dirt and rubbed it against Warren's trouser leg. "Grind some o' this duff into that whitewash on your clothes."

Warren frowned. "What for?"

Morgan thumped him on the back of his head, and Warren swatted at his arm. Morg made an actor's face like he was surprised, and then laughed at Warren's flash of anger.

"No more horseplay now," Wyatt said, putting his years into his voice. "You need to cover up any smell that don't fit with what's already here."

The two boys scooped up leaves and crushed them into their work clothes, the smell of the earth like the new scent of spring itself. When they finished, all the spite and banter was gone, as if the cleansing ritual had sunk beneath their skin and united them in a single purpose.

"Where're we goin'?" Warren whispered.

Wyatt shifted the gun to one hand, taking it at the point of balance that angled the barrel slightly downward. "Down to the low ground by the creek. Stay behind me and don't talk."

They followed him into the trees, attempting to match the quietness of his footfall in the dry leaves. When thunder rolled across the sky again, Wyatt stopped long enough to gauge that the storm was moving south of them. He turned and dropped to one knee, propping the rifle skyward with the butt of the stock planted on the ground. He pointed to a felled tree, and the two boys waited for him to speak. Instead he moved in a slow, cat-like crouch toward the log.

The wood was narrow between two fallow fields. Where the creek crossed through it, the undergrowth was thick with prime cover for bedding deer. When Wyatt settled in behind the log, Morgan and Warren squeezed in beside him. Their chosen spot commanded a view along both floodplains of the stream. There they waited—Wyatt with his eyes relaxed to catch movement, the two boys pivoting their heads at every sound.

Keeping his eyes fixed on the game trail by the water, Wyatt half turned his head and spoke in a low monotone. "First you got to know where to spend your time waitin'. Else that's all you'll be doing . . . is waitin'. Look yonder at that scuffed up juniper." Slowly, he raised his hand and pointed. "A buck scraped his antlers there. You see it? He chose that tree for the sharp scent of its sap. It sends a message."

The two boys' boots clawed for purchase in the dirt as they pushed higher to see over the log. "What's the message?" Warren whispered.

"This territory's taken," Wyatt explained. "He's claimed this place for his own."

Eager to please, both boys nodded, their faces bright and open, soaking up whatever Wyatt was willing to share. It was one of the few times that they had seen fit to agree on something.

"Next thing is to get nestled in," Wyatt continued. "Become part of the place. No moving . . . no exceptions. Deer see movement before anything else." Wyatt turned back to the hollow. The late afternoon shadows pooled and coalesced to make a dozen niches in which an animal could hide. He dropped his voice to the barest whisper. "And if you're skittish . . . tied up in a knot of nerves, they'll feel it . . . and they'll keep out of your range." He turned to look at his brothers with the unblinking stare that brooked no insolence. "If you can't control yourself, you ain't never gonna control nothin' or nobody else." Then he nodded once, and by this gesture alone the two boys knew they could do what he had asked.

The younger Earps struggled to become part of the unmoving landscape, while Wyatt remained still and content, like an extension of the log, the long barrel of the gun resting atop it as though there were no other purpose in this world than the one at hand. They had seen Wyatt target shoot, and they looked to his steadiness with the weapon as a paradigm of virtue, especially now, as the skill connected to something so practical as meat on the table. Listening to the steadiness in his voice made them feel important . . . something about being an Earp. Unlike the fearful allegiance they owed their father, their regard for Wyatt was more a yearning. They would do anything he asked of them, because in doing it, they believed they might become more like him.

Twilight darkened, and the birdsong tapered to a single meadowlark's flute notes coming from the field beyond the trees. Then a movement swept through the dimly lighted scene before them—three deer gliding through the trees, ghostlike, silent, their hooves not seeming to touch the ground. Two sleek does followed a stout buck with a proud rack crowning its head.

Wyatt gathered himself to the gun, his movements steady, like the settling of a liquid finding its level. Fitting his hand around the smooth walnut stock, he thumbed back the hammer and slipped his finger around the trigger in one motion. His eye lowered into place behind the sights. Then, sooner than the boys expected, the gun thundered, filling the hollow with smoke and surprise.

The gun's report lingered in the air as two of the animals bolted, crashing through the underbrush until they were swallowed up by the silence of the trees. But the largest deer lay still in the scuffled leaves, its antlers angling its head in an unnatural pose. Morg and Warren stared with slack faces, the lesson complete.

On the walk home, as a reward for their patience, Wyatt let them work the edge of the fields, giving each brother a chance at smaller game while the other flushed prey from the brush in the gullies. With the shotgun load, Warren missed twice, but Morg brought down a rabbit on the run. Wyatt, his pace only slightly slowed by the heavy buck yoked around his neck, gave a nod of approval but said nothing, knowing that Warren's festering jealousy could put the boy in a foul mood for days.

Morgan picked up his prize and handed the gun to Warren to try again, and the three brothers continued home. Behind Warren's back, Wyatt and Morg exchanged a brief look at one another, and in that moment Wyatt knew the passing of time was shaving away at the years that separated them.

CHAPTER 4

Spring, 1863: Earp farm, Pella, Iowa

In the fading light the three hunters hung the buck from the walnut tree, unaware that a traveler had appeared out of nowhere, standing in the yard as a quiet observer. Wyatt saw him first, then Morgan. Behind the man in the grass lay a duffel, and perched upon it was a wrinkled blue field-cap like the soldiers wore in town. He didn't speak until all three brothers took notice of him.

"Damn but you boys been growin' like weeds."

Warren ran to James and almost jumped on him before he saw the arm slung across his older brother's midsection by a dirty loop of rag. Morg approached, and the two boys stared at the dark stain on the shoulder of James's jacket. They stood embarrassed, as though it were a stranger who had arrived with sobering news of the brother who had once wrestled with them in the grass. This messenger smelled of whiskey and appeared to have traveled the dark side of the world.

James chuckled at their speechless state and splayed his hand atop each boy's head as he ambled past them towards Wyatt. "Looks like you're the one runnin' things, little brother," he said, offering his hand. Wyatt wiped his hands on his trousers. When they shook, James pretended to wince at Wyatt's grip. "Guess you ain't nobody's little brother no more."

"How bad is it?" Wyatt said, nodding at the bandaged shoulder.

"Oh, I'm only 'bout half-crippled," he said, tucking his chin into his collarbone, trying to examine his shoulder. "Took a Minié-ball at Frederickstown, but you can still count on being the right hand around here. Damned Rebs seen to it I'd never work a farm again." He kept a straight face for only a moment. When he laughed, he was the same James they had known before the war but for the whiskey breath. "Prob'ly worse news for you than for me."

"What about Virgil and Newton?"

"Hell, I ain't even seen 'em. I doubt Virge'll be back any time soon after getting the Rysdam girl pregnant. What was it . . . a boy?"

"Her family moved out west somewhere. She went with 'em, so we never heard."

James quietly laughed. "Damned war made a convenient backdoor for ol' Virge."

Wyatt said nothing to that. In truth, though Virgil had been the backbone of the farm, he was not as keenly missed as he might have been. Except by Wyatt. With an exaggerated groan, James stretched his back and took in the expanse of the winter-barren field across the road.

"Pa still slaving you?"

Wyatt followed his gaze. "I reckon so . . . me and Morg and Warren."

James turned at the dead tone in Wyatt's voice. "Things all right between you and Pa?"

"We're all right, I reckon." Wyatt's face betrayed nothing.

James adjusted the sling under his arm and put on a skewed smile. "Pa's got this contrary way of whippin' you into a man, but then once you get there, he still expects you to follow him around like a young pup." James pointed to the deer. "Was that there on his list of things for you to do?"

When Wyatt looked back at the deer, Morg and Warren did

the same. "Wyatt knocked 'im down clean with one shot," Warren said. James tousled Warren's hair.

"I kilt a rabbit," Morgan said. James jabbed a finger at Morg's belly, but the boy was too quick.

The kitchen door opened, and Virginia Earp stepped onto the back porch, squeezing a towel to each of her fingers. Behind her the light from the oil lamps outlined the stoop of her once-proud posture. The towel stilled in her hands when her eyes pinched at the number of Earps gathered in the yard. Her plain face drew up, and then her strong jaw went slack at the sight of James smiling at her. Holding the forgotten towel to her breast, she stepped toward him, her gaze stitching back and forth between his face and the sling over his shoulder. A fragile sweetness bloomed in her rough cheeks, and her mouth began to quiver.

"Oh, Lord," she breathed. "Jimmy." She hadn't called him that in years.

James picked up Warren and bounced the boy silly as he ran toward the house. "Hey there, Ma. I reckon they had enough o' me in the war."

"Lord in heaven," she whispered, her words thick and trembling. Then her voice took on its more familiar scolding tone. "Climb down off your brother, Baxter Warren!"

James let the boy down, and the three younger brothers watched as he managed the half embrace that was left to him. Virginia was crying by the time she led him inside. Warren stood wide-eyed, staring at the closed door.

Morgan turned to Wyatt with a twinkle in his eye. "Smells like Pa's corn liquor, don't he?" He made a wry smile at the deer. "Maybe James comin' home will help git us through this night."

Wyatt stepped past his younger brother and pried his skinning knife from the trunk of the tree. "Let's you and me finish dressing out this buck," he said.

It was fully dark when Nicholas returned from town. He smelled the aroma of roasting meat wafting from the kitchen, and by the pale light spreading from the window, he saw the offal glistening beneath the walnut tree, where the skinning and quartering had been done, the rope still crimped into a curl from its recent knot. The unpainted barn mocked him like the smile of a gaptoothed idiot, and he cursed under his breath—a rehearsal for the rage he would unleash inside the house.

Nicholas found Wyatt leaning over the basin, washing his face at the pitcher pump, but before launching into a reprimand, he stopped slack-jawed at the sight of James sitting beside his mother as she cut potatoes at the sideboard. Both mother and son smiled at him, waiting for a reaction.

"Well, good Lord," Nicholas said, quickly stiffening himself against any emotion. Stretching his neck up through his starched collar, he coughed up a rough sound deep in his throat and pushed the door shut. "It's about time they cut you loose. You're home for good?"

"For good or for bad . . . I reckon that remains to be seen." James rose to his feet and waited to see if his father would approach him. The elder Earp moved to the cupboard, and from the highest shelf he lifted down a clear jug of mash.

"You still brewin' up that poison?" James asked, eyeing the spirits. "Don't these Dutch farmers object to your liquor-making like the folks did in Illinois?"

"It ain't none o' their goddamn business," Nicholas growled. He took down a glass and poured it better than half full. James waited for another glass to be offered, but it was not forthcoming. "I'm the provost marshal for the district," Nicholas said, tugging at his coat lapel where the showy badge was pinned. "I reckon I can brew any damn thing I please." He downed the homemade whiskey in two gulps and smacked down the glass on the counter with a sharp rap. When he exhaled, some color came into his face. He poured himself another.

James crossed the floor to the cupboard. "I hear you're the one gets our boys ready for the war," he said. He stiffened the thumb of his good hand and stabbed it twice at the center of his chest. " 'Course, *I* been there." His eyes flared with challenge just before he took down a second glass and let it strike the counter in an echo of his father's gesture. "You want to pour for me?" he said, smiling. He gave no notice of his wound, but it was there for anyone to see.

Still holding the jug, Nicholas appeared to chew on something as he stared at his son. He tilted the jug and poured a half inch. James summed up the meager offering with an airy laugh through his nose, raised the drink to his lips, and threw it back with a toss of his head.

At his mother's bidding Wyatt stepped past them to the parlor doorway and called for his brothers to wash up. Nicholas still had not acknowledged him. When Morgan and Warren spilled into the kitchen, Wyatt retired to the dining room and stoked the fire in the hearth. Taking the sharpening stone from the mantle he began scraping the carving knife in long, steady strokes.

Talk of the war filled the kitchen, until Virginia carried little Adelia into the dining room and called the family to supper. Nicholas entered last and, avoiding Wyatt's eyes, took his seat at the head of the table. With the fresh logs crackling in the fireplace, Nicholas gave thanks for their bounty and for James's safe return, intoning it as though God had finally come to His senses. Then he opened the top button of his shirt and hooked his napkin into the crook of his collar, all the while eyeing the ill-gotten victuals spread before him.

Awaiting the proper signal to eat, Morgan and Warren watched their father prop his elbows on the table. The old man glared at them as though awaiting an explanation. Neither boy dared make a sound. In this tableau of family obeisance, Wyatt forked a slab of roast onto his father's plate and started on another for his mother.

"How is it you can take off huntin' when the barn ain't finished?" Nicholas said, still looking at the two youngest brothers.

Before they could muster an answer, Wyatt spoke up. "Looked like some rain comin' in, so I told 'em to quit. The three of us went huntin' instead." He served the venison to his mother's plate and nodded toward his brothers. "They got to learn some time how to get it to the table."

In the silence that followed, the space around the table seemed too small for the coming disagreement. Virginia set a jar of blackberry preserves beside her husband's plate, the grace of her simple movement like something swimming beneath the still surface of a pond.

"Nicholas," she said, "we can't keep eating stewed corn and cornbread. Try to enjoy the meal and be thankful for the meat . . . and for James."

Nicholas cleared his throat. "I reckon I can allow a day off for huntin' now and again." He glared at the meat. "Once a month," he ordained. He shot Wyatt a warning with his eyes and sniffed loudly, a signal that the affair was settled.

With their faces glowing at this new license to hunt, Morgan and Warren turned in unison to Wyatt. Holding their gazes, he lifted his milk as smoothly as a sacrament raised to the lips of a man certain of his salvation. He drank deeply before setting the glass back down.

"With James back," Wyatt said, "twice a month seems about right."

James choked back a whiskey laugh, the bawdy sound no less startling in this room than if the deer had sprung back to life on the platter.

"Nicholas," Virginia added quickly, "when we go to California, you'll need these boys to bring in wild game on the trail. Isn't that right?"

The father glared at Wyatt and set both hands on the table linen, his big fists curled like a pair of gavels. His face had reddened, and his nostrils flared with each wheezing breath.

"You're thinking you're too big for me to whip now?" Nicholas challenged.

Wyatt slowly placed his silverware in his plate, the light clink of metal on china as crisp as the cocking of a gun. "No, sir, that ain't what I was thinking," he responded, the rough certainty in his voice giving no hint of surrender.

James covered his mouth and rubbed at the patch of unkempt whiskers tapering down his chin, the sound like fingertips on dry paper. Only he had caught the play of words in his brother's reply. It was as close to humor as Wyatt ever got. Not so much what he'd said as what he hadn't.

"When we move out west," Wyatt said, nodding to his younger brothers, "we'll be ready."

Nicholas's face darkened, and his words, when they came, tore from his throat like strips of flesh. "Meanwhile, son . . . there's work to be done on this farm! I'll need to sell it for top dollar, and to do that I'll need a barn that don't look like a half-patched nightshirt."

Wyatt's farm-toughened hands rested loosely on the white tablecloth, the knuckles ridged evenly under his sun-browned skin. "Seems to me, if I'm man enough for that field of corn, I'm man enough to make a decision or two." There was no impertinence in his voice. He was demonstrating a point of reason.

As the family waited for Nicholas's reaction, the cherrywood clock in the hallway ticked with painful regularity, as though a half-wit sat in the next room diligently striking together two stones . . . oblivious to the monotony he imposed on the moment. Wyatt sat easily in his chair—the same way he sat a horse, as though he had earned the space he was occupying.

"I count on you to make decisions!" the elder Earp bellowed. "But not against my word!" He slammed both fists, and the plates and silverware rattled as if he had called down the thunder.

In the silence that followed, Virginia folded her arms on the edge of the table and leaned forward into her husband's view. "Then give them your word, Nicholas." Her voice was placid and rational, making her request all the more commanding.

"About *what*, woman!" he shot back, his voice trailing off in a whine.

"If *you're* not going to do it," she explained, "Wyatt needs to teach these two about hunting. And twice a month sounds right to me. How does that sound to you?"

Nicholas turned to the reflection in the windowglass and dragged his lower teeth across his upper lip. Everyone in the room knew that Virginia's calm could not be trumped. All that was needed was a graceful way for Nicholas to concede the point.

The old man turned to scowl at James. "Anything *you* want to add to this?"

Amused, James cocked his head. "Just a question." He hooked his good arm over the back of his chair. "When you went off to the war in Mexico . . . that story you used to tell us 'bout gettin' kicked by a mule . . . that true?"

Nicholas sniffed. "Caught me right in my Carolina chestnuts."

James held off a smile. "And wasn't it right *after* that when you sired Wyatt?"

Nicholas looked sharply at James, but seeing the mischief in his eyes, he did not bother to answer.

"Ain't it mules s'posed to be stubborn and all?" James wondered aloud. He was like an actor on a stage, sharing his private thoughts for the benefit of his audience. He cocked his head. "Reckon you can catch that kind a thing from a mule . . . and maybe pass it on?"

Everyone waited to see if Nicholas would respond to the crude joke. Virginia cupped a hand over his forearm, but Old Nick just sucked at a tooth and rotated his water glass on the tablecloth.

"You can hunt," he decreed, "but no more'n twice a month." He sniffed with finality, reached for a platter, and everyone went into motion at once. The sounds of serving spoons tapping on plates carried a blessed momentum that began to put the tension behind them. James buffeted Wyatt's shoulder with the back of his good hand, but Wyatt only picked up his fork and knife and sawed at a corner of his venison.

"You boys can rise early tomorrow," Nicholas said. "Get in another two hours on the barn before school. That'll square things this time."

Wyatt looked at Morgan and Warren, holding their eyes with his. "Yes, sir," he said and went about the business of eating his dinner in the same unhurried way in which he did everything.

CHAPTER 5

Spring, 1864: Oregon Trail from Pella to Omaha City, Nebraska Territory

The next year the Earps set out for the promised land of California, or as James liked to say, "as far west as a man could run from his past and still call himself an American." With Nicholas as wagon master—for he would take orders from no one—eleven families signed on with the Earp train. Charlie Coplea, a young bachelor neighbor who had unsuccessfully courted three women in the past year, asked to throw in with the Earps. When he walked, his left leg bent backward like a dog's, but he promised another pair of hands for the work that needed to be done on the trail. Unfamiliar with Nicholas's rigid demands, he agreed to work as one of the family and, as recompense, take his fill of Virginia's cooking.

While Nicholas fulfilled his role of captain from horseback, Coplea drove one Earp wagon, with Wyatt handling the other, trading off with Morgan or James when he rode out to scout for food. The hunting proved to be no easy feat, however, the overland route having suffered from the passage of those preceding them. Game was scarce. Many of the trees had been hacked down, and the water was sullied by the refuse and debris of ill-prepared crossings.

More often than not, Wyatt was forced to ride out of sight of the train to locate meat. On those occasions when he returned without a kill, no one voiced a complaint. Most of the migrating

42

families lived under the thrall of tales about marauding Indians and thought it a blessing to have any fresh meat at all.

In the evenings Wyatt tended to the draft animals, picketing them in the best available grass close to the wagon ring. Much of the work was essentially farm labor—the only difference being that it was mobile. Wyatt abided it, for he liked seeing new places. The stark land unfolded before him like the prelude to some grander story. Vast swales of river bottom gave rise to birds whose names he did not know. These he watched take to the air with a God-given grace in a liberation much like the one into which he was now stretching.

He began to catalogue every bluff and tapered defile as a landmark to remember, until they became so numerous and redundant that he began to understand just how immense this new country really was. That his gaze could reach so far across the endless land gave him a new grasp of vision. He felt at home here, a place where he could both expand and sharpen his vision, and he contemplated how he might one day profit by it.

Away from the rutted trail, the prairie was still raw and untouched, and Wyatt learned to see the land's components as untapped resources of income. A man with ambition and know-how could thrive in such a place. The ambition, he knew, was beginning to take form in him. As for the know-how, that would come in time.

They had barely forded the Missouri at Council Bluffs, when Wyatt was already considering wagon-mastering for his immediate future. Eventually the railroads would kill the enterprise, but for a time, he reasoned, it could be lucrative. Such a job relied on two physical elements at which he was a natural: handling horses and hunting. It was dealing with people that he wondered about. He watched his father's varied tyrannies. The explosive imperatives he imposed on these strangers bred hatred for the old man. There were better ways, Wyatt knew, to inspire allegiance. Fear might prod men to action, but it did not promote loyalty.

When Nicholas camped the train a mile outside Omaha City, Wyatt and Charlie Coplea took the two percherons into town to replace a bag of meal gone rancid. From a distance the town appeared as a stalled carnival on an otherwise desolate plain. Only the deep, lazy cut of the Missouri connected it to anything else in the world. Wyatt would always remember the idea that came into his head as he neared the town: *In a place like this, a man could make up just about any life he wanted.*

This was surely a comfort to some men—to know that, if who you were turned into flat disappointment, you could start again as somebody else in a place like Omaha. Not that Wyatt could imagine appropriating such a bargain for himself. He did not have the creativity for it. As his sixth-grade schoolteacher had once told him, he was too direct to playact.

"You ain't said a word all day," Coplea said, sidling his horse up to Wyatt's as they neared the town. "You ain't sick or nothin', are you?"

Wyatt turned to look into Coplea's simple face and shook his head at the uselessness of such a question. "You didn't take your meals with us today. Maybe I ought to be askin' *you* that."

Charlie turned away with a sheepish look on his face, and they slowed their horses to a walk and let the animals settle their breathing. "I might be sick o' being yelled at," he admitted. He turned back quickly to check Wyatt's expression. "I don't mean no offense to you . . . but your paw ain't a easy man to work for."

Wyatt said nothing. He kept his eyes on the nearest building ahead. A dog was chained there, its head lowered over its front paws. Only the dog's eyes moved to mark their progress.

"I don't reckon it's any too easy being kin to 'im neither,"

Charlie added.

Wyatt almost smiled. "Never dull, I'll say that."

Charlie's face screwed up like he'd been presented a book written in Chinese. "You ever think on headin' up a train like this'n, Wyatt?" Wyatt shrugged with a tilt of his head. Coplea started nodding even before he spoke again. "Hell, you'd be a natural at it."

"Maybe," Wyatt said.

Coplea's brow lowered as though any contrary thought deserved a debate. "Hell, yes. People'd wanna do what *you* asked 'em. Hell, they respect you."

At the emphatic whine in Charlie's voice, the dog raised its head and watched them pass. The horses' hooves clopped a syncopated rhythm for a time, until they turned on to the main street.

"You thinkin' on leadin' crossings yourself, Charlie?"

Charlie thought about that as he soaked up the town. "Nah . . . not me."

Music tinkled from a gray clapboard building where the street turned to sludge. People moved through the thoroughfare and along the walkways in every garb imaginable. It was strange to hear so many conversations mixing in the air after days of listening to sand catch in axle grease and squeal out notes that flew above the heavy rumble of wagon wheels like the cries of frantic birds.

Rough-sawn boards had been laid like child's work along the sidewalks, linking up at intervals to provide makeshift bridges over the mud slop from store to store. The men and women using them were like ants on a stick taking their turns in single file. Wyatt felt anonymous, as no one paid these newly arrived young horsemen any attention.

He reined up and watched, fascinated, as men, women, wagons, pigs, dogs, and all manner of livestock negotiated the sucking mire running through the center of the town. The stench of human waste hung in the air. He had never seen so many signs tacked to buildings, most of the lettering rendered by hands either uneducated or in haste. There was no charm to it. Nor was there a sense of community to the mass spontaneity of human activity all around them. It was as though the town had surrendered to chaos.

A group of men wearing leather-billed caps unloaded bulky crates from a freight wagon into a building, their swelling forearms bearing witness to a history of heavy work. And yet there was about them a debauched softness, too. Something far down the scale from the steel-tendon hardness of laboring every day, hours on end, in a sun-scorched field. Wyatt sized them up, as all men appraised one another when they met on the frontier. He did not underestimate them, but neither did he shrink from their brawn.

Across the street a plump woman, bare breasted and hair gone wild around her shoulders, leaned from an upstairs window and yelled to the men. When one of them called back and laughed, his voice boomed off the false-fronted buildings with the depth of a parade drum.

"Wade on in, Wyatt," Charlie sang as he booted his horse ahead. Wyatt watched the thick-boned percheron sink into the mud above the fetlocks and compromise its gait with a bandy-legged stiffness. It seemed that even to enter this raunch of Gomorrah required a token surrender of dignity, if only by the demeaning of a man's horse.

He clucked through the side of his teeth, and his mount lurched forward, eager to catch Charlie's horse. Wyatt held the steed back with a gentle word and the proper tension on the reins. He wanted to see everything about this town.

At the dry goods store they dismounted, but there was nowhere to tie the horses. Wyatt took Charlie's reins and dug into his pocket for the paper and money his mother had entrusted to him.

"I'll watch the horses," he said. "Here's the list for what we need."

Coplea pocketed the money and nodded toward his tack. "You keep an eye out on our rifles. There's shirkers here'd love to own our guns for us." Coplea hesitated at the door, kicked at the jamb, and lifted one boot to inspect its sole.

"It don't matter none," a voice called from inside. "Bring it on in."

As soon as Charlie stepped into the darkness of the one-room store, Wyatt swung the horses' flanks into the sunlight, where they would not cool down too fast. He put a hand on the butt of his over-and-under and tamped it a quarter inch deeper into its scabbard. His father had given him the gun when Wyatt was thirteen. Outdated then, it was still an unwieldy weapon, but he was not prepared to lose it in Omaha City.

"God . . . damned . . . son . . . of a bitch!" The words huffed out—like the breath of a man trying to talk as he swung an axe. Wyatt turned to the street, where a tall man with thick moustaches and a swag belly strode past him. His arms swung in stiff, aggressive thrusts, and his head hunched forward with single-minded purpose. His frog eyes bulged, though seemed to take in little. The knuckles of his clenched fists stood out like white pebbles. His boots sank into the mud and sucked back out, leaving open wounds in the street behind him. Wyatt followed the man's progress deeper into the town until his broad back disappeared in the mill of bodies.

A profane laugh turned Wyatt to his right. Three men stood in an open doorway under a crude, hand-painted sign that read "Last Kaintuck Whiskey East of the Rockys." Two of the men, seemingly pleased with their lot in life, wiped at their crooked smiles with the backs of their hands, while the grim man in front of them stared out past Wyatt, a long-barreled revolver hanging straight down from his hand like the stilled pendulum of a broken clock. Other men began to fill the doorway, and their collective banter was that of a circus audience come to witness the main event.

By the time Coplea brought out the bag of meal, Wyatt had moved the horses into the alley. Coplea stopped, looked around, and lifted his chin when he saw Wyatt. Charlie's face screwed up into a question as he set the bag on his bad knee.

"Better step back inside, Charlie," Wyatt suggested. Coplea let the bag ease to the rough-hewn bench under the window, balanced it there with one hand, and followed Wyatt's gaze to the men gathered outside the saloon.

On the far side of the street the tall mustachioed man had returned, this time walking along the pedestrian boards, his gaze jumping back and forth from his precarious footpath to the saloon cattycornered across the intersection. Swinging in his right hand was the same kind of pistol Wyatt had seen among James's relics from the war.

The world seemed to dissolve at the edges of a half sphere that lowered around the two antagonists, as an irreversible prophecy claimed them. As if by an audible signal, each man walked toward the other as though his momentum might decide the moment. Neither spoke. Or if they did, Wyatt did not hear them. He heard nothing but the sudden, sharp explosions—four of them—amplified all out of proportion between the buildings along the street.

The mustachioed man reeled in a half turn, fell to his knees, then tumbled forward into the slop of the street, his face slapping into the mud with blind indifference. The grim-faced man stood for a moment and then back-stepped, stumbling on the tread boards. As he scrambled to catch himself and stay upright, the gun fell from his hand and clattered to the thick planks with little more sound than the tap of a coin. The onlookers parted for him as if the touch of death were contagious.

He crumpled against the saloon wall then abruptly straightened one leg, which spasmed like a sleeping dog's. Blood spread across the front of his trousers, spurting in diminished arcs. Then he was still. The death scene cleared into crystalline detail as clouds of smoke melded into a common canopy and channeled away at the first opportunity of a breeze.

"God A'mighty," Coplea breathed, gawking at the still body lying in the saloon entrance. He turned to Wyatt, who stared at the dead man who lay facedown in the road. The man's hat was tipped forward, angled off the back of his head as though he were greeting someone.

Among the people gathering to the bodies, someone broke the silence with a summation so laconic as to constitute sacrilege. "Opened up his brisket, by God!"

Coplea looked away, took in several sharp breaths, and limped back into the alleyway where the horses waited. Wyatt watched him lean on the side of the building, both his arms stiff against the wall, his head sagging from his shoulders. Coplea's breath came faster now, and his body stiffened and arched forward. He backed his boots from the building just before his stomach emptied.

Wyatt turned back to the crowd in the street, where men on the outside wormed their way closer to see the body. More people hurried down the street, and those close by were yelling what they knew to those running to see for themselves. The feeling was almost festive. Then the knot of men in the street unexpectedly opened for a moment, and Wyatt saw the prostrate man's bulging gut torn open like a burst melon. Someone had opened his shirt. From the wound spilled a bright blue bubble of tissue not meant for the sun.

Wyatt walked to the sack of flour Coplea had abandoned,

heaved it to his shoulder, and carried it to his horse. He lashed the burlap tightly behind the cantle of his saddle.

"You all right?" he asked Coplea. Charlie nodded but said nothing. Wyatt checked the knots and waited for his companion to recover, but Coplea continued to stare down between his boots. "You paid already?" Wyatt asked.

Coplea nodded again and then looked at Wyatt, his eyes searching for something he did not know how to ask for. "There's more just inside the door." Wyatt started to retrieve it but turned back when Coplea called his name. The skin on Charlie's forehead was beaded with sweat. "You know . . . I done cut the meat out of every animal I ever kilt for food," he began in a whispery monotone. "But I ain't never seen nothin' like that." He spat and nodded past Wyatt toward the street. Wiping his mouth with the back of his sleeve, he shook his head. "You ever see anything like that, Wyatt?"

Wyatt turned back to the crowd and watched the postmortem antics of those left to the living. He felt strangely remote, as though he were witnessing the event before him from a private, unseen perch. He thought back to that moment when the two men had surged forward toward one another, as though making a show of their hostilities, each one to the other. Wyatt saw the flaw in it—a kind of vanity. The only show now was what this circus of a town was making of the two dead bodies. There was a more deliberate way to handle a fight, he knew, to ensure that the man handling it prudently would walk away.

The Earp campfire flickered through the wheel spokes at the periphery of the wagon ring. The train had fallen into its slumbered curfew with the spillover of bedrolls in every conceivable place. One man had draped canvas over his wagon tongue like a sloping tent, though there would be no rain. The stars spread across the prairie sky thick as the blades of grass beneath.

Wyatt sat cross-legged on a swatch of grass between two hog-sized boulders that hunched just below a rise. Behind him the horses stood still as churchgoers awaiting a pastor's word. The night air was still spring cool, and a pack of coyotes pooled their voices into a looping cacophony off to the west. The loneliness of the sound made him think of Virgil still chained to the war and unaware that his family had struck out from Iowa.

Wyatt turned to check on the stir and nicker of the horses. They parted to the sound of a low, gravelly voice, their starlit backs silver along the chine, weaving amongst themselves in liquid ripples. Nicholas chose his steps through the loose rock, his manner subdued and uncharacteristically attentive to the space around him.

When he reached Wyatt's position, he stood for a time looking over the dark rolling plain, neither of them speaking. An owl warbled from the creek bottom, and for a moment gave them a common thing on which to fix their thoughts. Nicholas sat on the lower rock.

"Coplea told me what you seen." Despite the vast landscape before them, the father's words hovered there like a third person, pressing, insistent. The world narrowed to a dark room bounded by stone, father, and son.

"Wyatt, there ain't nothing to do but accept the world the way it is and make sure you ain't at the short end."

Beneath the stars Nicholas's voice seemed less pedantic, as though conjuring up thoughts he himself had forgotten. Wyatt looked at him, but the rough silhouette of his father looked the same as it always had. He could not imagine this man on the short end of anything. Nicholas simply would not accept the humiliation.

"Wyatt, them men you seen today . . . you'll see more like 'em. Until a place gets civilized proper, anything goes with some. They'll wait till you turn around and steal your goddamn soul if they can. And they ain't gonna lose any sleep over your dead body lying in a gutter. To them . . . you're just a source of whatever it is they need. Whether it's your money or the blood-lust their drunken disappointments need to slake."

Wyatt tried to imagine himself standing in the slop of that Omaha street—the tall, bulge-gutted man stalking him, cold death in his eye. The more Wyatt's mind painted the picture, the more he felt disconnected from it. Not because it could not happen, but because he would not buy into the boiling fever of it. He would stand outside, looking in. Leveling a measure of sanity into the act where there was none elsewhere to be found. This, he understood, could tip the scales in a man's favor.

"Wyatt, look at me." The fire and brimstone was back in Nicholas's words. "If you ain't sure about a man's intentions, keep your goddamn eyes on him and be ready, you hear me? If you let a man get the best of you out here, he'll kill you. You be ready. If it comes to it—where you know he'll hurt you if he can—you kill him and to hell with everything you've been taught. The Bible ain't got the answers for every situation a man gets into."

Wyatt watched his father's face turn in profile as though he were studying the horizon for what lay ahead. Or maybe it was the past. Nicholas had always come out on top and been vocal about his methods, which had generally followed with the law . . . though not always. Supplied with pious platitudes on every subject, he nevertheless bent the rules when it was to his benefit. He had bootlegged liquor in Illinois, Virgil had once told Wyatt. Along with that trade had come the craft of barrel-making, a respected profession. There was good and bad in most every-thing, Wyatt figured. He thought no less of his father for the moonshining. It was a business venture, nothing more. No one had been hurt by it.

The wind at his back picked up and bristled the spring grass.

There was a sweet anise scent in the air from where the horses had been cropping the grasses. Wyatt scanned the plain, thinking how—with this sudden wind—now would be the time for an Indian to make a move, if only by a few inches. Nicholas seemed oblivious. Wyatt seldom saw his father contemplative like this.

When the breeze settled and the creek gargled again, the world before them seemed to open back up to its unending expanse. Wyatt wondered how much farther the land could unfold before they reached California.

"Coplea will take your place at midnight. Stay sharp, son. The damned Sioux might be beggars in the daylight, but they're a damned mite bolder at night, even this close to town."

"I'm awake," Wyatt said and touched his thumb to the hammer of the rifle in his lap. He let his eyes relax to include everything—checking for movement. There was none to see.

For a time they did not speak, and then Nicholas stood and walked back to the wagons. Wyatt swiveled and watched his father's dark hat and overcoat meld with the horses then dissolve through the picket line. There were times he could not stomach the man's arrogance, but Wyatt had seen that arrogance work in his father's favor too many times to dismiss it outright.

Wyatt rose and moved among the horses, speaking low to them with reassuring words. Then he returned to the rocks to think. Three hours till midnight. He liked having time to think about things. Nestling in, he kept his eyes and ears sharp, even as he let his mind roam back to Omaha City. He saw himself standing in the muddy street, watching the tall mustachioed man stalk him from straight ahead. And while he imagined dealing with that kind of crisis, he knew the intent of his actions would be as quietly aligned and familiar to him as the stars, fixed in their assigned places in the night sky. And he would do what he needed to do.

CHAPTER 6

*Summer, 1864: Oregon Trail—Nebraska through southern Wyoming,
across Utah and Nevada to the Santa Ana River Valley, California*
Well into Nebraska they entered the sandhills and followed the
lazy wind of the North Platte. Here the land seemed cleansed
and full of promise. Storms marched in dark columns across
the distant sky but could span the plain from one end to the
other without affecting the wagon train's immediate surround-
ings. Lightning forked and pulsated on the horizon in a silent
echo of itself, the grumble of thunder arriving sometimes half a
minute later. By the time one of these storms did wash over
them, they had watched its approach for hours. Between flash
floods, the river was wide and shallow—a mere ribbon of water.
The rolling dunes of grass seemed more of a river, boundless
and swaying as though pointing toward something better.

At Fort Laramie the Earp party was warned about hostile
activity from the Sioux, but only twice did bands of Indians
pose a threat. Each time they were a loose bunch, half-starved
and abject in their ragged animal skins. Neither encounter
amounted to much. Most of it posturing, on both sides.

On the first attempt at an attack by the Sioux, it was Wyatt
who, high on his sentinel's post, had spotted a skulking party
wending its way along a stream bed toward the horses. He fired
off the warning shot that set the camp into motion, foiling the
raid before it had begun. Still, the men of the train made much
of the confrontation and rode out to give chase. A farmer named

Chapman was shot in one of these forays, but it appeared to have been an accident, the hapless fellow felled by one of his own party in a moment of crossfire, though no one would admit to it. On the occasion of each attack, Wyatt remained with the livestock, for that was his job. Still, he remained prepared to fight. He was, in fact, heavily counted on for his hunter's reputation as a marksman. He kept his gun free of dust and grit by wrapping the receiver and lock in a strip of lightly oiled muslin. The barrels he plugged with small stoppers of cork. Each evening after supper he cleaned the weapon as a nightly ritual.

When the Rockies finally reared up like great jagged teeth from the floor of Wyoming, the migrants then had a significant landmark on which to fix their eyes. The wagons rolled on, averaging ten or twelve miles a day, but even after several days those mountains seemed no closer. Weeks went by where one day was hardly discernible from another, marked only by the steady plummet of morale under Nicholas Earp's stern manner of controlling the Iowa party.

Then, as if they had dropped their attention for too long, they realized the mountains were lifting them upward and looming over them like an abrupt challenge from God. Now the crossing became the dreaded uncertainty of which they had been warned, and the pilgrims looked to their leader like children lost in a wilderness.

Soon the terrain broke up into shelf and fissure, the land tilting ever upward. Nicholas showed no mercy to the draft animals, whipping them up and over every obstacle. As instructed, the men pushed at the rears of the wagons like doomed characters trapped in a fable that could end only in folly. If a wagon refused to go, Nicholas, still a stranger to these migrants, boldly climbed aboard to inspect its contents and threw out whatever he deemed expendable. The owners could only glare mutely at his back, their contempt for him building less on account of their losses than the peremptory swiftness of his decrees.

Nicholas, Wyatt knew, had been born for moments like this. To lead. To levy judgment. To reap scorn he cared about no more than the damned greeners foolish enough to waste their energy on such emotion. The timing was everything, and everyone who had signed on had to understand it. The mountains had to be crossed before first snow. Nicholas's pace was slow but steady, and he would not waver from it. Any complaints about the Earp captaincy were confined to diary entries or private conversations, never voiced to Nicholas's face.

Often Wyatt found himself on the receiving end of the train's silent resentment, as though he were but an extension of his father's brash ways. A scant few pitied him and went out of their way to show him extra kindness. Caring for neither treatment, he kept to himself. If he learned nothing else from this journey, it was not to confuse his own estimation of himself with anyone else's.

He had heard stories about the mountains, but none had prepared him for their raw beauty and sudden views of gaping spaces. The difficulties of travel aside, the Rockies were a world unto themselves, cool even in summer, rife with wildlife, and cloaked in regal evergreens that scented the air with a pleasing antiseptic cleanness that made him want to inhale deeply into his lungs. The roiling streams tumbling down the rocky slopes ran clear as glass, except where they pooled to green or foamed into brilliant white. Wyatt remembered his schoolteacher once talking about the gods of an ancient time living on an exclusive mountain, and now, on this pristine spine of the Rockies, he forever held a picture that served for that lesson.

By the time the train leveled out again on the flats of Utah, the Earp rule had taken its toll. Few spoke to Nicholas unless necessary. Charlie Coplea started taking his meals with the

Rousseaus. Even James broke free, declaring himself for Austin, Nevada, on the pretense that his old wound needed professional tending. Nicholas might have believed it, but the rest of the family knew that James, his store of whiskey depleted, would be seeking his medical aid from a saloon.

On the morning of his departure, James said his goodbyes to his family and then pulled his horse alongside the wagon Wyatt drove. He held out a bundle of burlap tied with brown cord.

"Thought you might need this," James said. When Wyatt took the gift and felt the heft of it in his hand, James turned his head away and held out his palm to stay Wyatt's protest. "Don't say nothin'. I got another . . . an extra I keep in my bag."

Wyatt untied the package and fingered the familiar contours of the Remington revolver James had used in the war. He had openly admired it, even asked to clean it on several occasions. A glow of pride spread from the center of his chest and coursed through him like a fever.

"There's balls and caps and a powder flask in there," James said. "Cleaning rod, too."

Wyatt nodded and set the gift aside on the plank seat. "When'll I see you again?"

James smiled and leaned on his pommel. "Can't say for sure, but the Earps always seem to come back together sometime." He coughed up a dry chuckle. "I ain't sure if it's a curse or a blessing." He winked and reined his horse away from the redundant churn of the wheel and scrape of axle. The last Wyatt saw of him was a dot on the horizon fading in the north.

Through all the discord within the train Nicholas kept his eyes stolidly on the trail west. Wyatt noted each phase of the social breakdown—marking the flaws in his father's ethic of leadership . . . as well as the flaws in the wagoners' expectations of him. But he also noted the occasional ruined wagons they passed, monuments to the failures that had come before them.

They were wooden ghosts, listing on bare axle hubs like ships run aground and stalled in a calm. But the Earps sailed on.

The arid stretch from Salt Lake took them southwest along the Mormon cutoff, across the austere flats of Nevada, and then the richly ochred Mojave, where the land was a skillet of rising heat. The fertile valley of San Bernardino provided a fitting climax to the epic journey. Reaching it in mid-December, the Earps hastily shed themselves of their fellow nomads and began scraping out their new start on the headwaters of the Santa Ana River.

Without a hard freeze in the sheltered valleys of southern California, Wyatt found himself quickly returned to the plow in an abandoned orchard field that had never known the farmer's passion to furrow. He deemed it his duty to settle the family into their new homestead. It would be a final gesture of obedience to maintain the appearance of familial ties—something he did mostly for his mother's sake. As usual, he took to the task with quiet dedication, his hands regaining their rough crust of callus as his heart hardened to his father's rule.

CHAPTER 7

Winter, 1865: San Bernardino, California

On the afternoon of New Year's Eve, the Earps took their wagon into San Bernardino to join in the holiday celebrations planned by the locals. The occasion drew people from miles around to mingle on the esplanade. The music was festive, Mexican tequila in abundance, and betting on horse races fast and loose.

Nicholas pretended to be pulled into the wagering against his will, but Wyatt knew gambling to be the reason they had made the trip into town. He watched with interest as his father shouldered his way closer to the race entries to assess their attributes. Each time Nicholas laid down a coin on the barrelhead, he pointed to the very steed Wyatt had favored by private appraisal. Despite the gulf widening between father and son, Wyatt was often reminded of their commonalities.

In the plaza the anticipation of the race bets escalated to a near frenzy, each man declaring his horse a winner through the euphoric prophecies of tequila. A tittering audience of colorfully dressed *senoritas* only fueled the male performances. The mayor and several other village officials managed to bring a semblance of order to the drunken chaos, and finally all bets for the first race were declared closed. At the mayor's signal the small band of guitars and trumpets fell silent. Then the crowd quieted. All eyes were on the two racers lined up at the starting mark.

A swarthy man in a purple vest with gold embroidery called out the starter's cadence in Spanish, and a gun popped above the heads of the onlookers. The cheering broke out of a sudden and propelled the two riders and their mounts out of the semi-circle of audience like a wave pushing them forward. It was a short sprint the length of the plaza, around a stone well-house and back. Even before the horses could be reined in, the winners converged on the bet-takers like starved beasts claiming their share of a downed prey.

"Wyatt, git over here and set with us a spell." Charlie Coplea stood awkwardly in a brown suit, white shirt, and red silk tie. His dull brown hair was oiled and combed close to the skull—a futile effort to iron flat the curls that forever twined around his simple face. He walked his hat brim through his fingers as he held the hat flat against the front of his coat. He shifted uneasily from his good leg to the other, like a man testing his weight on ice.

"Damn, Charlie," Wyatt said, examining Coplea's clothes. "You running for mayor?"

Charlie's face flushed, and his gaze lowered to the ground. "Want you to meet somebody, Wyatt." He gestured behind him, and Wyatt followed his gaze. Amid the crowd dining under the cantina *ramada,* a slender Mexican woman sat alone at a table looking back at them. Her coal-black eyes stared at Wyatt with a confidence that belied her small stature. "I done told her who you are. How we crossed the divide together and all. Come on, I'm good for a drink."

Coplea waved Wyatt to follow and then limped a weaving route through the tables. Wyatt stood for a moment, considering the invitation. Coplea had not spoken to any of the Earps since Nicholas had cursed him as a "deadweight biscuit eater" in front of the other pilgrims. Wyatt ran his fingers through his hair, re-fitted his hat, and pushed through the crowd toward the table.

The woman was not a woman, but a girl in women's clothes

and women's jewelry on her fingers. A golden luminescence lifted off her dark skin—warm and sweet as fresh-churned butter. Her face was severe, with hard shadows in the hollows beneath her cheekbones, but softened by the fullness of her eyes. Her hair, black as ink, fell behind her in a train that reached below the seat of her chair. Though she looked down at the cup set before her, Wyatt felt her attention on him, as though she were peering at him through some clever arrangement of mirrors. When her eyes came up, they surprised him with their effortless utility—like precision tools meant to pry into his mind and expose his private thoughts.

"Wyatt, this here is Valenzuela Cos." Coplea looked at the girl and shrugged awkwardly at the obligation of introductions. "This here is Wyatt." Charlie waved his hat toward a chair, and they both sat.

The girl looked out at a race taking shape in the plaza, but her eyes showed no interest. As she raised her cup to her mouth, she turned those dark eyes on Wyatt again, a faint smile lifting the corners of her mouth. The smile disappeared behind the cup's rim as she drank. Against the pockmarked ceramic vessel her fingers were long and silk-smooth. She set the cup back on the table and returned her attention to the plaza.

"Helluva country, ain't it, Wyatt?" Charlie babbled.

Wyatt nodded to Coplea, who turned his hat by increments on the tabletop, careful to keep it away from his beer glass and the unlit candle glued upright in its own wax atop a flat stone.

"Cómprale un trago a tu amigo, Char-dree."

Charlie's head came up, and he stared at the girl, his eyebrows pinched together. Smiling, she glanced at his beer mug.

"Oh . . . yeah . . . sure . . . how 'bout a drink, Wyatt?"

Wyatt nodded to the girl's cup. "What's she having?"

Coplea made a face and tentatively leaned toward the girl's cup. "Some kind o' tea, I think."

"I'll have some o' that."

Wyatt dug into his trouser pocket for the few coins he had brought, but even as he sorted through them in his palm, the girl reached across to his hand and closed his fingers with her own.

"Eres nuestro invitado." Her voice was a smooth purr that became a texture moving across his skin.

He looked at her arm stretched across the table and thought of the grace and muscle of a catamount. Her grip was firm, yet it was a woman's grip—its strength coming not from the tautness of tendon but from the certainty of its intent. She seemed older than her years, as though the events of her past would tell a story about hardships most men would not know.

He was half sure she was a whore, but then again Wyatt recognized in her the very thing that he prized in himself: this girl was clinging to a resolve to take hold of a better life. He wagered she would find it, too. Women with that kind of beauty usually did. She released his hand and looked at Coplea, who rose instantly and looked around, leaving his hat on the table.

"I'll go find us a waiter," he mumbled as he wandered into the crowd.

Not wishing to embarrass himself with his child's grasp of her language, Wyatt sat back and focused on the music of the *mariachis.* The lively notes washed between them like a border river breaking over shoals while the two of them sat on opposite banks, and he dared not yell above the rapids. With such a clear gulf between them, he should have felt safe and content, but somehow he didn't. Stirring inside him was an uneasiness about their aloneness within the crowd. When he glanced at her, she was smiling as though privy to his thoughts.

"Me dijeron que manejaste los vagones a través de las montañas."

Wyatt offered up a smile of surrender and shook his head.

"¿No?" she said.

"No *Español.*" He dipped his head and raised a hand palm up from the table.

"I have heard that d'jou led the wagons here to California." Her use of his language was startling and musical, the words coming effortlessly from the delicate curves of her lips. Wyatt studied her face as if seeing her for the first time.

"You speak Amer'can."

"If I have to," she said and smiled a smile that did not include her eyes.

Wyatt nodded to the empty chair. "Charlie know that?"

The smile widened, but she sat comfortably and said nothing. Wyatt thought about that for a time and then remembered her question.

"It was my father who was wagon master."

"But d'jou are the oldest son?"

"That's right . . . for a while anyway."

She nodded and looked away, pleased about some point he had apparently missed. The gun in the plaza went off again, and the thunder of hooves was drowned out by cheering.

"*Los norteamericanos,*" she said, looking at the bettors, "they love their money."

Wyatt turned and hooked an arm over the back of his chair. It was a crude piece of furniture made of rough juniper dowels still covered with the shredding bark.

"Seems to be a lot of your kind out there, too."

Her smile turned crooked, and her eyebrows lowered. "My kind?"

He saw the error in his choice of word. He doubted there was another person in the village like her. Hers was the kind of face a man remembered in the middle of a night. She seemed as complete and autonomous as an animal running wild in its native land.

"Don't Mexicans like to make some money when they can?"

She dipped her head. "I think they like to lose it more." Wyatt waited for her to explain, but she just settled her dark gaze on him, as she drank from her cup. Lowering the cup she turned her head to face him directly. "Do d'jou like to gamble?"

"I might," he said, "if I had the money for it."

She reached toward him for the second time and opened his fingers. Her fingernails raked across the calluses of his palm with a dry scraping sound. When she lifted her cup again with both hands, Wyatt realized that Coplea was standing across from them.

"She read my fortune, too, Wyatt. Hope yours looks better'n mine. Valenzuela says I'm not to git rich in this lifetime."

Wyatt felt the girl's stare on the side of his face. The tickle in his hand lingered, causing him to close his fingers into a fist. Just then a cup of amber water appeared before him.

"I already paid for it, Wyatt," Charlie assured him.

Wyatt looked up at a smiling Mexican waiter and nodded. Picking up the lukewarm tea he sipped. It tasted like water that had collected in an old boot. Keeping his face expressionless he set down the cup. When the girl smiled at him, he tried again and took it in three swallows to be done with it.

"I reckon I'll be going," Wyatt said, standing. "I'm obliged for the drink, Charlie." He did not look at the girl until he had pushed his chair to the table. "*Señorita.*"

"*Valenzuela,*" she corrected, holding his look with hers. "*Ha sido un placer.*"

Wyatt looked at Coplea, who smiled and shrugged. "I got no idea, Wyatt." Wyatt nodded and walked to the plaza, feeling the girl's stare on his back as he entered the crowd.

The shadows of the buildings had pooled across the esplanade, and men stacked tree limbs and broken crates into piles on the hardpan of the street. Soon two open bonfires blazed, and the band broke into a lively fandango. The space between the fires became a stage for those bold enough to initiate the dancing. All the women dancers were Mexican, but their partners were a mixed bag. Wyatt recognized one, an Anglo freight hauler who drove a route past their land on the way to Yuma. So drunk already that the rhythm of the music eluded him, he nonetheless lifted sluggish boots in a pitiful attempt to match the cursive spins of the dark-haired *señorita* orbiting wildly around him. When at last he tripped and collapsed into a heap, she simply laughed and kept flashing her skirt, turning with the music. It was like a celebration, the solo performance establishing the completeness of a female in the matter of dance, where a man was tolerated but unnecessary.

Nicholas stood on the far side of the dance arena, his hands in his overcoat pockets. He stared numbly at the dancers as though he were observing unfamiliar creatures swimming beneath the surface of water. Wyatt's mother bent behind him, talking to Warren and Adelia. Morg stood a little to one side flipping a length of rope he had picked up somewhere.

Just then Wyatt felt a hand slip through the crook of his arm. Tensing as the slender arm wrapped into his and clung as tightly as a vine, he turned his head and was startled to see the Mexican girl's black eyes so close. A sweet scent rose from her— something he had not noticed earlier—like the wild fragrance of a pungent root. Wyatt scanned the faces around him, looking for Coplea, but the man was nowhere to be seen.

"Stay and see the fireworks with me," Valenzuela said, her directness now both facile and commanding.

Wyatt nodded toward the tangle of fire-lit dancers where his mother and father stood. "Reckon I'll be heading home soon. I came with my family." When she said nothing, Wyatt kept look-ing at her, studying the quiet confidence in her eyes. "What about Charlie?"

She tilted a flat hand over and back in a slow flutter, her gaze fixed on his eyes. "Char-dree *es* . . . Char-dree."

Wyatt turned back to the dancers and laughed to himself. "He ask you to marry him yet?"

"Of *course*. All men ask me that."

Wyatt turned to appraise her expression. "I ain't."

Valenzuela Cos pursed her lips into a coy smile. "Not yet."

He waited to see if she would let the smile spread over her face. She did, though not the way he had expected.

"Besides, I doubt I'm good marryin' material," he said. "I don't aim to stay around here for too long."

"Nor do I," she replied.

Two men brought fresh bundles of sticks and tossed them on the fires. When the flames leaped skyward, Wyatt felt the heat press upon his face. The intense light brightened the adobe walls bordering the plaza while prematurely darkening the twilight sky. The girl held to his arm so tightly, he could feel his pulse throb against her fingers like a telegraph he could not shut off.

"I asked Char-dree to invite d'jou to our table."

"I figured it wasn't Charlie wantin' to have tea with me." He watched her confident eyes study his face. It was like being stroked with a soft pelt of fur.

"D'jou have strong lines in your face," she said offhandedly and touched the angle of his jaw. "What do d'jou call that color of hair?"

Wyatt frowned at her question. "I don't know. Sort o' yellow, I reckon." He tried to picture the lightness of his hair next to the black ink of hers. Her darkness was like an energy escaping the boundaries of her body—some primordial ingredient of character possibly unknown to men.

"Are d'jou afraid of me?"

A whispery laugh issued from his nose. "I prob'ly oughta be." He breathed in deeply and exhaled. "Truth is . . . I ain't real sure what I think about you."

"D'jou've never been with a girl?"

He knew what she meant, but he tried to conjure up an answer that might sidestep the query, as if he had misunderstood her meaning. Nothing came to mind.

"*Should* I be afraid of you?" he said and stared into the dark wells of her eyes.

When she neither answered nor looked away, he understood for the first time that there were some women it might be impossible to lie to. It was this kind of woman, he guessed, whom men most feared . . . and desired.

"Tell d'jour family d'jou are staying for the fireworks," she whispered.

They lay wrapped in a coarse blanket on a rise among the barren limbs of a peach orchard. The shower of exploding rockets from the celebration now over, the sky was dazzling, reduced now to its natural ink, pierced with pinpricks of light in infinite number. Wyatt looked at the stars and breathed in the scent of Valenzuela Cos's hair. He liked the strong texture of it. Like horsehair. And the warmth of her body. It enfolded him in an almost maternal way now, as though she were protecting him from his own thoughts.

She had been his guide, moving in ever-confident gyrations that spoke of her experience. And his lack of it. Yet there was no embarrassment. She saw to that. She moved her skillful hands about his body and helped him with gentle cues that made him feel a part of decisions she had already made. Then, with a fierce start, she had tightened her legs and raised her face to the sky, her mouth formed into a rictus, a sound squeezing from deep in her throat. Her desperate breathing had locked in place, and she shuddered the length of her spine, sitting over him like a will o' the wisp riding bareback in the night air. He had spent himself half a minute before, and she seemed almost to expect it, yet it did not deter her from the place she was going. It had been an otherworldly escape he would have liked to make with her. Which, like everything else, she seemed to know, too.

She leaned forward, bringing her mouth close to his ear. "Next time," she whispered, "we will go there together."

It was the last thing she said before curling against his side and falling asleep. Wyatt, though, did not know how to sleep with such a person lying next to him. Least of all one so beautiful. He stroked her, unable to get enough of the smoothness of her skin, the curve above her hip, the firm mound of her buttocks. He turned his head toward an amber glow in the east. The moon was in its fourth quarter, rising late. When it showed, it was the color of a dirty gold coin held up to a candle flame. As it rose, its color deepened to ochre and then orange.

"*La luna de adobe,*" she murmured and rose up on an elbow, exposing her young breasts to the cool night air. He watched her tuck the blanket around her . . . and then him.

"What?"

"We call that 'the adobe moon.' "

Wyatt frowned and turned to study it. "Why do you call it that?"

"The color, I think." She looked back at the richly hued crescent ascending from the far end of the earth. "It is the moon of our people. Other people say the moon is made of gold or diamonds or wishes or this and that. Ours? It is made of what is available to us. Like our homes. We make our homes with mud. It is what we have."

"You don't have any wishes?"

"We all have wishes. But in the end, we must settle for what we have."

They watched the skewed sliver of rust light hover among the stars like a horseshoe hooked over a nail. Behind them, somewhere distant, two coyotes howled and yipped for a time, connecting to one another in the night. The gaping hole of the universe swallowed up the sounds, making this California valley seem small and inconsequential. And the two of them all the more so.

"I want a sight more than a house of mud," Wyatt said. "And I aim to get it."

"Maybe."

He turned around to look at her, his back to the moon now. "I reckon I will."

"And if not, you will settle for what you have," she said, her voice flat with pragmatism. She took in air and let her breath escape as a sigh. "The adobe moon is better than no moon at all."

He had nothing to say about that. Lying back, he propped his head on the pillow of his arm. He could not see the desolation of this land as she did. Only its inventory of opportunity. He had felt it on the wagon trail, the burgeoning movement of bettering himself, swept up in the current of enterprise. For him this layover at San Bernardino was just a temporary stall. There was too much out there waiting. Wyatt watched Valenzuela's face as she came to terms with a moon that somehow held sway over her. He cleared his throat, trying for some pragmatism in his voice.

"I ain't got much money with me. What should I be paying you for tonight?"

Valenzuela Cos gave no answer, save with her hand, which now roved boldly over his body. He felt his manhood stir again, and the reprise of their lovemaking was somehow even sweeter now that he knew more of its secrets.

This time as she rode him, the sickle moon hovered white next to her face like a piece of jewelry granted her by the heavens for this one occasion. Together they entered that netherworld of pleasure, each feeling the desert around them retreat to the fringes of their circle of passion. When she arched her body and shuddered, Wyatt looked up at her face. Her eyes filled with tears, and the moonlight touched the wetness of her uplifted face, transforming it into streaks of quicksilver.

CHAPTER 8

Spring, 1866: Earp farm, Santa Ana Valley, California; coach line from San Pedro to Los Angeles; freight-hauling from San Bernardino to Prescott, Arizona Territory

Wyatt had come out to the barn early to put an edge to the scythe. With that job done, he hung the lantern from a nail and unwrapped the Remington revolver James had passed down to him. Later, after Old Nick had left for town, he planned to engage in some target practice, but for now, with the chambers empty, he stuffed the barrel into his waistband and ran through the repetition of jerking the gun, cocking, and holding steady on a feed sack propped against the workbench.

When he heard a trotting horse slow to a walk outside, he stopped in mid-draw, straightened, and quieted his breathing. Someone dismounted and walked the horse to the barn. When a man's silhouette darkened the doorway, Wyatt lowered the gun to hang by his knee.

"Well, goddamn," the man said, "look at you."

Wyatt slipped the gun back into place against his belly, his eyes never leaving the man's outline against the morning light. He was more than half sure it was Virgil by the way the man held his head erect—a hint of pride to the jut of his chin—but there was a thickness of hair and body that Wyatt did not recognize. Only when Virgil let go with the rough laugh that scraped up from his chest—like a man starting to cough—could there be no doubt.

They approached one another and stood close enough that Wyatt could smell the sweat and woodsmoke from his brother's clothes. Eye to eye they were the same height, the same span of shoulders, their hair the same tawny gold, and for all the distance the war had put between them, each felt this mirrored effect. They clasped hands stiffly, letting muscle convey their fraternal affection. With Virgil's arrival, Wyatt felt the integration of his family settle into a solid unit—like snapping the breech shut after loading his over-and-under.

"You're all right?" Wyatt asked, stepping back to arm's length.

"Never got hit once, thank God."

"You seen Pa?"

"Nobody but you so far." Virgil looked out the door and breathed in and out deeply through his nose. "How's the climate for prodigal sons?"

"Ma'll be glad to see you." Virgil's blond hair was touched with copper-red, sun streaked the same way Wyatt's hair colored in summer. "You here to stay?"

"Hell, no. I'm here to see you . . . see my brothers." Virge looked around the barn at the orderly arrangement of tack and tools. The harnesses were soaped and gleaming in the lantern light. Each stall was properly shoveled and hayed. "Still slavin'?"

Wyatt looked away from the question; now that he had quit schooling, he worked full days. "I figure I owe it . . . for a time anyway."

"I'm working for Banning," Virgil announced. "Stage line b'tween here and Los Angeles. And sometimes down to Prescott." Virgil saw the change in Wyatt's eyes. "Might could help get you started as a swamper with Banning."

Wyatt turned to the nearest horse and looked into the big dark eyes that stared back at him. "I've been thinkin' on something like that."

Virgil laughed. "You'd be good at wrangling. I never knew a

cannier judge of horseflesh. Banning says knowin' your horses gives a man the advantage of never expecting more from an animal than what it's capable of giving." Virgil raised his chin at Wyatt. "Hell, that's you all over."

The two brothers studied the row of equine muzzles hooked over the stall gates—two percherons, two draft Morgans, a bay gelding, a chestnut mare, and the Thoroughbred—giving them time until the awkwardness of Virgil's compliment passed.

"Still racing the Thoroughbred?" Virgil asked.

Wyatt crossed his arms over his chest and shook his head. "Locals won't bet ag'in' 'im anymore." He stepped close to the racer, and it stretched to blow a pool of warm air on Wyatt's neck. "Lonely at the top, ain't it, Salem?" He spoke to the horse no differently than to Virgil.

With the flat of his hand Virgil slapped the dust off his trousers. "What about Morgan and Warren. They ain't big as you, are they?"

"Morg's getting close."

Virgil let his gaze rove over the barn again. "Might be it's their turn here, Wyatt."

Wyatt moved back to the door and stared toward the house. With the growing dawn, the kitchen lamp was now snuffed. Morg and Warren would be finishing up with breakfast, and their mother would be packing ham and biscuit lunches for their day at school. The door to the house opened, and Nicholas stepped out, stopped on the porch, and directed his attention to Virgil's horse tethered outside the barn. He stuck his pipe into his mouth and puffed aggressively, the smoke seeming to take the shape of his clouded thoughts.

Wyatt nodded to the porch, and Virgil turned to look out the door. Unseen, they observed their father's proud posture, stiff and unrelenting like a soldier on sentry duty.

"Want me to check with Banning?" Virgil said, his voice quiet and contained.

"Yeah," said Wyatt, "check with 'im."

When Virgil stepped out the door to let himself be seen, Nicholas stood his ground, staring at his son through the tobacco smoke he generated.

Virgil made a little snort through his nose. "Well . . ." he said to no one in particular and cleared his throat. He walked from the barn in a direct line to the house.

Wyatt watched his brother's back, the ease of his carriage. He had been to war, and it showed in his stride, in the glide of his shoulders. Virgil said nothing as he climbed the steps to gain the same level as the old man. Only Nicholas's head turned to track his newly returned son, the rest of him remaining anchored in place, his bearing imperial. Seeing how his brother stood several inches taller than Nicholas, Wyatt realized for the first time that he himself must tower over his father in a like manner.

When Virgil spoke and held out his hand, Nicholas hesitated for only a moment then turned to face his son squarely. He said something Wyatt could not hear and took Virgil's hand, and they both went inside. Wyatt blew out the lantern and walked to the house. As he crossed the yard, he felt a little taller than he had at dawn, walking to the barn. But more than that, he felt his steps infused with a new purpose. And a new direction.

After two months with the Banning company—loading and unloading luggage, shoveling horse manure, hauling grain from the feed bins to the holding corrals, greasing axles, and repairing everything on the coaches that had vibrated loose or broken—Wyatt worked his way to the better matched responsibilities of wrangler. Once among the horses, his easy manner of controlling the more temperamental animals quickly marked his worth among the other hands.

Banning, a robust fellow with a strong moral code that he openly shared with all employees, grew to like Wyatt, not only for his work with the horses, but also for his quiet manner among men. Despite grumblings from the veteran drivers, the stage line owner gave Wyatt his first experience at handling a coach on the run from the San Pedro harbor into Los Angeles proper and back. Banning gloated in his unprecedented decision to hire a eighteen-year-old driver, for Wyatt never lamed a horse, upset a passenger, or lost luggage . . . not even a single piece of mail. Furthermore, he never failed to meet his schedule.

But there was better money in the freight lines, and so the two Earp brothers signed on with the Taylor Company, which made regular runs to Salt Lake City and Prescott. Due to his age, Wyatt again stepped onto the low rung of business, while Virgil picked right up driving behind a triple brace of horses. Just as he had at Banning's, however, Wyatt was soon graduated from the menial work of loading crates up to the position of driver.

On the occasion of his first route, Wyatt, following Virgil's wagon out of San Berdoo, whistled a signal and pulled up at a lone ranch at the east end of San Timoteo Canyon. By the time Virgil had pulled his team over and stepped down to the road, Wyatt had thrown a lead rope over the neck of a stout dun mare and was walking it from the traces, watching the rear hooves as he stepped backward to assess a subtle limp.

"What is it?" Virgil asked, unable to keep his big-brother irritation out of his voice.

"This'n'll never make it to Prescott," Wyatt stated simply. "Fetlock's flared up. She ain't lame yet, but . . ."

Frowning at the horse, Virgil was unable to detect which leg showed an injury. "Well, how bad is it? Why don't you switch off with your spare?"

Seeming not to listen, Wyatt studied a ranch house beyond a

row of peach trees.

"What are you aimin' to do?" Virgil said, holding the annoyance in his voice.

"See if I can trade off."

Now Virgil turned his frown on the house. "This here's the Clanton place. Word is, they're runnin' stolen livestock through here. Hell, Taylor thinks they got a few with *his* brand on 'em, but he can't get the sheriff to come out here on a hunch. Taylor's lost three good draft horses in the last month."

Wyatt looked deeply into Virgil's eyes. "That right?" He coiled the lead rope as he continued to size up the ranch. "Then let's go see if we can get one back."

When Wyatt turned and started toward the house, Virgil hurried up alongside his brother. "I ain't sure Taylor's gonna like this."

"He'll like it less if we pull into Prescott a day late and a horse short," Wyatt said, pulling the mare over to the ditch by the Clantons' gate. He knelt, sank his hand in a small pool of water, and churned the mud with his fingers. Cupping a fistful of soft, brown mud, he moved to the mare's rump and ground the clay mixture into the *T* branded there, spreading the smear as though the animal had lain down and rolled in a small wallow.

"What the hell're you doin'?" Virgil asked.

Wyatt kept working the edges of the mud stain. "Gettin' this'n ready for the auction block."

They had not walked half the distance up the entrance road before two riders came out to meet them. The one leading came on hard, kicking his boot heels into his horse's ribs. He appeared to be about Wyatt's age, curly-haired and short, with beady eyes that jumped back and forth between the Earp brothers. The other one—clearly a brother to the nervous one—was closer to Virgil's age and seemed to maintain a perpetual dense expression of mild surprise.

"You boys're trespassin'," the younger one barked. "This here's Clanton land." He straightened in his saddle, punching his chest with his thumb. "And I'm a Clanton."

Wyatt ignored the rancher's ill-mannered introduction and swept a hand toward the mare. "Might'a found one o' your horses," Wyatt said, hitching his head back toward the freight teams. "Out on the road yonder."

Checking the surprise on his face, Virgil could not help glancing at Wyatt. He stepped forward and offered his hand to the older Clanton.

"Virgil Earp," he said. "Me and my brother are makin' a freight run to Prescott."

The younger Clanton squinted at the two rigs stalled on the canyon road. When he looked back at Wyatt, the skin around his eyes tightened, making a fan of lines across each temple.

"I'm Phin," the older Clanton said, reaching across his horse's neck. He shook Virgil's hand. "This here's Ike." Phin's face wrinkled as he appraised the mare. "I don't think that—"

"Might be ours," Ike interrupted, pretending to study the horse's markings. His quick eyes angled away from the smear of mud on the horse's rump. "Think I remember that white blaze around the eye."

Phin now stared stupidly at the horse. "Guess we could ask Pa," he offered.

Ike turned quickly to scowl at his brother. "I can handle this, aw right?"

Wyatt tossed the coil of lead rope to Ike. "Can you boys sell me a horse? Something stout enough to harness to my rig? I don't like crossin' the Mohave without a spare."

Ike looked suspiciously from Wyatt to Virgil and back. "Yeah, we can prob'ly do that." He turned in his saddle, stiffening one arm on the cantle. He nodded toward the outbuildings. "Come back there to that holding pen beside the barn. I'll bring up a mount and then we can talk some business."

With the Taylor horse in tow, Ike and Phin rode to the pen and dismounted at the gate, but when Wyatt came abreast of them, he kept walking past the holding pen to a larger corral that extended across the grassed floodplain of the creek running through the bottom of the canyon. Two dozen horses were spread out over the pasture, each looking well fed and fit for work. When Virgil came up beside him, Wyatt kept his eyes on a knot of horses idling in the shallow water.

"Look at that big sorrel gelding," Wyatt said quietly and nodded toward the creek. "That look like a Taylor brand to you, Virge?"

Virgil narrowed his eyes. "Been altered, but . . . hell, yes, that's the big *T,* all right."

Wyatt climbed the fence and started across the meadow.

"Now, wait a minute!" Ike yelled. "Those out there ain't for sale."

Wyatt kept walking. At the creek he studied the brand, stepped slowly into the water and began talking to the sorrel until he was able to stroke its neck. Then, in an instant, he took a fistful of mane, threw a leg up over the spine, and brought the gelding on at a comfortable gallop. The two Clanton boys dismounted and stood flat-footed at the fence. Neither wore sidearms, but from each of their saddles the stock of a Winchester carbine jutted from a leather scabbard.

Virgil opened the gate, and Wyatt rode the new mount out of the corral, coaxing it to a stop before the Clantons. "Looks like you boys found one o' ours. Seems a fair trade, don't it?"

Ike tried for a laugh, but he was unconvincing. "*S* over *T.* That's our San Timoteo brand."

Not bothering to check the mark again, Wyatt just shook his head. "Somebody's burned over the *T,* that's all. We're obliged to you for holdin' on to 'im."

When Wyatt offered his arm, Virgil clasped it and swung up onto the sorrel's haunches, and together the Earps started down the dirt track to the road where their wagons and teams waited.

Out of earshot, Virgil glanced back to see the Clanton brothers in a heated argument. "Well, at least they're too busy fussin' at each other to wanna shoot us. But I wish you'd let me know when I ought'a bring my artillery along. I felt naked as a jaybird back there. We're damned lucky Old Man Clanton didn't greet us at the gate with a scattergun."

When they reached the road, Virgil walked straight to his rig and strapped on his cartridge belt and holster and unlimbered the company shotgun from under the driver's box. Wyatt harnessed up the new off-wheeler, all the while keeping the Clantons' gate in sight. His shotgun was propped within reach on the sidewall.

"Where's your pistol?" Virgil asked.

Wyatt clipped in the trace-chains and straightened, looking over the sorrel toward the Clanton Ranch. "Right here." He patted the small bulge beneath his shirt at his waistband.

"You had that all along?" Virgil said, his voice working up some anger.

"Better to have it than not," Wyatt said.

Virgil stared at his brother for a time, shook his head, and marched off for his wagon.

In Prescott, at the Red Desert Saloon, Virgil and three seasoned drivers pressed Wyatt into the mandatory celebration that marked his crossover into what freight-haulers called "independent captain of the horse's ass." Ushering his younger brother to the bar, Virgil stood drinks for everyone and explained to Wyatt that by tradition, he must down every drink bought for him. Before an hour passed, Virgil and a big Texas muleskinner carried Wyatt to a cot in a back room of the saloon, where he lay sick when he wasn't groping for the back door to heave up his gut. Finally, when the stomach cramps would not let him rise, he made use of a chamber pot he found under the bed.

In the morning when Virgil came to fetch him for the return haul to San Berdoo, Wyatt's face was the gray-green of tree lichen. "I don't think I can sit up," Wyatt mumbled, "never mind drive a team." He squeezed his eyes shut to the open curtain his brother had flung aside.

Crinkling his eyes, Virgil laughed and shook his head—goddamned man of the world that he was. "Best thing to do is have another drink right now," Virge counseled.

Wyatt opened his eyes and slowly raised his head to a notion that would have been laughable did he not feel so sick. Virgil gave him a helpless shrug.

"I ain't joshing you. Keep you from comin' out of the drunk too fast."

"I can't come out of this drunk too fast to suit me."

Virgil coughed up his deep rumbling laugh. "You'll grow to it."

"I ain't sure I want to."

"Hell," Virgil chuckled, "every man's gotta learn how to drink."

Wyatt laid his forearm over his eyes and sank deeper into his misery. "I can't see that it ever does a man no good to surrender his good senses."

Having no reply to that, Virgil left the room. He was back in a few minutes with a shot of whiskey and a tall glass of lukewarm beer. He set both on a table by the cot and turned to look out the window, giving his brother some margin of space for dignity. Something stirred on the floor in the corner of the room, and Wyatt tried to focus on a man getting to his feet.

"Who the hell is that?" Wyatt said.

"Helped carry your drunk ass in here," the man snarled, answering for himself. Then he laughed. "You California boys don't appear to hold your liquor any too well. I figured you to puke your life away last night."

"Big George, here, is from Texas," Virgil explained. "Runs the route from El Paso."

Ignoring the man's insults, Wyatt swung his legs to the floor too fast, and the nausea erupted from his gut like boiling soup. He grabbed for the pot that reeked of the night's vomitus and managed to spew most of the burning fluid where it belonged. Virgil could not help turning to witness the whiskey demon's hold on a brother who took such pride in self-control.

"You look like hell," Virgil said, a rare tenderness in his voice.

"Smell like it, too," said George.

"I oughta look like hell," Wyatt groaned. "Figure I spent the night there." He frowned at the unlikely remedy on the table. "You sure about this?"

"It's the common cure. Just drink it and let's get going." Virgil stared at Wyatt's misery for a time, opened his mouth to speak, but then closed it. "I'll be outside," Virge said. "I already harnessed your team."

The disheveled Texan poured water into a basin, bent, and scrubbed his whiskered face. He dried with a dirty towel and peered into the wavy mirror wired to the wall. Under his eye a gray scar caught the morning light. It lay flattened like a leech attached to his skin.

"You boys should come over to Texas some time," he said. "We'll teach you how to drink." George snorted, tossed the towel on the washstand, and walked out.

Wyatt stared at the whiskey again and shook his head. He tested his legs by crossing to the washbasin. Staring at the grim image in the mirror, he saw that his shirt was stained and clotted with the putrid rejections from his stomach. There was no water left in the pitcher. Peeling off the shirt, he submerged it in the basin that the Texan had used. After wringing out the material, he repeated the process. When he had cleaned himself and wormed his way back into the wet shirt, he considered walking outside and bracing up for the job waiting for him, but nausea turned again in his gut. He sat down on the bed and, after thinking about it for a long minute, downed the whiskey in two forced gulps. This he chased with half the beer before he was convinced he had made a mistake.

Virgil lifted him up onto his wagon and patted his knee for encouragement but got no response. When Wyatt took up the reins, his arms trembled. He was weak and dizzy, his hands as colorless as the underbelly of a fish.

"You gonna make it?" Virgil asked. Wyatt looked at his brother but said nothing. Big George from El Paso was perched on his wagon seat, practicing his gloating grin.

"Hey, California boy!" he laughed, snapping his reins. "Come over to Texas, and I'll buy you a round!" Wyatt watched the Texan's heavy wagon trundle east down the road.

"Don't let him bother you," Virgil called out from his wagon. "Hell, he's always got a burr up his ass."

Any hope Wyatt held out for pushing through his misery was lost in the first leg of the trip. Every mile of jostling on the plank seat plunged him deeper into his suffering. For two days the driver's box seemed but the anteroom to death itself. He put nothing but coffee into his stomach.

Not until the third day did Virgil dare approach his brother for a talk. Wyatt was working his way around his team, checking each horse's hooves. Virgil moved quietly past him to the creek, knelt, and dipped his canteen below the surface. The silence between them was something new, but Wyatt seemed in no mood to repair the rift. Virgil rose and slowly screwed down the cap as he watched Wyatt reach up to stow his farrier's rasp in the toolbox. Still working on the fit of the canteen cap, Virgil ambled over.

"Every man's got to have his first drunk, Wyatt. Thank God we only got to do it once."

Virgil waited for a reply as his brother walked around his wagon checking the lashing. When Wyatt had made the full circuit he fixed Virgil with a solemn stare.

"Any man who would repeat that experience by his own will is a damned fool."

Virgil started to speak but thought better of it. Wyatt picked up the grease bucket and rounded the wagon again as he dabbed the swab at the wheel hubs.

"If there's any more freighter traditions I ain't yet met, you can take 'em for me." Wyatt handed the bucket to his brother, but Virge seemed not to notice.

"Well . . ." Virgil muttered, but he said no more. He gave Wyatt a gentle slap on his upper arm and moved back toward his wagon. Wyatt walked to his team and checked the bits.

There was something to be gained from every experience, Wyatt knew, and if a man did not take clear notice of it, he was walking blind along the lip of a ravine where he ought not to be. He climbed up to the driver's seat to wait their departure and took this time to catalogue the lessons that had come his way in the last few days. First, no man's solemn word was without its liabilities. Not even Virgil's. A man didn't carry his own instincts for nothing. If he didn't abide by the private set of rules God gave him, he might as well be living someone else's life.

And last, though Wyatt did not yet know in what business he would seek his fortune, it would most likely be through transactions with other businessmen. For such dealings, a man needed to be sharp enough to hold the upper hand. The sobriety he now intended to swear by would certainly afford him that. It only made good sense.

CHAPTER 9

Spring, 1867: Freight runs from San Bernardino to Salt Lake City and Prescott; then to Julesburg, Colorado, to supply the railroad grading crews in southern Wyoming

Wyatt settled into the freighter's life, covering the routes to Salt Lake City and Prescott, until, due to his age, he was occasionally forced to yield the driver's box to an older employee. He sat in to take the reins only when one of the men was sick or incapacitated, which happened not enough for his liking.

Hearing about an opening for a driver in another company, he hired on with Charles Crisman, but within weeks Crisman negotiated a grading contract, leveling the way west for the Union Pacific Railroad as the rail crews laid down track into southern Wyoming.

Relocating to Julesburg, Colorado, Crisman offered considerably higher wages to select members of his old freighting crew— Wyatt among them. Increased pay, no matter how it came, had to be considered a sign of progress. "Go where the money is"— that had always been his father's credo. And beyond the financial improvement, there was also the satisfaction of moving around, seeing new places. He liked not knowing what was ahead. Not knowing made room for the possibility of striking it big in some unforeseen venture. Keeping his options open and circulating, he decided, was the best way to encounter opportunity.

The railroad camp was filled with a rough lot, and though the backbone of the grading crew was a stout team of Belgian draft horses, still the daily labor was exhausting. Wyatt drew from his farming years and worked with an economy of motion. The laborers around him noted it—sometimes grudgingly and other times admiringly. Whenever the train whistle blew to signal the workday's end, most went to the tent saloons to relax. Most often, Wyatt rode off over a hill to find some private time before the chow lines opened. If he could not nap, he set up empty food cans and practiced his pistol handling with the Remington.

Every manner of man seemed to pass through the camps at some time, but only those with hard bark lasted more than one paycheck. Toughness, Wyatt learned in the railroad's employ, had multiple definitions. There were men who could drive iron spikes with a thirty-pound sledge all day. Some carried tongs and, without complaint, lifted their share of the fourteen-hundred-pound rails in a team of twelve. There were others whose endurance showed at the all-night gambling tables.

A remote rail camp on the move was the perfect arena for a skilled card player. The laborers—when they were not working—grew bored, and their pockets were filled with cash on a weekly basis. Not only was the average rail worker a novice with cards, but he lacked the skill to disassociate his emotions from his luck, be it good or bad. Ripe pickings for a professional.

Before sitting in on a game, Wyatt followed his inherent credo to be nobody's fool—especially where money was involved. From a distance he studied the methods of these sharps and engaged in the private tutorial of soaking up the education they unknowingly provided. That professionals of the green cloth cleverly turned the odds in their favor was a given. Sometimes it was by sleight of hand, other times a lookout or a "winner" was strategically planted in the crowd. There were more ways to mark a deck of cards than the average man could fathom. Even if a dealer never lost and his winnings were known to be illicit, he was generally accepted so long as his methods were not discernible. But if his shady dealings came to light, his only recourse might be a handy belly gun to hold the attention of his disgruntled customers while he made a hasty exit.

Professional gamblers moved on after a night's killing, to be replaced within a day or two by new ingratiating countenances. The camps, Wyatt came to understand, were stopping points on a circuit for such men. Wyatt bided his time, cutting a deck only with the laborers he knew.

Inside a gaming tent west of the Medicine Bow Mountains, a loud-mouthed Swedish roustabout took a seat across from Wyatt and, on foolish bluffs, lost four straight hands to a line foreman. On the fifth hand, after lying low on the previous bets, Wyatt took the pot, and the big blond-haired Swede glared at him with a closed-mouth smile stretched across his face. As Wyatt raked the money toward him, two meaty hands clamped down on his wrists.

"I vonder just vhat you boys godt going here," the Swede challenged. Well-practiced in the art of intimidation, he stared at the foreman and then at Wyatt.

"You saw the cards I laid down," Wyatt said. "Now get your hands off me and my money."

The big man showed his teeth. "You sons of bitches vork togeder, yah?" He kept his grip on Wyatt. "You are cheater. You and—"

Wyatt jerked his hands free and cracked the man's nose with a slashing blow of his right fist. It happened so fast that the others at the table had no chance to react before Wyatt stood and landed another punch that burst the big roustabout's lip and sent him falling backward off the crate on which he'd been sitting. Taking his time, the Swede rose up from the ground, paying no attention to the blood pouring down his chin. A demonic smile spread around the pink saliva glistening on his teeth, and in a methodical, fluid movement, he slowly circled his fists before him, like a man carefully coiling a length of yarn.

"Now Stefgard teach you some-tingk about da fine ardt." He circled around the corner of the table, his eyes hard and hungry.

Wyatt lunged and threw a right, but the laborer's meaty left forearm took the brunt of the blow. In the instant that followed, the Swede advanced, jabbing twice, making Wyatt's head snap backward each time in quick succession, flashes of yellow-orange light filling his head. As Wyatt backed up to recover, Stefgard followed. Two more jabs, and Wyatt's vision blurred again. Next came a right cross out of nowhere that put him down. He stayed there long enough to let his head clear. Surprisingly the man allowed him the respite.

"You stay down, I take money. You get up, Stefgard give you more lesson."

"It ain't yours to take," Wyatt said, getting to his feet. He swung a roundhouse right only to feel the blow shunted by that big forearm again, just before the lights went out in his head.

Three men were dragging him through the tent flap into the cool night when he awoke. They dropped him in the camp thoroughfare, and Wyatt lay there looking up at the blur of stars trembling against the boundless black of the sky, his face burning hot and cool at the same time. He raised his head enough to see that his shirt was torn and bloody, but the effort set the camp spinning, and his head fell back into the muck.

"I'll give you this," said a voice from nearby, a clear Irish lilt giving the man's words a mix of warmth and amusement, "you've the kick of a spike-hammer in that bony fist o' yours, my friend, but your fighting skills? They're about as crude as the Swede's gamblin'."

Embarrassed to be seen as he was, Wyatt tried to prop himself up on an elbow. Standing in the doorway of the tent was a man thicker than the roustabout. The Irishman lifted his eyebrows and clamped a cigar between his teeth. Wyatt squinted as the man walked out to him. He had the swagger of a fighter himself.

"That Swede in there, he's got a big mouth all right, but, see, he knows a thing or two about the pugilistic arts. I've seen him in the ring a time or two, and . . . you're not in the same class, boyo." He offered his hand and lifted Wyatt to his feet.

"I ain't done," Wyatt mumbled.

The man winced. "You're not going back in there, are you now?" He spread his hands before Wyatt's shirt. "Look at you, son."

Wyatt set his teeth but would not look down at himself. "I won that money square."

"Aye, you probably did, but you won't be taking it off him this way." When Wyatt said nothing, the big man took on an expression of worry. "Look . . . I'm a fighter myself . . . John Shanssey . . . I know a little about this kind of thing, laddie. You left your mark on him with those first two blows. Why not leave it at that?" When the man offered a hopeful smile, his face widened, giving his chin the breadth of an iron bell.

"He's got my money," Wyatt said, his voice a low gravelly hum. "I ain't done."

Shanssey raised both palms and pushed gently at the air. "Whoa now, lad. I can see you've got the heart for it. And you do keep your wits about you. But this Stefgard . . . he's had some training in fisticuffs." The Irishman lowered his hands, produced a fresh cigar, and extended it.

Wyatt ignored the offer. He touched two fingertips to his lip and then checked his fingers for blood. Wiping his hand on his trousers, he stared at the Irishman blocking his way. Shanssey stood no taller than the tent entrance, but he was almost twice Wyatt's girth. The thick-necked boxer traded his easy smile for a look of inspection as he leaned closer.

"I don't see anythin' damaged that won't mend. We'll need to close those cuts though. Come with me. Can you walk?"

"I can walk."

Wyatt took two steps before his legs buckled. The last thing he remembered was trying to catch himself on Shanssey's thick forearm.

He awoke on a cot in a tent stitched together with mismatched colors of canvas. The cuts on his face had been patched, each one smarting like a bee sting. He looked down at his stocking feet, and then he leaned and spotted his boots standing side by side beneath the cot. By the chorus of crickets chirring lazily outside the tent, Wyatt knew he had not slept through to dawn. He threw his legs over the side of the cot and sat up, and right away the expanded space inside his head warned against standing.

Just then the Irishman pushed in through the tent flap carrying a bucket and a striped, bloody rag, which Wyatt recognized as a part of his shirt. "Look here now, son," Shanssey said around the cigar clamped in his teeth. "You'll want to let that patch-up job take." He set down the bucket and, with a hand gently clamped to each of Wyatt's shoulders, eased him back to the cot.

Taking the cigar from his mouth, he poked it toward Wyatt. "I'll tell you what. You get what sleep you can before breakfast. Then in a few days, when you feel up to it, I'll teach you how to protect yourself and how to counter a man's blow. You'll find that most of it's in the footwork. You'll be helping me out in the bargain. I'll be needin' a sparring partner. What do you say?"

From out in the night they heard the Swede's big booming voice, complaining about the cards he had been dealt. Wyatt turned his head to the direction from which the sound had come, and he stared at the wall of the tent, the muscle in his jaw knotting.

Shanssey managed a grim smile and shook his head. "If you go back there, son, I can fairly promise you the same outcome." He leaned to put his face in Wyatt's line of sight. "Why not learn to do it right?" Clamping the cigar between his teeth, he brought up his arms and performed a smart flourish of strokes with a speed that belied his bulk. His blocky fists whipped through the air like flying bricks. Then he smiled around the cigar and held out his hand to seal the deal.

Wyatt searched the man's beseeching eyes, wondering about the goodwill that could be packaged inside such brawn. When he gripped the fighter's meaty hand, Shanssey's smile expanded, slicing across his wide face like a split melon.

"We'll train together, and we'll both benefit from the work." He nodded in earnest to the cot. "For now you get some rest. We'll think about the Swede later. Agreed?"

In this man's gracious presence, Wyatt relaxed and let his eyes close. Suddenly his body felt like dead weight, and his need for reprisal with the Swede freefell into the void of sleep.

In the late afternoon of that same day, Wyatt found Shanssey behind the supply tent where he had roped off a square of sod for training. It was the business end of camp where the engineers and surveyors had set up a forward outpost for the next day's progress. Wincing at the crescents of purple pooled beneath each of Wyatt's eyes, Shanssey tried to cover his smile by idly scratching his broad chin. Wyatt stopped outside the rope.

"This ain't goin' to work," he said, "if you plan on insultin' me."

Shanssey dropped his hand and chuckled. "Easy there, lad. I'm smiling at your pluck. Damned if there isn't at least a little Irish blood running through those ice veins of yours." Wyatt's set jaw refused to relax. The brawny pugilist walked to where he stood. "It's a hard case you are, boyo, that's the God's plain truth of it. I didn't expect you so soon . . . that's all."

"Reckon I'm ready to get started," Wyatt said.

Shanssey's face took on the earnest glow of a child. "You've some hard bark on ya. Not a bad way to be out here." He threw a hand toward the camp. "But, lad, you're going to have to learn to recognize a friend when you see one." The Irishman stooped under the rope and pointed to a crate, where a small leather case sat on top. "Sit down there, and I'll treat those cuts for you again. Then we'll get down to business."

The training began with footwork. After an hour Shanssey was able to coax Wyatt off his flat feet onto his toes, but he could not persuade him to dance.

"You've got to stay mobile, Wyatt. Make your opponent unsure of where you are and where you're going to be."

"I can move when I need to," Wyatt said.

"Can you, now?" Shanssey raised his fists, and his torso and head began to bob like something rising and falling on the waves of a river. "Then show me!"

Wyatt assumed the stance, his left foot in front, his fists raised before him. Rocking forward and back, forward and back, he rotated stiffly to follow Shanssey's effortless circling. The Irishman's left arm flashed, and a brisk slap stung Wyatt's cheek above his damaged lip.

"See, I followed your rhythm," Shanssey explained. "You told me right where you'd be."

Wyatt began to bend his knees and weave.

"That's it. Now mix it up. Get your head movin'. Surprise me." Shanssey unleashed another jab that only partially connected. "That's it, that's it!"

Wyatt himself threw a quick punch, but Shanssey blocked it, and, stepping inside it, pulled a straight right a half inch from Wyatt's chin. Both men stopped as still as a photograph, with the tacit understanding that the blow, had it been delivered, would have sent Wyatt sprawling.

"A man will instinctively back away from a fist coming at him. Learn to use your opponent's momentum against him." Shanssey repeated the move in a slow, dreamlike performance. "Slip inside. Hit him while he's coming at you. Like this. Hit me!"

Wyatt threw a halfhearted jab, and the big man weaved his way inside to pull another punch. Again they froze together for an instant as the lesson burned into Wyatt's consciousness. Shanssey lightly patted Wyatt's cheek and backed away, and the training continued.

They worked for a week before sparring. To spare his hands any damage, Shanssey produced pairs of padded gloves for these sessions. Though the gloves provided protection to knuckles, they allowed a man to hit harder at his opponent's head. Wyatt took his blows, but he learned from them. Shanssey said he was quick to learn the things new to him . . . if not nearly so quick to let go of old habits. Soon Wyatt became adept at turning a defensive move into an aggressive offense, and a few of the surveyors began to while away their twilight hours by watching the two fighters at work, pulling up crates and barrels to form a makeshift spectators' section. It wasn't long before proper crowds began to gather, and all privacy was lost. Even Stefgard, the braggart Swede, stopped by once or twice to spectate, but he never stayed long.

Adopting the new Queensberry rules that were slowly making their way into American boxing circles, Shanssey prepared for his future as a professional fighter, giving Wyatt a unique opportunity to learn the ropes. The Irishman was clearly the more accomplished boxer, but the Earp name went around camp as a raw-boned fighter who could take a lot of punishment and deliver a vicious blow. He had sand. Hell, nobody else volun-teered to climb into the ropes with John Shanssey. Not even Stefgard.

The jewel of Wyatt's reputation was his unshakable coolness. Onlookers never failed to note it. This and an acquired knowledge of the Queensberry rules ushered Wyatt into the role of referee for the Sunday matches set up by the gamblers. He presided over seven bouts, only one of which required settle-ment by a decision. Those on the losing end of the wager predictably grumbled, but no one challenged Wyatt's word.

"Well, Wyatt," Shanssey exhaled as he climbed out of the ring after a victory over a German spike-driver. "Did you learn anything from this one?"

As they walked, Wyatt unrolled the cuffs of his sleeves to his wrists and secured the buttons. "I reckon if he'd connected more'n that one time, you'd a got into some trouble. Fella could hit."

"Aye . . . bugger had the kick of a mule." Shanssey looked at Wyatt and waited.

"Them men tauntin' you to stop circlin' and go to fightin'," Wyatt went on, "I reckon you had to teach them something about choosin' your moment."

"Indeed, lad. But it weren't the crowd I was teaching. It was the damned German." Shanssey laughed. "Did you see how he let the crowd egg him on to be more aggressive?"

Wyatt nodded. "Didn't help him none when he charged you."

Shanssey slapped Wyatt on the back and squeezed the slop-ing muscle that ran from his neck to his shoulder. "I do believe you are acquiring an education, Wyatt."

CHAPTER 10

Spring, 1869: Southern Wyoming with the Union Pacific Railroad
When the east and west grading crews finally met in Utah and the rail lines connected to span the country, Wyatt considered the points of the compass. He could stay on and work on the spur-lines, but the fact was, he was tired of the camp. And he was not going to get rich gambling with men who squandered the better part of their money on liquor and whores. He was ready for a change. Something with a more substantial future.

As the grading and survey crews loaded their instruments and gear into a boxcar, Crisman's foreman beckoned Wyatt aside where the draft horses were picketed. The man stood looking off at the horizon with his hands slipped into the rear pockets of his trousers. Wyatt stepped in front of him, and one of the Belgians stretched its neck forward and blew air on Wyatt's shoulder.

"Earp, you done a fine job for us . . . especially with the horses. You know how to handle a team." The foreman smiled at his boots. "Hell, they seem to *wanna* work for you." When he looked up at Wyatt's face, his smile broke off. "I'm done with these rail camps and ready for something a bit tamer . . . something that don't involve a warm beer and a cold tent at night. There's plenty of freightin' needed in the rail towns poppin' up along the line. I'm hopin' you might wanna take a run at it with me."

When Wyatt did not reply, the foreman shrugged. "Well, think about it. I won't leave for a few days." From inside his shirt he pulled out two envelopes. "Here, this come for you."

Wyatt took the offered envelope, stamped and postmarked. He recognized Virgil's handwriting and slipped it inside his shirt.

"And this . . . this here is for you," the foreman said, shaking the envelope by his ear as if it might rattle. "A little bonus I'm giving to only a few." The man made a crooked smile and shook his head as though he had been caught in some petty crime. "Aw, hell . . . it's a flat-out bribe to get you to stay on with me. Wages will be better freighting into the bigger towns."

"How much?" Wyatt asked.

The man squinted off to the horizon again and inhaled deeply through his nose. "I think I can up your monthly pay by ten dollars." Then he thrust out the second envelope as if he had forgotten he was holding it. "Either way, this here is yours. You earned it."

Wyatt took the envelope and weighed it in his hand. "Can I think on it?"

The foreman nodded once and offered his hand. Wyatt took it and felt the man's gratitude telegraphed through the strength of his grip.

"Till I pull out for Rawlings," the foreman said. "Either way . . . good luck to you. You've been a good hand."

Wyatt nodded and held up the bonus envelope as a gesture of thanks. "I'll let you know."

After work he sat on a pile of surplus ties, pushed back his hat brim, and studied the envelope from Virgil. *Peoria, Illinois*, it read. He opened it and flattened the letter on his thigh.

Wyatt,

This is a long shot to reach you. A fellow who quit freighting for the railroad came thrugh here and told me you been working for the Union Pacific. If you're waring down from hard labor

and the wether like I did, there are some opportunaties here in
Peoria and Beardstown that might intrest you. These bisnesses
need protection from trouble makers. Thare is good money and
mostly it means looking like a hard case. I figure that might be
something you'd be good at.

If you come out by rail to St. Louis, stop off in Beardstown
and look up John Walton at the Walden Hotel. I met him just
after the war. I told him about you. He has several profitable
enterprises going. If John has got nothing for you there, come on
upriver to Peoria and join me. We might just sew up this town
between the two of us.

Ma and Pa have settled down in Lamar, Missouri. Pa is up
to his usual—running for office, running bootleg whisky, start-
ing up some kind of bisness to put a good face on it.

If you get this, let me hear from you.

Your brother,

Virgil

Before leaving, Wyatt gave notice to the foreman and sold the
gear he had accumulated for his job. With the extra pay, he
bought a packhorse to accompany the roan mare he had
acquired through a winning hand of poker. He bought provisions from the sutler who stocked the nearby forts, and then
said his goodbyes to John Shanssey over a pot of Irish coffee the
pugilist had brewed in his tent.

When they shook hands, Shanssey asked, "So, are you pulling
out right away?"

"Just about," Wyatt said. "I've got one piece of business to
tend to."

Shanssey squinted at the expression on Wyatt's face, but
Wyatt said no more. He only nodded once, turned, and walked
out the tent.

Wyatt found Stefgard in one of the tent saloons connected to
a row of whoring cribs. The burly blond was arm wrestling, tak-

ing all comers on one-dollar bets. The onlookers laughed and taunted the man currently losing to the Swede. Wyatt circled the crowd and made his way to a bench where the doves sat disgruntled over the men's choice of entertainment.

"Well, hello, Wyatt," purred a slender woman with teasing, green eyes. She sat up straighter and pushed a curl of hair from her forehead. "Are you looking for something more pleasin' than squeezin' another man's hand on the table?"

Wyatt set his hat on the nearest table and remained standing. "Just going to set a spell, if you don't mind." The whore squirmed along the bench and patted the rough plank next to her hip.

When Stefgard slammed the challenger's arm to the tabletop, a roar of approval filled the tent. Money changed hands, and Stefgard drained half a pint of beer.

"Who iss next?" he dared. "Who vill face Steffo? Steffo hass steel cannonballs right here, by God." He grabbed his crotch and contrived a manic smile. "Vat you boys got down dar? I tink maybe you got little hum-mink-birdt eggs!" Stefgard's booming laughter filled the tent.

"I'll have a go," Wyatt said, rising from the bench.

The whores turned to see Wyatt's face but said nothing. The bartender stopped wiping the long plank bar. Everyone in the camp knew of the beating Wyatt had taken from the Swede, and now this new contest put an expression of uncertainty on most of the faces.

"Ah, iss da little piss-ant come back for anudder lesson from Steffo." He sized up Wyatt with a sneer. "You tink you got da muscle for diss, little piss-ant?" He propped his elbow on the tabletop, opened his hand, and smiled enough to show his teeth.

Wyatt's face showed nothing. "We'll do this standing up," he said.

Stefgard coughed up a laugh and let his hand fall flat to the table. He cocked his head.

"You vant fight Stefgard again? You make badt schoolboy. You not learn lesson goodt?"

Wyatt picked up his hat and walked to the table, the soft padding of his boots on the dirt floor the only sound in the tent. He stopped across from the Swede.

"You gonna talk or fight?" Wyatt said evenly.

The Swede crossed his arms over his thick chest. "You vant put money on fight?" Wyatt opened the front of his coat, and every eye before him locked on the Remington pistol stuffed into the waistband of his trousers. A few men stepped back, and the space inside the tent went still and quiet again, the only movement amongst the crowd being the slow drift of tobacco smoke in the dark quarters.

"I'll take just what's owed me," Wyatt said. "What you do with the rest is your business."

Moving in an unhurried fashion, he picked up a stack of coins from the table and dropped it into his hat. The Swede made a grab for it, but Wyatt's move was too fast. Stefgard missed and half slipped off his stool, hitting the table with his chest and upsetting his beer. By reflex two of the men sitting at the table backed away to avoid the spill, looking sheepishly at Wyatt as if belatedly asking for his permission to move.

Stefgard pushed up from his knee, staring at Wyatt's gun all the while. "So da little piss-ant brings gun to do what he can't do widt hiss fists. Iss the way of da cowardt, yah?" He searched the room for agreement, but no one paid him any mind. Every eye was on Wyatt.

"I'll be outside," Wyatt said. "If you come out there with a gun, you better aim on using it. Otherwise"—he tapped the walnut grips of the pistol—"I'll set this aside, and we'll take up where we left off."

Stefgard's chest pumped up, and the guarded slant of his

eyes relaxed. "Yah? I tink I put you down for goodt dis time."

Wyatt counted out a number of coins, inverted his hat, and dumped the remainder onto the table. The coins spilled across the tabletop, rolling in random arcs, the sound humming on the wood surface until the last coin toppled into silence. Stefgard made no move to recover them. Wyatt pocketed his share of the money and walked out.

All bets were placed for Stefgard to win, the winnings based upon how long Earp would last. When a self-appointed handler took charge of the money and led the procession outside, Stefgard rode out with the flow of bodies like a hero caught up in his own parade. More spectators poured into the muddy thoroughfare, asking questions, and flashing money to be included in the betting. Wyatt took off his coat and shirt and draped them over the side panel of an idle buckboard parked between tents. He handed his revolver to the old hostler who lived in one of the passenger cars on the tracks. When Stefgard removed his blouse, a few spectators involuntarily sucked in a whisper of air. The Swede had forty pounds on the young Earp.

When John Shanssey arrived on the scene, he quickly took charge, steering the event toward the formality of their Sunday bouts by adopting Queensberry rules and a referee. The bloodlust of the crowd was high, but Shanssey prevailed, and gloves were doled out to each fighter. They decided upon six rounds and a fifteen count when a man went down. A reluctant rail crew foreman was pushed into refereeing, and the bartender agreed to serve as timer.

When the proper space was paced off and cleared, the foreman nodded, and the bartender clanked an iron ladle against an empty whiskey bottle, and the fight commenced. The crowd of onlookers raised a rowdy roar as both men circled, fists aloft, eyeing one another for an opening. For three revolutions neither man broke the monotony of the circling, and the general cheering turned to taunting. Wyatt's concentration was complete, his focus locked on his opponent, as Stefgard laughed and jested with the crowd.

"Someone go make coffin for piss-ant! Steffo put him into ground!"

"Git to it, Stefgard!" someone yelled. "I got a week's pay ridin' on round one, goddamnit."

After two more revolutions by the fighters, a man yelled an insult to Sweden. Stefgard's forehead tightened to rounded mounds of flesh; his eyes squeezed down to angry slits. Lunging, he threw a left jab just as Wyatt reversed direction, slipped the punch, and drove in hard with a right before the Swede could cover up. In the shuffle Stefgard lost his footing in the mud and went down. The crowd groaned. Two men stepped forward to help the Swede up, but the foreman ordered them back.

Slowly Stefgard rose, glaring at Wyatt. "You von't touch me again, little piss-ant!" His pale face went hard and glowed with rekindled heat. Hunching forward and weaving his big fists in the air before him, he moved steadily toward Wyatt with a new momentum. Feinting twice, he sidestepped and struck Wyatt a jarring blow to the ear, following that with a series of jabs that backed Wyatt to the edge of the available space. The men standing there pushed him back toward Stefgard. The Swede dodged in close and connected with a powerful right.

Wyatt went down hard, slapping the mud with his back. The crowd roared its approval. Stefgard backed away, trying to bob on his feet in the mire. As the foreman began a count, Wyatt stood and faced the men who had thrust him back into the ring space.

"You'll keep your hands off me, or I'll bring some o' this fight your way!"

"Fight is dis way, piss-ant," Stefgard taunted. Wyatt turned to the Swede and assumed the boxer's stance. Smiling, the Swede straightened and propped his fists on his hips. "Vat you tink, boys? Do I beat him into pile uff broken bones or take pity on young hot-head piss-ant?" He looked to his left as if to take an assessment of the crowd's pleasure . . . but it was a ploy. Even as someone began shouting an answer to his question, the Swede charged, his forearms crossed before him to ward off blows. He used his weight to barrel into Wyatt, and the two fighters went down together, taking onlookers with them.

The bartender set up a racket clacking the ladle against the bottle as the referee followed the fighters into the notch that they had cut into the crowd. Both officials yelled for the men to disengage, but Stefgard continued to pummel Wyatt with repetitive blows to the head.

By the time the foreman wrestled Stefgard away, Wyatt's face was cut and bloodied and one eye half closed. His other eye gazed into the sky in an unfocused glaze. Two men pulled him up and tried to thrust him into the arena. Wyatt rolled off their hands, spun, and struck one man squarely on the nose, producing a fountain of blood that spilled down the front of the man's shirt.

When the ref came back for him, Wyatt was standing on his own. The Swede pranced heavily around the confines of the fighting space, pumping his fists above his head as though already claiming a victory. The foreman leaned to Wyatt's ear in quiet conference.

"You're cut up pretty bad . . . you want me to call it?"

Wyatt hinged his jaw from side to side. "I'm all right," he said, his eyes fixed on the Swede. The ladle clanked against the bottle, and Wyatt staggered forward on wobbling legs.

Once again Stefgard came at him swiftly, but this time Wyatt ducked the first fist. The second caught him full-force on the chin, and he stumbled back into the crowd. Greedy hands clutched at his upper arms and back, and again he was hurled forward. After two steps, Wyatt reversed direction and came at the men who had pushed him. His first punch put a man on the ground, and the second sent another man sprawling into the ones standing behind him.

The referee grabbed Wyatt from behind and struggled to guide him back toward the arena. There he released the young fighter, quickly stepping back to avoid Wyatt's wrath.

"Keep the goddamn crowd off me," Wyatt said hoarsely. But before he could turn back to the fight, Stefgard charged again, driving him deeper into the spectators, who parted more nimbly than before. The two fighters crashed into the gate of the wagon where Wyatt had hung his clothes, and they went down, the Swede on top. On his knees, Stefgard straddled Wyatt and began pounding his face in a relentless rhythm.

The foreman grabbed a handful of the Swede's pale-blond hair and pulled him back into the makeshift ring. "No hittin' when a man's down!" the referee warned. He returned to Wyatt, checked briefly for signs of consciousness, and then proceeded to yell over the celebratory shouts of the onlookers. "One! . . . Two! . . . Three! . . ."

At the sixth count Wyatt stood and leaned on the wagon gate. In the bed of the wagon lay a cast-off sledge hammer, the heavy head plugged by a three-inch stob of broken shaft, the rest of the wood handle stretching more than half the width of the wagon.

A foul-smelling bearded man put his face into Wyatt's and yelled, "Either quit or git back out there and take your due." He took Wyatt's arm and tried to turn him. Another man grabbed the other arm and together they tried to disengage him from the wagon.

Wyatt stretched forward, fitted his gloved hand around one end of the long hammer shaft, and turned, swinging in a vicious arc that connected with the bearded man's skull. The solid rap of wood on bone was audible above the din of the crowd, and the men around him drew back.

When Wyatt stepped back into the arena carrying the sledge handle, the glee in Stefgard's face dropped away. The referee raised both palms to Wyatt and cocked his head deferentially.

"Wyatt!" came an iron voice from his right. He turreted his head to see John Shanssey's face gone stern. "Queensberry rules, Wyatt. Hold to the book and wear him down."

Wyatt looked back at Stefgard, opened his gloved hand, and let the club drop to the mud.

The din of the crowd surged, as if to push both men forward by the strength of its collective sadistic pleasure. When Stefgard charged again, Wyatt sidestepped and struck a downward blow behind the Swede's ear that put him down. The crowd responded with anger, the sound sweet to Wyatt's ears. It empowered him, and he moved in to finish the job.

"Let him git up, Wyatt!" the referee ordered, stepping into his path.

When the big Swede rose, half his face was covered with mud. He staggered for a moment and then tried ineffectually to scrape the muck from one eye with a glove, which only made matters worse. Cursing, he grabbed one glove lacing with his teeth and managed to pull out the knot. Then the other. To the uproarious approval of the crowd, he pulled the gloves from his thick hands and cast them aside. Wyatt worked at loosening his own gloves as he watched Stefgard begin to breathe in deeply, filling his chest like a bellows. Before Wyatt could get a glove free, the Swede, abandoning all caution, charged at him with an animal growl hissing through his bared teeth.

As Wyatt was hurled backward he felt Stefgard's fingers grinding mud into his good eye. When they hit the ground, Wyatt tried to cover himself. The blows he took to his head brought bright flashes of light, and the shouts of the crowd began to retreat into a room filled with water. Then a large bell pealed inside his skull, and all his senses faded to black.

How much time had passed, Wyatt did not know. Shanssey was kneeling beside him, gently dabbing a wet cloth to his eye. The crowd milled about in a chaotic mix of buoyant conversations. Wyatt pushed away the Irishman's hand and levered up on an elbow. Squinting through the grit in his eye, he could make out Stefgard stuffing his trouser pockets with coins. Wyatt tore off his gloves to check his pockets and, finding them empty, stood.

"Wyatt," Shanssey called to his back, "they've already given him the win."

Most of the laborers were crowded around the bet handlers as names were read from a list and bets paid off. Stefgard stood talking to the foreman and two other men. Wyatt leaned down, picked up the sledge handle, and made his way to the Swede.

At his name, Stefgard turned. His smile snapped off as he eyed the wooden haft hanging by Wyatt's leg. The foreman stood for a moment as though he might speak, but thought better of it and took two steps backward.

"Some o' that's my money you're holding," Wyatt said in a low monotone.

"You haff lost fight, piss-ant. Now be like man and take vat comes." He patted the pocket at the front of his hip. "Vinner take all."

"You've got my poker winnings. And I figure you throwed out Queensberry rules, so I reckon we'll split whatever's left."

Stefgard turned to the man next to him and chuckled, but the bystander remained mute, his attention fixed on Wyatt. The wood club flashed and made a dull thud on Stefgard's head. The big Swede sank heavily to his knees and flopped face-down into the mud. Wyatt knelt and dug a handful of money from the

Swede's pocket. After counting it out, he stuffed a portion into his own trousers and threw the rest into the mud. Before standing, he lifted the Swede's head by his hair, turned his face away from the mud, and let his cheek slap back into the slop.

The knowledge of the Swede's demise spread through the crowd, and men jockeyed for position to have a look at the pugilist's inert body. Then all eyes settled on Wyatt, who stood defiant against what any man might say.

"You ain't got no call to be usin' a club in a fistfight," barked a big man in a plaid shirt. "Queensberry rules was agreed on." The man took a step toward Wyatt and stopped. Two others joined him to make a flank, each man's face taut with challenge.

"Reckon those rules weren't workin' out so well for anybody today," Wyatt replied. When the smooth grips of his revolver slipped into his left hand, he turned to see the hostler standing beside him. The feel of the gun was money in the bank. The men in the crowd looked down at the stillness of the weapon, and Wyatt felt the momentum of the confrontation stall. With an easy swing, he tossed the broken hammer shaft into the bed of the spring wagon, where it clattered against the side panel. He transferred the gun to his right hand, and the crowd quieted.

"He's earned it," someone called out. "Let 'im keep it. Besides, now we don't have to listen to the goddamn Swede crow . . . for a while anyway." Only a little laughter rose from the ranks.

Wyatt watched the faces in the crowd and waited to see how this would play out. When the men went about their business, he stuffed the pistol into his waistband, its cool metal pressing reassuringly against his skin. He walked to his clothes, where Shanssey waited.

"You look like hell, son," the Irishman said and lifted a bucket of water.

Wyatt dipped his hands into the bucket, bent forward, and washed his eye and face. Then he stood for applications from Shanssey's vial of astringent.

"There's nothing here to be ashamed of, Wyatt." The Irishman spoke quietly and kept his eyes on his work. "You two boyos are not in the same weight class, that's all. And the Swede . . . he's been at this game for a lot of years." Shanssey set vial and cloth on the buckboard and pulled a silver flask from his hip pocket. He took a long pull and offered the bottle to Wyatt.

Wyatt shook his head. "I ain't ashamed. I got my money back."

Shanssey returned the flask to his hip and cracked the wide smile that narrowed his eyes. "Well, you throw one lively goin'-away party, I'll give you that. Tell me, was the money worth all the trouble?"

Wyatt looked at his friend for several seconds before answering. "It was *my* money."

"Yes, but was it—"

"Maybe you ought to ask the Swede that question."

Looking back at Stefgard in the mire, Shanssey smiled and nodded. "Aye, maybe so."

That first night on the trail, Wyatt camped in a high meadow surrounded by tall pines. He looked up from his bedroll at the early evening stars and thought about the years of sleeping in rough camps, whore tents, and way-station bunkhouses. There was nothing undignified about raw labor, but he now felt done with that. As if he had paid the proper dues that might elevate him to a business that did not involve breaking his back. He was ready for that . . . and the money that went with it.

The moon rose, a smoldering disk of ochre glowing behind the trees. He wondered where Valenzuela Cos might be now. What would she think of him pulling up stakes and heading east for Illinois? Being on the move at least held possibilities that were not evident in his present situation. Certainly there would be no mud houses or tents waiting for him there.

He sold his horses in Granger and took his first journey by train to St. Louis, watching the plains move past him as if he were afloat on a swift river of grass. When he thought of the grinding pace of the wagon trek to California, this trip by rail felt like irrefutable evidence of the world opening up to uncountable opportunities. And by joining Virgil in Illinois, Wyatt calculated that a time had come for some of the Earp brothers to take a piece of the new promised land. It was time to capitalize.

CHAPTER 11

Spring, 1869: Beardstown, Illinois

He took the stage up the Illinois River to Beardstown, where the Rock Island Railroad was laying track down the main thoroughfare of the village. It was three o'clock in the afternoon when he stepped from the coach onto the street, and the cloudless sky was like a blue porcelain bowl hovering above. The citizens went about their routines, paying little notice to the rail crews. At a German gunsmith's shop Wyatt bought balls, powder, and caps and asked the smith for directions to John Walton's hotel. The man's face seemed to cloud over with sudden mistrust.

He pointed. "Go to da intersection, turn left, and keep valkin' till you haff almost come to da edge of town. Den just follow your nose. You vill smell it before you see it."

The hotel was an old two-story building, neglected and barren of any adornment. The main lobby had been converted into a second-rate bar, where two patrons stood talking to a portly bartender. The three turned as one to look at Wyatt as he entered. Off to Wyatt's right another room opened up as large as the barroom. There three women sat in open nightgowns talking casually as if they were sisters conversing in the privacy of their home.

Wyatt stepped to the bar six paces away from the two drinkers, set his saddlebags and duffle on the floor, and waited for the ruddy-faced barkeep to approach him.

"I'm looking for John Walton."

The man's red-veined eyes hardened. "What for?"

Wyatt showed no change of expression. "You Walton?"

"No," the man replied curtly and raised his chin to point at Wyatt. "You buyin' a drink?"

"I'm looking for Walton. I was told he owns this place."

Keeping himself at arm's length, the man wiped his hands on his apron. "We can play this game all day, so you'd better tell me what you want with him. You with the law?"

"I was told he might have some work for me."

He stared at Wyatt, looking him up and down as though reassessing his features. "Name?"

Before Wyatt could answer, the heavy scuff of boots turned both their heads to a barrel-chested man just then pushing through the front door. The newcomer swaggered to the entrance of the side room, propped a hand on either side of the door frame, and leaned in to survey the women's lounging area. He frowned, wrinkling his fleshy brow and broad nose. With his thick shoulders and narrow hips, he presented the silhouette of an ox.

"Where's Lilah," he growled to the women in the side room.

Wyatt could not hear the reply, but it did nothing to improve the man's demeanor. He scuffed to the bar and leaned on the polished top close enough to Wyatt to bump shoulders. With the side of his boot he kicked aside Wyatt's saddlebags.

"Gimme a cold beer!" The bartender turned and swept down a mug from the shelf. "And it better be cold this time! If it ain't I'll pour it in your ear!"

Wyatt sidestepped to remove himself from the man's rancid scent. He waited for the barkeep to set down the drink.

"What about Walton?" Wyatt said.

The bartender gave Wyatt a deadpan face. "He still ain't here."

"Where the hell is Lilah?" the ox interrupted. "I wanna see her . . . now!" He glared at the bartender over his mug as he downed half his beer. Slapping the mug to the bar, he belched. "What room's she in?"

The bartender snatched a towel from a rack and wiped at the spill around the man's mug. "You got to pay up front before you can go up to a room. And you can't pay till one of the girls accepts your offer. You know how it works, Pinard."

"Well, it ain't workin' too well, is it? 'Cause she ain't down here, and she's the one I want." He dug into his pocket and slapped down two gold dollars under his meaty hand. He leaned forward and lowered his voice to a menacing rasp. "So just tell me which goddamn room, you big tub o' lard."

"Nobody goes up before they're told to," the bartender said. He began folding the towel and turned around to face the back counter where the bottles and glasses were lined up. Wyatt saw the butt of a pistol protruding from a stack of folded aprons on a lower shelf.

"Hey!" Pinard yelled. The bartender froze with the folded towel in his hands. "You turn around with that goddamn shooter in your hand, an' I'll blow a hole in that fat gut o' yours."

Pinard leveled a Navy Colt's revolver at the man's back. The bartender's forearms levitated to a horizontal position out to his sides, and he turned around slowly.

"Mr. Pinard, we got enforcers on each end of the upstairs floor. If you go up by yourself, you're going to have to deal with them."

Lowering his hands, the bartender made a smart turn to his right and began to march toward the far end of the bar. Wyatt reached out and grabbed his arm, forcing him to stop.

"I've asked you twice," Wyatt said to the side of his face. "Don't make me ask again."

The bartender managed a contrite nod. "Come back at

eight," he mumbled.

Pinard let his gun clatter on the bar top, and then he drank the rest of his beer. Wyatt picked up his gear and walked out into the street to search for a better class of hotel.

When Wyatt returned to Walton's brothel after dark, a lively string of piano notes spilled into the street from the saloon. Reentering the dimly lit bar, he now found the room filled with laborers from the rail crews. A groundswell of male voices underscored the music. The same red-faced man served at the bar. A few women circulated through the crowd, and everywhere they mingled, the men grabbed at them with rough hands. The air was stale with alcohol, sweat, and cigar smoke.

A bald man with bushy, gray eyebrows and a beer mug in his hand was trying to dance with an unwilling female partner, who tried to hold him at arm's length to avoid the spillage of his drink. Finally she kicked at his shin, and his beer shot upward to rain on a table of drinkers behind him. One of the baptized stood up, spun the offender around, and knocked him off his feet with a blow to the side of the head with his pistol barrel. The drunken reveler dropped like a sack of bones and lay unconscious on the pinewood floor. The crowd opened a space around the fallen man, and conversation stopped. No one moved for a moment as the music rattled on with its inane momentum. Then, when the piano player became aware of the lull in the room, he lifted his fingers from the keys.

A young man with smooth cheeks and sympathetic eyes knelt to examine the older man. "You got no call to go beatin' on a old man," he said, looking up at the man still holding the gun. When the bully made a snarling laugh, Wyatt recognized him and the Navy Colt's in his hand.

Pinard took a step forward. "You want me to ring your bell, too, sonny boy?"

The younger man said nothing and lifted the limp body by the armpits, dragging it toward the side room where the women had lounged earlier in the day. Pinard laughed and returned to his table. Wyatt watched a man in a brown suit behind the bar raise his chin to the piano player, and the music picked up with the same rollicking tempo. The conversations picked up again to a steady murmur.

After Pinard sat, a broad-shouldered man seated next to him leaned in close to speak into his ear. When both men rocked back in their chairs and laughed, Wyatt recognized the other man by his raucous crow and the ugly flat scar on his cheek. His cruel smile brought back the alcoholic blur of Wyatt's initiation into the freighters' fraternity in a Prescott saloon. It was Big George, the driver from Texas who had found sadistic pleasure in Wyatt's drunken misery.

Wyatt stepped to the crowded bar and waited as the bartender conferred in low tones with the brown-suited man. After seeing Wyatt's approach, the bartender turned away, giving Wyatt his back. The other man, wearing a frown of curiosity, walked toward Wyatt, his expression opening into a smile before he had traveled half the length of the bar.

"You've got to be an Earp," he said, his words stretched melodically by a soft, Southern slur. The warmth of his smile spread upward into his slate-blue eyes. "I'm John Walton."

Wyatt reached across the bar to take his hand. "Virgil told me to look you up. I'm Wyatt."

Walton tightened his grip and let his eyes wander freely over Wyatt's torso and arms, and then he turned their clasped hands to examine Wyatt's knuckles. "Hell, yes. I'm glad you did." Walton released his grip and propped both fists on his hips. This time when he smiled, he showed two rows of small teeth that matched the other small features of his face. His red-brown hair curled on his head and trailed down his jaws as bushy muttonchops that were less brown than red. "Let me buy you a drink, Wyatt."

"You got coffee?" Wyatt said.

Walton narrowed his eyes as though he had just heard a sensible idea. "Hell, yeah!" he said and held up a forefinger to hold Wyatt in place.

As Walton stepped away, Pinard wedged in next to Wyatt. On the other side of Pinard, Big George dropped his forearms onto the bar top. Both men slapped down empty beer mugs. Wyatt removed his hat and laid it on the bar.

"Hey, tub o' guts!" Pinard called out. "Give us a fill!"

The bartender approached, keeping his eyes anywhere but on Pinard. When he picked up the empty mugs, Pinard grabbed for his apron, but the portly man stepped back and broke free.

"When's Lilah comin' down?" Pinard growled. He grasped the edge of the bar and leaned in to glare at the bartender.

"I don't keep up with the girls' schedules. I just pour the drinks."

Pinard and George watched Walton walk past them balancing two steaming cups. When he placed one before Wyatt, the big Texan squinted and then roared with laughter.

"I'll be damned! Hey . . . it's the California boy! And you still ain't learned to drink."

Walton turned to the Texan with a question on his face. Then he turned back to Wyatt, who looked straight ahead and sipped his coffee.

"Hey! 'California boy'! It's me . . . Big George Peshaur. Remember?"

Wyatt lowered his drink and spoke to the mirror. "I remember you," he said in a flat tone.

Pinard gave Wyatt a dismissive glance and leaned his face into Walton's. "Hey, whore-man, go tell Lilah to get herself down here. I'm a payin' customer, and I want some service."

Walton managed a politic smile. "Why don't you choose one of the other ladies, Tom?"

" 'Cause I want Lilah. She ain't supposed to be tied up this long. Now go and tell her."

"Well, Tom," Walton began with a pained expression, "the fact is, she doesn't want to be with you, see? Have a go with one of the others, all right? I'll give you a dollar off."

Pinard widened his grip on the bar, and in doing so his elbow jutted outward, spilling Wyatt's coffee. Wyatt set down his cup and faced the man.

"Mister," he said evenly, "that's the third time you've trespassed on my space."

Pinard put on a look of mock wonder. " 'Trespassed'? What're you . . . a preacher?"

"That's 'the California boy,' Tom," Peshaur laughed. "Careful or he'll puke on ya."

Pinard worked up a vicious smile of yellowed teeth streaked with tobacco stain. "Well, California boy, wanna see some trespassin'?" He coughed up a clot of phlegm and sucked in his cheeks. When he took in a deliberate breath through his nose and tilted backward as a prelude to spitting, Wyatt caught him with an uppercut in the chin, making the bully's teeth click like the dry snap of a pistol. Pinard's head snapped back as he stumbled into Peshaur and fell. He hit the floor hard, and a circle quickly opened on the floor. When the music stopped, the bystanders leaned in to see Pinard flat on his back, moaning.

Wyatt stepped into the empty space and waited, the coffee stain on his shirtfront glistening wet in the dim lamplight. He glanced at Peshaur to see if he would take up his friend's fight, but Walton had the Texan's attention with a short-barreled pistol cocked in hand.

Pinard lifted his head and gently probed inside his mouth with his fingertips. "Goth-thammit . . . my thongue." Blood trickled from one corner of his mouth. His eyes found Wyatt and instantly filled with a white-hot fury. But before his right hand could get to the gun in his waistband, Wyatt stepped forward and brought his boot down over both wrist and abdomen. The man squealed and kicked as if he'd been stabbed. When he gripped Wyatt's boot with his free hand, Wyatt pressed down harder, pushing the air from Pinard's lungs, and in the same moment snatching up the revolver from the man's waistband.

"You goth-thammed thunovabith!" Pinard bellowed.

Wyatt stepped back, holding the gun by its frame with the butt forward. He turned his head to the bartender and tossed the revolver to him over the bar. Pinard pushed himself up to his feet and made a show of being huffing mad. Wyatt widened his stance, letting only his expression deliver any warning.

Pinard pretended to examine his wrist, and then suddenly he charged. His size slowed him, giving Wyatt time to sidestep and deliver a numbing blow that put Pinard on the floor again, this time with a loud crack from one of the rough boards. The conversation in the room dropped away to nothing.

When Pinard was able to sit up, Wyatt leaned down, pinched his ear with a vicious twist, and led him toward the front door, the man whining like a scolded dog. The crowd moved like a wave to the door and windows to watch Pinard be heaved into the street, where he skidded on his belly in the dirt. Wyatt waited until Pinard was able to rise to his hands and knees, but the man only hung his head and raised one hand tentatively to his ear. Blood drooled from his mouth, and a low moan issued from his lips.

When Wyatt walked back into the saloon, the men at the door parted to make a path for him. Someone offered to buy him a drink, but he declined. Big George Peshaur remained at the bar, where Walton—his gun now put away—tried to placate the Texan with a complimentary beer. Peshaur glared at Wyatt but said nothing.

"Wouldn't mind trying that coffee again, John," Wyatt said, stepping to the bar. Walton, seemingly delighted over the recent events inside his saloon, snapped his fingers to his barman and held out both cups until the man retrieved them.

"Listen, Wyatt," Walton said, his voice fairly singing with good spirits, "let's you and me go back to my office and—"

"Hey, whore-man!" Peshaur interrupted, pulling at Walton's shoulder. "Give me Pinard's gun, so I can get it back to him."

Walton pursed his lips in thought and checked Wyatt's face for input. Wyatt's expression remained unreadable as he watched the bartender set down fresh coffee.

"I would prefer that Pinard cool off before he retrieves his arms," Walton said.

Peshaur laughed. "I don't think you'll want 'im coming back here for his pistol, will ya? I'll hold it for him for a while."

For several seconds Walton scratched his fingernails along one of his long sideburns. Finally he reached down below the bar and laid the Colt's revolver on the polished countertop. "All right," he said, "tell him I don't want him back in my establishment. You can tell him that's official."

Peshaur lifted one corner of his mouth. "You bet!" He raised his mug and gulped down the beer in one breath. Then he exhaled heavily, picked up the gun, and left.

Wyatt set down his cup and looked at Walton. "Better give me that shooter behind the bar."

Walton frowned and stared into the steadiness of Wyatt's eyes. "You think there'll be more trouble?" When Wyatt said nothing, Walton removed a pocket model Colt's from inside his coat and offered it butt first. "Use mine."

Wyatt nodded his head toward the bartender's shelf. "The Remington," he said. Walton put his gun away and retrieved the longer-barreled pistol. As he offered it to Wyatt, a gun roared in the street, and glass shattered in the front window, scattering shards across the floor, just as the back wall spat out a sound like the sharp blow of a hammer. The piano had started up, but now it quieted. Almost every man in the room sprawled flat on the floor as the women raced for the side room.

"Hey, Califo'nia boy!" called Pinard's shrill voice. "Get ou' heah, you thonovabith!"

Wyatt checked the loads on the Remington and looked at Walton. "This your gun?"

Walton's eyes were large as quarters. "Hiram's . . . my bartender."

Wyatt called over Walton's shoulder to the barman. "How fresh are these loads?"

"Just this morning," Hiram said.

Wyatt let the hammer off half cock and pulled it back quickly all the way. He did this again and then eased down the hammer.

"It's reliable," Hiram assured him. "Never jammed. Never a misfire."

Keeping out of sight Wyatt walked toward the front window. The sound of his boots crunching on broken glass seemed magnified inside the unnatural silence of the saloon. Easing his head around the doorframe he spied Pinard standing alone in the middle of the street, his pistol leveled from his waist at the hotel's front door. Searching the far side of the street, Wyatt spotted Peshaur in the shadows of a store awning catty-corner in the next block. Both his hands were in sight gripping an awning post.

"What'sa matter, Califo'nia boy?" Pinard yelled, getting his tongue working again. "You yellow?" He lowered the gun beside his leg. "Get on out heah! I got thumthing fo' you."

Wyatt turned to see Walton crouching at the side of the bar.

"You got any law here?"

"They won't come down here," Walton whispered, "unless there's a killin'."

Wyatt watched Pinard another few seconds, checked the street again, and cocked his gun.

"Wyatt," Walton said, now with urgency in his voice, "if you kill him, it'll make trouble for me with the law."

Wyatt leaned back to the window and watched through the glass as Pinard glanced down the street toward Peshaur. Taking this opportunity, Wyatt pivoted and stepped through the door onto the boardwalk with the Remington pointed down beside his leg. Pinard's shot came unexpectedly, and right away the door lintel cracked. Wyatt raised his weapon smoothly, aimed low on the torso, and fired. A plume of smoke temporarily blurred his vision as he thumbed back the hammer again, but Pinard was down, his Colt's out of reach in the street. Wyatt swung the barrel of the gun to the corner of the intersection. Peshaur was gone.

The saloon patrons began to trickle out onto the street, fanning around the prostrate man and gawking as if he were some unfamiliar creature just dredged up from the river. Walton stepped beside Wyatt, cleared his throat, and swallowed audibly.

"Is he dead?"

"No," Wyatt said, watching Pinard writhe in the dirt of the dark street.

A boy holding a stack of newspapers stepped down from the walkway where Peshaur had stood. "Better get the doctor," Walton yelled to him. The boy stared for a moment, then ran off.

"What about the law?" Wyatt said. "Will they look into this?"

Walton looked back at Pinard and licked his lips. Several men had lifted the groaning man and started carrying him up the street.

"Maybe," he said, turning back to Wyatt. "What do you want to do?"

"Why don't we go see if we can finish a cup of coffee."

CHAPTER 12

Summer, 1869: Beardstown, Illinois, to Peoria by keelboat

Sipping coffee in the small office, Wyatt sat opposite Walton at his desk as the hotelier peeled away bills from a three-inch roll and pushed them across the desktop. "I doubt that stain will come out, Wyatt. Let me at least buy you another shirt."

Wyatt set down the cup and shook his head. "I might take it from Pinard . . . not you."

"So what are your plans, Wyatt?"

"Headin' to Peoria to see Virgil."

Walton sat back, propped his elbows on the arms of his chair, and steepled his fingertips. Lightly bouncing his fingers against his pursed lips, he stared down at the papers on his desk.

"No chance you'd consider staying here to work for me?"

Wyatt hitched a thumb back toward the saloon. "Out there?"

Walton parted his hands to point at the ceiling. "Upstairs. I need a good enforcer."

Wyatt looked into his coffee. "You mean . . . for your whores."

Walton nodded. Wyatt looked around the room.

"You own this place?"

Walton frowned at the bare walls and shook his head. "I run it. Manage the saloon and the whores. There's good money in it."

Wyatt faced the window where the factories and warehouses stretched beyond the commercial district and appeared as colorless as a tintype. "Reckon I'm looking for something with more of a business future to it," he said and looked back at Walton. "I don't see how banging on the heads of drunks is gonna help me do that, John."

"Do you have a horse?" When Wyatt shook his head, Walton cocked his head to one side and pushed out his lower lip. "Well," he said, "if you're set on going to Peoria, I'm taking some of my girls up there in two days. How'd you like to go along? We've got plenty of room."

"In what?"

"I've got a fifty-foot keelboat." He smiled. "I need one more pole man."

Wyatt took another sip of coffee. "How much does a man make poling up the river?"

Walton raised his eyebrows at Wyatt's interest. "Four dollars a day. Six days."

Wyatt set down the cup and settled deeper in his chair. Threading his fingers together over his stomach, he gazed through the window again. Beyond the warehouses he could see the open air over the Illinois River.

"Been cooped up in a train and a stage most of a week. Might like bein' on the river."

Walton half stood and reached across the desk to shake hands. Straightening, he added two more bills to the money on the desk and pushed it on Wyatt.

"Buy two shirts. I want a natty crew when we pull into Peoria. And get some good gloves."

Wyatt pocketed the money. "What about this shootin'? Shouldn' I talk to the law?"

Walton shook his head. "Long as nobody's dead. Pinard works for the Rock Island Railroad. *They* might raise a stink, but they'll raise it with him, not me." He shrugged. "Somebody'll kill the sonovabitch soon enough. That or he'll learn he's not the cock of the walk around here and move on."

"They all learn it sometime or other," Wyatt said.

The going was easy near the river banks where the current was sluggish, but the abundance of snags was tedious. Still Wyatt liked working in the cool air coming off the water. East shore in the mornings, west in the afternoons—the long ferry in between to keep the boat out of the heat.

It felt good to work his muscles as he pushed the pole from bow to stern and then walked his pole cabin-side up the deck to start the cycle again. At night they tied fore and aft ropes to stout trees on the bank, and the poling crew played cards while the whores whispered about feminine toiletries and fussed with their hair after a day of preparing the cabin cribs for Peoria.

On the second day out during the noon break, the youngest whore—little more than a child, she seemed—approached Wyatt where he sat alone on the larboard deck with his back against the long cabin. He was eating cheese and bread and a jar of cooked apples.

"You're Wyatt?" she said.

Wyatt looked up and stopped chewing. Up close the girl appeared gaunt yet resilient, as though she had lived more years than he had guessed. He drew his boots beneath him and looked down at the food laid out in his lap, thinking he ought to offer her something to eat.

"Please, don't get up," she said. She backed to the low gunwale as though she might sit on the rail, but after peering at the dark water she changed her mind. Putting her back to the cabin she slid down beside him. "I'm Sarah," she said matter-of-factly. "You're the one shot Tom Pinard?"

Wyatt looked at her for a long five seconds. "After he shot at me."

The girl's mouth and nose were small, and this, he realized, made her appear fragile. Her skin was wrapped around her facial bones with clean angles—until she pulled her upper lip into a childish snarl.

"He needed shooting. He was real hard on Lilah. Busted her lip twice."

Wyatt screwed down the lid on the jar. "I expect he was hard on a lot of people."

She turned her head to look squarely at him. "Yes," she said and kept staring. "So, is this what the eyes of a killer look like?"

He tore off a piece of the tough bread and chewed it into submission as he noted her self-amused expression. "Far as I know, didn' kill him."

"Now that you're working for Walton, are you gonna take care of us?"

"I'm just earning my way upriver. Once I get to Peoria, I ain't sure what I'll do."

She flopped her legs out on the deck and tapped her shoes together like a little girl unconscious of her actions. "Can I call you 'Wyatt'?"

"I don't mind." He gave her a sidewise glance and then looked out over the water. "How'd you get mixed up in this line o' work?"

Her feet stopped tapping, and she gave him a sharp look. "Is that a problem for you?"

Wyatt shook his head. "Nothin' wrong with bein' a whore. Just seem young for it."

They listened to the mooring lines stretch from shore. The river flowed steadily past them as though they were still making their way slowly to somewhere.

"Guess I was born into it," she said. "My mother is Jane Haspel." When Wyatt showed no reaction, she added, "She runs one of the biggest brothels in Peoria."

Wyatt did not know what to say to that. She caught him

frowning, so he nodded.

"Your brother worked for her," she said, as if that somehow justified her situation. "He looked out for us. Not no more though. He works for Vansteel now, protecting *his* women."

Wyatt tried to imagine Virgil working in a whorehouse, but with the sun glinting off the ripples in the water and the breeze blowing pleasantly across the deck, he could not make the picture materialize in his mind. "Just how old are you?" he asked her.

"Almost fifteen," she said without hesitation. She smiled at his surprise. "I grew up fast."

Wyatt began wrapping the cheese and bread together, glad to be doing something with his hands. "I reckon you did," he said as gently as he knew how.

"Can I use your name?" she asked, the question dropping out of nowhere like a flicker of lightning flashing in a blue sky.

"What?" he said, frowning.

"If we get boarded by the law, can I say I'm your wife? They might go easier on me."

Wyatt stared out at the trees on the horizon, feeling the skin on his forehead crease into tight furrows. "I reckon you can, if you need to . . . long as there ain't nothin' bindin' to it."

She smiled, pulled her knees to her chest, and hugged her arms around her shins. "I won't henpeck you," she said and laughed. "Sarah Earp." She turned her full smile on him. "How's that sound?"

"Sounds all right, I reckon, long as you understand it's just a loan. I might need it back."

Sarah poked his ribs and giggled. "Are you thinkin' on gettin' married any time soon?"

Wyatt shook his head. "No plans to."

She buried her face in the folds of her dress between her knees. "Maybe you'll marry me," she said, her little girl's voice muffled by the material.

When she looked up at him, he felt his face flush with color. He kept looking at that far shore, trying to think what to say without hurting her feelings.

"If I ever do get married, I hope it'll be to someone as pretty as you . . . but older."

She laughed as though he had said something illogical. "Well, *I'll* get older, Wyatt."

He conceded that with a nod. "Yeah . . . I reckon we all will."

Wyatt found the Vansteel House in the Bunker Hill district of the Peoria waterfront. It was a squalid section of town with the stench of gin mills and slaughterhouses and breweries and a class of people who seemed not to abide by any standard of appearances. The docks teemed with boatmen and roustabouts who labored in the sun, while the streets and sidewalks just a block away appeared more like a darkened cave, where a more primitive breed of people thrived. Every man and woman Wyatt passed seemed worn out by some travail of city life.

At one in the afternoon he walked into Vansteel's saloon and waited for the bartender to see him. The aproned man glanced at Wyatt, went back to his conversation with a customer, and then immediately turned back for a second look. Wiping his hands with a towel, he came slowly down the length of the bar with his head cocked to one side and a question on his face.

"Looking for Virgil Earp," Wyatt said.

"He's prob'ly asleep. Who're you?"

"I'm his brother."

The man's inspecting gaze traveled down Wyatt's torso and back to his face. "I figured." He pointed to the upstairs landing. "Last room down the north hall. There's no number."

Climbing the stairs, Wyatt heard the bartender mumble the Earp surname as he resumed his conversation with his patron.

Wyatt could feel the two men's attention on him until he turned down the dark hallway. At the end door, he paused and heard a soft purr of snoring that could not have been Virgil. Wyatt frowned, considered the numbered doors behind him, and then knocked on the unmarked door.

When it opened, Virgil stood squint-eyed in his long drawers. A red-tinted moustache had begun to fill out over his upper lip, and his wheat-straw hair was mussed as though he'd just stepped inside from a stiff wind. His skin was paler than Wyatt had ever seen it.

When recognition hit him, Virgil's face lit up, and his eyes danced with light, like the sun playing off the river. "Holy Jesus," he said, dredging up the familiar laugh from deep in his chest. He pulled Wyatt into an embrace, and over his brother's shoulder, Wyatt met the dark watery eyes of a lithe, black-haired woman looking back at him from the rumpled sheets of a small bed. "It's about time," Virgil laughed, bracing Wyatt at arm's length. "Get on in here while I get dressed." The woman pushed up on an elbow, exposing one breast.

"I'll just wait outside," Wyatt said.

"Oh." Virgil laughed and looked behind him. "This here is Rozilla." He walked to the bed and covered her with the sheet. "This is Wyatt, Rosie. You 'member I told you 'bout 'im."

"Ma'am," Wyatt said and nodded. The woman offered no more than a blithe stare.

"She a French lady," Virgil said and winked, as if some joke were inherent in the claim.

Wyatt backed through the door. "I'll go see if I can get some coffee at the bar."

"Hell, Wyatt, she won't bite . . . 'less you want 'er to." Virgil laughed and fanned his hand at the air. "All right . . . go on . . . I'll be down directly."

Wyatt had finished his coffee when Virgil came down the

stairs wearing a blouse with stitch marks showing where the material had ripped in front. He poured coffee at the bar and carried it to Wyatt's table by the front window. Sitting down, he lowered his brow.

"What the hell happened to your hands? Not back at the plow, are you?"

Wyatt checked the blisters on his palms. "Poled upriver for six days with John Walton."

Virge snorted. "What, that old gunboat of his? It's supposed to be for pleasure, not work."

"Paid pretty good," Wyatt said. "Figured I could use the money."

Virgil frowned over his coffee. "There's better ways to make money than pushing a damn boat up a river. Walton make you any job offers?" When Wyatt nodded, Virgil said, "And?"

"I wanted to see what you had in mind."

Virgil shrugged. "Same kind of work as Walton's, but the pay's better."

Wyatt looked at the moth-eaten buck's head mounted above the bar. Then he wiped at the table and inspected the dust on his fingertips.

"Ain't much of a place," he said.

Virge squinted. "I thought you liked saloons."

"I do," Wyatt said and nodded at the spare furnishings. "This'n could stand some work."

Virgil spewed air through his lips. "Beats bumpin' your ass on a freighter's buckboard." As he drank, Virgil narrowed his eyes to a smile over his cup. Setting down the cup, he leaned forward on his forearms and lowered his voice. "Sometimes you gotta bust a head or two, but mostly it's lettin' a man know you don't mind doin' it. Once you get a reputation, that'll do most of the work for you." He sat back, relaxed, and pointed at Wyatt. "You already got the reputation. People around here just don't know it yet."

Wyatt looked around the room again. "Why don't we open up our own place? You and me . . . maybe James. Fix it up nice. Get a better class of people as customers."

"Well, for one thing, James is somewhere up in Oregon workin' bars," Virgil said. Then he surveyed the interior of the saloon as though he had never paid attention to it before this moment. Frowning, he blew air again. "You got any idea how much it costs to rent a place like this . . . let alone purchase it? Hell, we'd be in debt for the first ten years."

"We could build it," Wyatt said. "We built the barn in Iowa."

Virgil made a pained expression and pushed his coffee aside. "Hell, Wyatt, we'd be just one more saloon against all these others. And the price of property in town . . ." His voice trailed off, and he shook his head. "Why don't we just make some money bein' hard-asses for a while?"

"I ain't talkin' about here," Wyatt said. "We can buy up some land in one o' the new railroad towns. They're springin' up all across the prairie. We just got to find the next boom and get there early before the prices jump."

Virgil smiled and canted his head. "You always had ambition, son." He laughed and shook his head. "I like it here right now. It suits me." He glanced toward the upstairs landing. "Even got a woman wants to take care of me."

"That'd be the one from France?"

Virgil nodded. Wyatt tilted his cup and studied the dregs of his coffee.

"You know a woman by the name of Haspel?"

"Jane Haspel," Virgil said. "I worked her place before here. How d'you know her?"

"Her daughter was on Walton's boat." He set down the cup and met his brother's eyes. "Said she wasn't even fifteen," Wyatt added.

"Yeah . . . well . . ." Virgil's mouth tightened into a humorless smile. "I hear you were fourteen when you tried to run off to the war." He shrugged, tried his coffee, and frowned. "Cold," he said, pushed back his chair, and started to get up.

"I shot a man in Beardstown," Wyatt said.

Virgil stopped and sat back down. "You kill him?" When Wyatt shook his head, Virgil stared out the window and thought for a moment. "In Beardstown . . . it prob'ly won't amount to much." He turned back to study Wyatt's face. "What happened?"

"Fellow pushed too much. He shot first."

Virgil's eyes turned hard. "Well, you might not want to make a habit o' that."

"What?"

Virgil's eyes remained cold. "Lettin' the other'n shoot first."

They stared at one another for several seconds, and in that time Wyatt felt their family bond tighten like the integrated parts of a finely crafted gun. If Virgil had been there, Wyatt knew, in Walton's saloon, there would have been two Earps for Pinard and Peshaur to deal with.

"By the way," Virgil said, leaning and hunching a shoulder to reach into his trouser pocket. "I wrote Ma and Pa in Missouri . . . told 'em you might be comin' East. Pa wrote me back, and included a letter for you." He opened an envelope and withdrew a folded paper, which he flattened on the table. Then he rose and walked his cup back to the bar.

Wyatt spun the paper around and recognized his father's florid script.

Wyatt,

I am currantly holding the office of town Constable here in Lamar and plan to take the position of Justice of the Peace. If you can see your way clear to come here and take over as Constable, I can see how it would be faverble to all us Earps. I have talked to the town council, and all you have to do is step in when I step down. I believe this job will suit you.

I have got my hands into a few other bisnisses and all are doing well. Thare are good bisniss oportunaties here for all of us in Missouri.

Your mother sends her kind regards and hopes you can join us. Write me soon with your anser so I can tell the council.

Your father, Nicholas P. Earp

"Wants you to go to Missouri," Virgil said, settling back into his chair. He sipped from his steaming cup and set it down on the table. Virge raised his eyebrows. "I've been thinking of goin' for a visit myself, maybe in the winter. I'd like to make some more money here first." He gazed out the window at the summer day, at the trash scattered along the curb. "This place is dreary in winter." He scowled at the street and smiled at Wyatt. "So . . . are you goin'?"

Wyatt stared at his own hand resting on the table. He rapped his fingertips in a single sequence like a quick shuffle of cards.

"Might," he said and turned to the street scene outside. "Long as I'm here, I'll look over your setup . . . see if I can find some card games. Maybe stay a coupl'a weeks. Might go see the grandparents in Monmouth and then head to Missouri from there."

Virgil made the quiet laugh that rumbled up from deep in his chest. "You're a ramblin' soul, brother. I doubt you'll ever settle down."

Wyatt looked up at the dusty spiderwebs hanging from the exposed floor joists of the landing. "If I do, it won't be in Peoria."

CHAPTER 13

Early fall, 1869: Lamar, Missouri

In the window of the Lamar Mercantile, a mannequin gazed blindly out into the main street and stopped Wyatt cold. Sitting the fine chestnut blaze he had purchased in Monmouth, he considered that he might be staring at some image of his own future. He reined his horse to the edge of the boardwalk and stared through the glass. The nut-brown shade of the mannequin and the span of the shoulders could have been his own. He dismounted and studied the rich black color of the outfit. The shirt beneath was royal blue with widely spaced stripes and bands of gray that crisscrossed in a pleasing pattern. He cupped his hand to the glass to read the price tags. All told, the suit and its accoutrements cost more than a new pistol and Sharps rifle combined.

He let his focus adjust to his reflection in the glass. The Illinois-to-Missouri beard showed a reddish tint and a hint of wildness that he deemed inappropriate for his new job. The door opened, and the storekeeper emerged like an old friend, inviting him inside.

"Where can I get a shave?" Wyatt said. The man pointed out the tonsorial parlor, and Wyatt nodded his thanks.

An hour later he returned to the mercantile smelling of rose water. After an awkward moment of narrow-eyed scrutiny, the storekeeper's face dawned with recognition.

"Oh, yes . . . the gentleman looking for the barber. May I say, sir, the moustache is most becoming."

Wyatt looked around the store. "Wouldn' mind trying on that black coat in your window."

"That's straight from Chicago, sir, and those lapels are the newest fashion." Wyatt waited for the man to sort through a rack of half a dozen identical coats. "Would you like to try the matching trousers and vest, too?"

Wyatt removed his hat and set it upon a stack of dungarees. "Won't hurt to try."

"And the shoes?" The man held up a pair of walnut-brown Brogans polished to a high sheen. Wyatt shook his head and glanced back at the mannequin.

"Maybe the hat."

Until today he had never thought of spending money like this on clothes. Now he saw the haberdashery as a tool as valuable to his ambitions as to his personal liking. Like purchasing a finely crafted gun, there was purpose to it.

"I have a room in back where you can change, sir," the man offered and handed over the stack of folded goods as though it was the finest hour of his day.

Wyatt held the material as if he'd been handed a baby. "What about the hat?"

From his vest the storekeeper produced a cloth tape. "If I may, sir," he said and rose up on his toes to measure Wyatt's head. "I'll get the hat from stock for you."

Fully dressed in the storekeeper's goods, Wyatt stood before a long mirror and saw in his reflection an unexpected persona: a figure worthy of wearing a constable badge. The deep black of the cloth appealed to him, dignified but not showy. He had seen bankers and land investors similarly dressed and had noted how they handled themselves. Wyatt could see a successful man dressed this way only becoming more successful. Or a man just setting out with an ambition more likely to make his mark.

The clerk lifted a new hat from its box and tried to settle it on Wyatt's head, but Wyatt took it from him and mounted it himself. One look in the mirror, and the dark mantle of a man stepping boldly into his future was complete.

When he walked from the store with his trail clothes bundled under his arm, he felt the town of Lamar condense into a manageable domain. He had made the right decision in coming here. He could sense the money. Lamar did not exhibit the spark of the western boomtowns, where there was the constant sound of new construction and lively piano music filling the streets from the gambling houses and saloons. Here in Lamar there was a quieter momentum, a solidity of community, where businesses could burgeon behind closed doors on the foundations of family traditions in place for generations. And, unlike Peoria, it was a clean place without a darker side of the town hidden at the fringes. He mounted and walked his horse through the late afternoon to the house where he had been told the Earps lived.

For a moment his mother stood speechless in the doorway and then, shedding her stoic inspection of him, she stepped forward and buried her face in his shoulder. When finally she pushed away from him she could not speak until she had wiped her tears from his new coat.

"Lord, just look at you." That was all she could get out before the tears welled again.

Nicholas stopped in the doorway, his face flushed. "Well . . . you look tougher'n a plowshare . . . even in that banker's suit." He opened the door wider and stood in his commanding pose. His vest parted, unbuttoned, and his starched shirt hung outside his dark trousers. The shirt was wrinkled where the waistband had pinched the material into a watershed of creases. Even so, with a silver constable scroll shining at his breast, he was ever the man in charge.

At the sight of Wyatt, Morgan and Warren whooped, but when they shook his hand, each studied his face as though trying to recognize something familiar in his eyes. Morg had shot up lean and straight, his good humor still showing in his crinkled eyes. If unsmiling, he looked more like Wyatt than even Virgil did. Warren's excitement seemed to surface as a temporary interruption on his rebellious face. He was constantly in motion, his dark eyes cutting back and forth between father and older brothers as though stitching together patches of the family quilt.

Adelia hid behind her mother until Wyatt offered his hand. She buried her face in the folds of her mother's dress and then as quickly spun and threw her arms around Wyatt's legs. When she let go, she stepped back and bit her lip.

"Are you a preacher now?" she said. Virginia and Morgan laughed, but Warren scowled.

"Not hardly," Wyatt said. "But I *will* be a constable."

Nicholas finally gripped Wyatt's hand and pumped it. "Might have to change the name of this town to 'Earp,' " he crowed, his teeth flashing white against the tangle of grizzled beard.

"Man at the barber shop told me you're runnin' a bakery," Wyatt said. "You're gonna be justice of the peace and a baker, too?"

"Got to have your hand into more'n one piece o' the pie," Nicholas said. "Easier to do when you got family. Have you been by the bakery shop?"

When Wyatt shook his head, Nicholas fingered his watch from his vest pocket and opened the face. "Mother," he announced, pushing his shirttails down into his waistband, "we'll want to hold supper till we get back." He began buttoning his vest, and Wyatt watched the way the old man could still display authority in the simple motion of his hands. "Baxter Warren, get my coat from the bedroom."

"Morg and me'll go with you," Warren said.

135

"You boys will get back to your studies," the old man ordained.

Warren leveled dead eyes on his father, but Nicholas remained oblivious to the surly stare. The room went painfully quiet until Warren scuffed off to the back of the house, his narrow shoulders seesawing with a parting message that brought a smile to Morgan's face.

Inside the bakery Nicholas slapped the front counter and yelled to the backroom, where the clatter of metal pans and baking sheets spilled out like the jolting of a tinker's wagon. "Who's running the store here?" Nicholas barked. The racket ceased, and the old man turned his head to watch Wyatt's face.

Through the connecting doorway came a thin, dark-bearded man wearing a soiled, white apron cinched at his waist. He stopped, his gaze piercing and curious as it settled on Wyatt. A gentle smile broke across his narrow face.

"Wyatt," he said simply, his voice as unexcitable as a man who had seen most of what there was to see.

Wyatt knew the voice of his half-brother before he recognized the face. They gripped hands across the counter, Wyatt nodding with gratitude for another Earp who had come back from the war.

"Nobody told me you were here, Newton," Wyatt said. "You look . . . different."

"Well, Wyatt," Newton said quietly, "it's been what? Nine years? I'm married with a family now. Got a little girl pretty as a prairie flower." He carried his grin down to his apron. "And I'm covered with sweat and flour." He hitched a thumb to the room behind him. "These ovens are beginning to feel like purgatory."

Right away the easy manner of their talk bridged the gap of time that had passed, and Wyatt felt his respect for his oldest brother revived as if not a month had gone by since seeing him.

It had been Newton who had taught him how to shoot and clean a rifle, how to field dress a deer, and how to harness a team of horses for plowing.

Nicholas tapped a knuckle against the glass of the bread display cases. "Give 'im a sample."

Newton bent and looked over the selections, finally choosing a fist-sized roll with a dark glazed crust. He tore a piece of newsprint and wrapped the bread, just as if Wyatt were a customer. Wyatt peeled away the paper, smelled it, and tasted. Nicholas wore a wide grin as though he himself had done the kneading and the baking.

Wyatt began nodding as he chewed, and Newton's easy smile spread up into his face to squeeze his eyes to crescents. "Ma is a good teacher," Newton said, stepping around the counter to join them.

Wyatt had always considered his half-brother less wild than the other Earp boys. It was to Newton Wyatt had entrusted many a private matter before the war. Newton held a quiet pride and lacked the stubborn streak Wyatt saw especially in Virgil and Warren. People had always liked and respected him, because there was nothing hidden about him. He was smart. And he was personable without being too talkative. When Old Nick stepped back into the kitchen, the two brothers strolled out to the walkway that overlooked the town square.

"What about your wife?" Wyatt asked. "Does she work here with you?"

Newton crossed his arms over his chest, leaned against the awning post, and shook his head. "Jennie . . . she's got her hands full at home . . . bein' a mother and all."

Wyatt rewrapped the roll and studied the contented smile on Newton's face. "I'd say that just about suits you fine. Easy to figure you for a husband and a father."

Newton gazed out at the picket fence around the courthouse

and began to nod. When he finally looked back at Wyatt he said, "Suits me down to the bone." He waited, expecting Wyatt to say more, but now Wyatt was surveying the town. Newton pushed himself from the pole and squeezed his brother's arm. "So, you were freight hauling . . . and then grading for the railroad. You look strong." He slapped Wyatt's shoulder. "You ready to be the law in this town?"

Wyatt looked up and down the square at the orderly flanks of business establishments and at the peaceable nature of the pedestrians moving through the commercial district. The main roads had been recently graded. Scant horse droppings dotted the thoroughfare. Wyatt felt a long way from the sprawl of canvas tents and slipshod shacks slapped together in the rail camps.

"I'm ready," he said.

CHAPTER 14

Late fall, 1869: Lamar, Missouri

Wyatt received his badge from the mayor in the presence of the city council and the leading merchants of the community, some of whom had brought their families. All the Earps were there to see father and son accept their appointments. The ceremony was informal in the town hall, yet Wyatt never smiled, not even when the newspaperman approached him with notepad in hand.

"Have you worked in the law before, Mr. Earp?"

Wyatt shook his head. "Reckon I'll be learning as I go along. I expect the job will suit me."

"How is that?" The reporter kept writing as he asked the question. When he looked up, he followed Wyatt's gaze across the room. "Oh, that's Sutherland's daughter," he offered. "He runs the hotel, and she runs the desk sometimes. You have an eye for aesthetics." Wyatt frowned at the word, and the man leaned in closer. "Beauty," he amended.

"What's her name?"

"Rilla, I think . . . or Aurilla." The reporter made a point of poising his pencil at the ready over his notepad. "Mr. Earp, I'm curious what you think you can offer to the position without any real experience. You are young to comprise Lamar's complete law enforcement."

Wyatt nodded at a fair question. "The job requires some grit and probably some political know-how. I reckon I'm lacking in one, so till I learn it, I'll concentrate on the other."

The writer opened his mouth then closed it. The look Wyatt gave him was sufficient to answer his question about which attribute Wyatt already possessed.

"If I may be candid, some wonder if you are going to be a repeat performance of your father." The man made a nervous laugh. "Old Nick could be . . . well . . . gruff."

"I ain't my father, if that's what you mean. I learned from him both ways: what to be, what not to be. I believe I can do the job. I reckon you'll be the judge of that in the long run."

Wyatt slipped his hands into his pockets and looked over the man's head at the town's elite. " 'Course, if you print that, you'll have to deal with my father." Wyatt looked at the reporter. "And me."

The pencil stopped scratching, and the man gave another nervous laugh. "I believe that's the first time I've seen you smile tonight," he said. "I had the sense you might not be comfortable in a gathering such as this."

Wyatt turned his attention to the Sutherland girl. "I had my doubts coming in." He nodded. "But these seem like the kind of people worth knowing."

The reporter followed Wyatt's gaze to where Aurilla Sutherland fussed over a shawl draped around the shoulders of the mayor's wife. "Might I call on you from time to time, Mr. Earp? I'd like to keep our readers up to date on the goings-on inside the constable's office."

"I'll be available." Wyatt looked the man in the eye. "You got your job to do, just like me."

They shook hands, and Wyatt watched the reporter cross the room to the refreshment table, where he began to interview the mayor. Though the newspaperman had some of the qualities of a proper woman who had never soiled her hands, Wyatt figured he could tolerate him. The reporter knew how to put a man at ease in conversation, and there might be something to learn from that.

A melodic laugh pulled his attention back to Aurilla Sutherland. Her smile transformed her face, like a bright flower blossom opening after a rain. Though he did not speak to her that night, he did learn that she liked horses. Each time one of the citizens shook his hand, he pushed her from his mind to concentrate on the person before him. Learn the name. Remember it later when he would patrol the streets. It was part of the job to know people.

More than once when he returned his gaze to the Sutherland girl, he caught her studying him. And each time, she looked away at nothing and let a smile linger on her lips. That smile pulled at a memory. It was the way Valenzuela Cos had received him when she believed he had led the wagons over the Rockies. But on this Missouri girl, the smile was more a portent . . . something more relevant to his future. She was his kind. An American. And no whore.

One week into the constableship, Wyatt adjusted his expectations. At best the job was lackluster—serving papers for court appearances, seizing personal property from men who could not satisfy debts, shooting stray dogs, shooing hogs off the street, and locking up drunks. For the rowdy and inebriated, Wyatt made use of an abandoned stone building as a jail. For a better cut of prisoner, he made arrangements through the town council to rent out a room at the Exchange Hotel, where nineteen-year-old Aurilla spent her afternoons behind the desk.

Wyatt waited for an opportunity to house a prisoner at Sutherland's, and it came with an Irish tanner named Kennedy, who could not pay his creditors. While Wyatt filled out papers on him at the city office, Kennedy paced to the front window and stared out at the busy street.

"Mr. Kennedy, if you'd like to rest a spell, you can use the cot there," Wyatt offered.

The tanner turned from the window. "How's a man to make bond when he's unable to meet his debts? That's what I'd like to know."

Wyatt opened a drawer, filled his ink well, and went back to his writing. By the time he had completed the form, the tanner was pacing the floor, so that he could alternate glaring out at the unjust town and at the constable who worked at a snail's pace. For the fourth time, Wyatt extracted the pocket watch from his vest and opened the face.

"One fifteen," he said. "How 'bout we walk over to the Continental for a meal."

The man's perpetual scowl tightened. "I don't have the money for that."

"You're a guest of the town for a spell, Mr. Kennedy."

In the hour they spent eating, Wyatt listened to the travails of an independent tanner, who had struggled against the newly incorporated tannery operating on Clear Creek. Wyatt nodded at each point, reducing the man's dilemma to the lessons that he might one day employ in his own ventures, whatever they might be: *When choosing an enterprise, study the odds first. Know what you're up against. Then back yourself up with people you trust.*

Wyatt was thinking of his brothers—Virgil, Morgan, James, and Warren. And half-brother, Newton. Maybe they would all go into business one day, but before broaching the idea, he would need to pin down that business. Meanwhile . . . there was Aurilla Sutherland.

When Wyatt finished his meal, he checked his watch again, returned it to his pocket, and looked out over the restaurant as he spoke to his prisoner. "What about some pie, Mr. Kennedy? You're not likely to get any pie on the regulation meal doled out by the city."

The tanner's face wrinkled, and he stopped chewing. "Ain't I on the city plan now?"

Wyatt nodded at the man's plate. "For the meal. The pie's on me."

Confused, the tanner pinched his eyebrows into a peak as Wyatt ordered for them.

It took the better part of an hour for Wyatt to finish a single slice of pie. Then they took a leisurely walk back to the constable's office to get the papers. From there they strolled the two blocks to the hotel. Wyatt stopped at the last store window and checked his reflection. The tanner stared at Wyatt's back.

"Earp, I think you are the slowest man at his job I have ever come across."

Wyatt turned. "You in a hurry to get locked up?"

Kennedy's cheeks inflated as he exhaled. "No," he admitted. "I reckon not." When Wyatt stepped into the hotel, the tanner followed. At ten minutes past three, Wyatt set down the papers next to the registration book. Aurilla Sutherland looked up from her work, and her eyes widened with surprise.

"Oh . . ." she said and blushed.

"Afternoon," Wyatt said. "I've got some papers here on this man. He's to be accommodated tonight on the city's tab, if you have a room."

She took the papers and scanned the contents of the document. When she looked back at the constable, she allowed a modest laugh to show that she was flustered.

"I've just come on duty," she said. "Let me check the register." Her finger slid down the page. "We've sometimes used number thirteen for female prisoners. Will there be a guard?"

Wyatt waited for her to look up, and then he turned to the tanner. "Will you be trying to run off tonight, Mr. Kennedy?"

Kennedy opened his mouth but said nothing. Wyatt turned back to Aurilla Sutherland.

"Reckon I'll keep watch," he said. "Just to keep things official."

Wyatt studied her as she reread the legal papers. Her hair— several shades lighter than his—shone atop her round face as if she had just run in from the rain. Her skin looked cool and smooth as a china plate. Compared to the whores of the railroad camps and Peoria, Aurilla Sutherland was spun out of royal cloth and had materialized in this world like a mother's sweet song to her child.

"Mr. Kennedy is not a dangerous man, Miss Sutherland. Just a little low on money at present. Just the same, I'll be on duty while you're here."

"All right," she replied, and then, carrying the beginning of a smile, she looked away to the panel of keys hanging in rows on hooks. Wyatt admired the straightness of her back and the way her neck rose erect from her shoulders. Most of the town women twisted their hair into some kind of painful knot and secured it with a long treacherous pin, only to cover the whole affair with a frivolous hat. He liked Aurilla's simple style. And he liked it that she had handled the prisoner's accommodations without her father's help.

After shutting Kennedy in his room, Wyatt took a chair in the lobby and read the newspaper as he listened to the sounds of Aurilla going about her work: the rustle of her dress when she moved, the scratch of her pen, her light step. Now and again she made a faint humming sound in her throat that accompanied certain phases of her bookkeeping. Three times he caught her looking at him, and on that third time, she finally smiled as she went back to work.

Her replacement, a short, stooped man with long, gray sideburns, came in at seven, and she briefed him about a few details—the new occupant in thirteen being one of those. When she wrapped her cloak around her shoulders, Wyatt stood and intercepted her at the door.

"I'd be proud to walk you home, if you don't care."

"Aren't you on guard duty, Mr. Earp?"

"I got to get Kennedy's supper. I don't reckon he'll run off in the next ten minutes."

"Can't someone from the restaurant bring over a plate?"

"Could . . . but I don't mind."

Her eyes were so clear he might have been looking up at the scattered blue of the sky through springwater. Unlike his own, that blue seemed to contain its own source of light. Valenzuela Cos had told him that his eyes were washed out like blue-tinted ice.

"My house is not on the way to the restaurant, Mr. Earp."

"Don't mind that either."

"Someone usually walks me home. I imagine he'll be here any minute."

Wyatt nodded and kept his eyes on her. "Are you expecting him for certain?"

"Well . . ." She looked through the glass in the door. "I don't suppose 'for certain.' "

Wyatt looked out at an evening made for walking. "Well, it's for certain I'm here."

She looked into his eyes, and he wondered if she saw ice there. "Yes, you are," she said and presented a smile that changed her face into something from which he could not look away.

After the droning heat of the woodstove in the lobby, the autumn night was a blessing. They walked the first block in silence, each enjoying the change of atmosphere. Wyatt knew her house was only two blocks distant, so he listened to their footsteps tap on the boardwalk like a clock ticking away their time. Moving in and out of the glow of the street lamps, he kept his eyes straight ahead, glancing at her only in the shadowed interludes.

"You're not curious about who usually walks me home?" she said.

"I reckon you'll tell me if I need to know."

"I have a feeling it wouldn't bother you one way or the other, no matter who it was."

"I'd be pleased if you'd go for a ride with me sometime. Just us . . . on horseback."

She laughed at the sudden change in the conversation, and the melody in her laugh seemed to him as personal as if she had touched his hand. "Do you really think your prisoner will remain in his room just because you want him to, Mr. Earp?"

"I'm satisfied he'll stay put. I reckon all my prisoners will have to sit tight long enough for me to walk you home."

She laughed again. "It doesn't sound like you will be our constable for too long, Mr. Earp. I imagine the town will want its prisoners locked up more tightly."

Wyatt thought about that and nodded at her good sense. "Well, could be I don't want to always be a constable. I might like to do something a bit more profitable."

"Oh, really? And what might that be?"

"I'm still thinkin' on that."

"So you have ambition."

He looked at her. "Yes, ma'am. I reckon that's why I'm walkin' you home."

"So you intend to do this often?"

"As often as I can."

"Then you'll have to do away with the 'ma'am' and 'Miss Sutherland,' Mr. Earp. Why don't you call me 'Rilla'?"

They reached the Sutherland house just as two young men stepped off the porch to the stone walkway. Rilla stepped through the open gate and turned to Wyatt, who stopped in the road.

"What about that ridin'?" he said.

She lowered her eyes and smiled but did not get a chance to answer.

"God, Granville! Where'd you get that outfit? Are you preaching somewhere tonight?" Laughter bubbled up from the two men approaching from the house. Then the laughter cut off sharply, and they slowed their walk.

"This is Constable Earp," Rilla announced. "These are my brothers, Burdette and Frederick." Wyatt shook hands with them in silence.

"Where's Gran, Rilla?" the taller brother said.

"Mr. Earp walked me home. I haven't seen Gran."

The two Sutherland boys looked toward town, then back at Rilla and then briefly at Wyatt. The silence seemed to belong to the brothers, so Wyatt waited to see what they would do with it.

"Well . . ." Frederick said. Without another word they passed through the gate and started for town. Wyatt could hear their muted whispers on the crisp, cold air. He turned back to Rilla.

"Reckon you better call me 'Wyatt,' " he said.

"All right. But maybe with my brothers it ought to be 'Constable Earp' for a while." She flashed an apologetic smile. "You have brothers, don't you, Wyatt?"

He nodded. "Newton is the oldest." He nodded down the street toward the square. "He's working in my pa's bakery. James is somewhere in Oregon. Virgil is in Peoria. I've got two younger brothers livin' with my folks." Wyatt stepped backward into the dirt lane. "Time for me to take some food to my prisoner. You might think about that ride with me."

Rilla smiled, looked down at her shoes, and brought the same smile back up to him. "Good night, Wyatt. Thank you for the escort."

He pinched the brim of his new hat and started down the street. In front of the barbershop the two Sutherland boys stood in the middle of the street with a third man with sloped shoulders and trousers a little too short for his long legs. As Wyatt approached on the boardwalk, they turned in unison to watch him. They followed his progress past the post office until the third man disengaged from his friends and walked a line to intercept Wyatt. When the man stopped six feet from the boardwalk, Wyatt turned and faced him.

"My name's Brummett," he stated flatly. "I'm the one who walks Aurilla home." His voice cracked on the last word. He cleared his throat and swallowed. "Meanin' . . . nobody else does."

Wyatt made a concerted effort to keep the hardness out of his voice. "I already did."

Brummett hesitated too long and tried to compensate for his failed script by pouring some venom into his voice. "She's spoke for."

Wyatt glanced at the Sutherland boys, who had not moved from the middle of the thoroughfare. He stepped down from the boards into the street and lowered his voice to be heard by Brummett alone.

"She don't appear to know that."

Brummett gestured toward Wyatt's lapel, then curled his lip until his teeth showed. "That badge mean you can carry a gun?"

Wyatt paused, letting himself settle from the man's surly tone. "It does."

"Easy to talk big with a gun."

"I don't need a gun to talk. You'd best go cool off, Mr. Brummett. You're disappointed and frustrated and about to make a mistake."

People slowed on the boardwalk to watch the development. Brummett straightened his spine and started to step forward, but stopped when one of the Sutherland boys called out.

"Gran, come on down to the billiards parlor with us."

Brummett turned at the waist, but it was Wyatt who spoke to them. "I don't want to arrest your friend over something personal. Best get him off the street." Brummett took a step back as if the words had physically pushed him. He did not retake the ground he had given up.

The brothers didn't speak as they approached and carried out Wyatt's request, but Brummett began making a bigger fuss. He needed to do this, Wyatt knew, to save face. Wyatt listened to the abusive words and watched the three figures move away down the street.

In almost any other context, Wyatt would have knocked the joker on his ass and had done with it. But as it was, he knew he had played his first political hand like a seasoned officer. With less than a month into the job, he didn't need any marks against him with the council, not over a woman. And he didn't need Rilla to hear about him laying this jaybird out in the street.

When he looked toward the boardwalk and nodded, the bystanders moved on, and once again alone he felt the prudence of his discretion. He had handled this in a proper way. This would get back to Rilla, he knew. He gazed down the dark street toward her house, recalling that Brummett had referred to her as "Aurilla" . . . not "Rilla." He thought about that as he walked to the restaurant.

CHAPTER 15

Early winter, 1869—fall, 1870: Lamar, Missouri

Two days before Christmas Wyatt and Rilla rode out to a juniper flat that sat high over Clear Creek. Rilla sat her bay gelding with a fluid grace, the certainty of her control reminding Wyatt of the way she had led him through the steps at the Christmas dance three nights before in the community hall. There she had been gently instructive without being commanding. On the big gelding she moved as easily as the steed's dark mane, swaying naturally to the horse's gait and melding with its passion for speed and open space.

They stopped for lunch at a broad beach, where Wyatt broke up ice near the shoreline with a found barrel stave and picketed the horses near the water's edge. As Rilla spread out the few provisions that she had folded in a cloth, he built a driftwood fire and heated water in the trail pan he had packed to make coffee. He liked the way she did not overdo the meal: biscuits, ham, and a small jar of preserves. He saw to the coffee and watched her sort out the meal on a checkered cloth, her cheeks flushed in the biting air. She had worn sensible clothes for riding: a union suit, a man's trousers, and a knitted sweater under her woolen overcoat. Even bundled up so, her irrepressible relish for being alive radiated from her face like a jewel shining from the folds of a black velvet bag.

"You ride like a Indian," he said.

"*An* Indian, Wyatt." She always smiled when she took the opportunity to improve his speech. He knew it was not for her pride but for his ambitions in the community. He had told her he needed to know how to talk to men who had been properly educated.

"You ride like *an* Indian," he corrected. "Reckon I talk like one."

She laughed. That he could make her laugh was a miracle to him. There was no sound he liked better. When she saw the way he was looking at her, she walked to him, rose up on her toes, and kissed him. Stepping back she smiled and touched her fingertips below her nose.

"Your moustache tickles," she laughed and canted her head. "But I like it."

"Are you cold?"

She held the smile and shook her head. "Indian make good fire," she said. Wyatt laughed quietly, another miracle to which he was growing more accustomed. "Wyatt, next time we go to a dance, why don't you bring along your horse."

He had knelt to the fire to rearrange the partially burned sticks. "My horse," he echoed, looking up at her, his eyes pinched with a question.

"The two of you know what you're doing together. I believe you were born to ride." He pushed at the coals with a stick. "Of course, it will hurt more if the two of you step on my feet."

"I reckon I can get better at it with some practice. How are your feet?"

She gave him the look that he was certain no other man saw. "Did you like dancing?"

"I liked being with you."

"But did you like dancing?"

"I like riding better."

She crossed her arms under her breasts. "Wyatt, you are the most direct man I've ever known, but you're starting to sound like a politician."

He smiled. "I liked the dancing fine. If you can stick with me on it, I can learn it."

She knelt beside him and slipped her arm through his. "I'll stick," she said.

In less than a month, standing before Justice of the Peace Nicholas Earp, they exchanged vows to become man and wife. Virgil had arrived in time to see it happen, bringing with him the willowy young French woman from Peoria—Rozilla. Her accent charmed all the family except Nicholas, who was perpetually confounded by the exotic alteration of her words. Though still pretty, there was a jaded look about her, as if she had already suffered more disappointments than most women would ever know. Sometimes when Wyatt looked at her, he thought of Valenzuela Cos, who, like Rozilla, had been scarred but still held to a dream of a better life.

The newlyweds moved into a room at the Exchange, where Rilla continued to work behind the desk of her father's business. Wyatt liked the arrangement. And he liked Lamar. The prospects for improving his life seemed set into motion.

In the spring Virgil took up managing the bakery in town, and appeased his parents by taking Rozilla as his wife. Newton traded the ovens for farming, with plans to expand the family shop to a grocery. Through that greenest of summers, the prosperity of the Earps appeared to be on the verge of blossoming.

When Aurilla grew heavy with child, Wyatt made a down payment on a house on a small lot next to half-brother Newton and his family. There on the outskirts of town the birthing would take place. Wyatt knew he was blessed to have his hard-edged life touched by someone like Rilla, but now the coming of the child ushered him into a new sense of self-worth. The raw life of the boomtowns and railroad camps was far behind him now. He had sown his oats with whores and gambling and fighting, and now he set his eyes on a path for a more substantial future, a course inspired first by Rilla, and now by the baby.

In the early fall on a crisp day, with the sky as clear as a great blue ceramic platter, Wyatt came home from work early driving a wagon load of wood he had sawn and split in the woods north of town. It was well after dark when he had finished stacking it by the house. When he went inside, Rilla worked at the sideboard putting together the evening meal.

"We were just trying to decide if you were a constable or a woodcutter," Rilla said and then turned to show him her smile. She kept looking at Wyatt as he sat and pulled off his gloves.

" 'We'?"

She placed a hand on her belly, the movement as gentle as a holy ritual. Setting down a serving spoon, she walked to him with both hands pressing to the swell of her dress. Wyatt placed his hands on hers, and she bent and kissed him. Her smile dissolved when she read his face.

"I run into a coupl'a boys who'd been hunting up north of town. They found a liquor still set up back in the woods, and they took me to it." Wyatt removed his hands from her and tugged off a boot. When he started on the other, he said, "Looks like it might belong to Gran Brummett." He set the boots on the floor and looked up to see Rilla's censorial eyebrow arch as it always did whenever he shared with her the misdeeds that went on in Lamar. "It's a big operation. Word is . . . your brothers are in this with him."

Now she became very still, and her forehead creased like a washboard. "What did you do?"

"What I had to do. It's out of the town limits, so I handed it over to the sheriff."

"What will *he* do with them?"

"It'll go to court. Probably just a fine. The sheriff will have to bust up the still."

She walked back to the counter and began serving their plates. The sharp tap of the spoon on the cookware seemed to serve as a surrogate message for the words she would not say.

"Upholding the law is what I do, Rilla. The town pays me for it."

She brought the plates to the table and sat. Wyatt tucked his cloth napkin into the crook of his collar, but Rilla only folded her hands in her lap and stared at him.

"It doesn't seem fair," she said quietly. Her gaze lowered to the steaming food before her. "You told me your father has moonshined everywhere he has ever lived." Her luminescent eyes came up briefly to meet his. "I've even heard people here talk about the quality of *his* liquor."

Wyatt held his fork motionless above his plate and waited until she would look at him again. "If it had been Pa's still, I would'a done the same thing."

Rilla's face relaxed. She rested an elbow on the table, lowered her head, and pinched the bridge of her nose between her eyes. "I know you would, Wyatt," she whispered. When her hand came down she smiled. "I really do." She reached for him, and their hands met across the table. With the squeeze of her grip, he felt her love enfold him with a level of trust he had never before experienced with another human being. At times like this, the walls of their little house seemed like a stone palisade, an impassable boundary that could shut them off from every trouble the world could throw their way.

Wyatt started on his meal, and Rilla followed suit. "I reckon my pa prob'ly is runnin' a still out there somewhere. If he is . . . he never talks about it." He chewed and looked north out the window.

"Well, I hope Gran and my brothers don't have to stand

before *him* . . . in *his* courtroom," Rilla said more to herself than to Wyatt. "Wouldn't that be ironic?"

Wyatt bit off a mouthful of bread baked in his family's bakery, and then he chewed for a time, until he began nodding. "Be a hard nut to swallow." Slicing at the piece of ham on his plate, he dismissed the trivial details of the moonshine operation. "I'm going to run for constable again in the elections."

She looked mildly surprised. "You are?"

"Thought I'd see if I could get voted in this time . . . 'stead o' slippin' in through the back door. If I can hold the position another year, then I'll figure out a business that'll help us prosper. All I need is the right idea and the right people to back me."

"Everyone respects you, Wyatt. You have a good reputation in Lamar. I was here when your father was constable. You're not like him. You handle things calmer . . . calmer but stronger."

From anyone else, such a compliment would have meant little to him. People were forever trying to gain favor with the ones in charge. But Rilla's voice always carried a ring of certainty.

He nodded toward the swell of her stomach. "You reckon I can conjure up that calm when that little baby decides to pay a visit?"

Rilla's smile spread across her face. "This baby is going to wrap you around his finger."

" 'His'? Sounds like you might have this birthin' all figured out," he said, knowing that, being a woman, she probably did have some way of knowing it would be a boy. "If I'm still the constable, maybe I'll have something to say about how things work around here."

"You'll still be the constable, Wyatt. You'll see."

★ ★ ★ ★ ★

On a cold night in November, after cleaning the dishes, Rilla went to bed without a word, just as she had the preceding night. With the birth approaching, she seemed to need the extra rest. In the parlor Wyatt struggled to compose the newspaper notice that he hoped would get him elected to another term. Within minutes, without Rilla's help to find the proper words, he gave it up and carried the oil lamp to the kitchen, where he flattened a newspaper on the table and disassembled James's pistol, laying out the parts in the same order in which he would, in reverse, reassemble it.

Running the wire brush through the barrel, he felt the abstractions of laboring over the newspaper card dissolve with the tangible exercise of cleaning the gun. The heft of the frame in his hands was a reward in itself. He treated the gun with care and respect, not only because it had been James's weapon, but because its mechanics guaranteed his well-being. One day he would call on the gun to reciprocate, and for that occasion, it would need to be as ready as he was.

A mewling sound from the bedroom stilled his hands. Suspending his breathing, he listened for anything else he might hear. Rilla's breathing had gone ragged, and her muted voice was a raspy whisper as she spoke, as if someone else were in the room with her. Wyatt laid down the hardware, crossed the floor, and quietly pushed open the door. The grip of her fist on the bed sheets stopped him cold.

"It's too early," she said. The voice that squeezed from her chest was as unfamiliar as the look of agony distorting her face. "I can't do this."

Wyatt felt a match strike against the pit of his stomach. "Rilla?" He pushed through the door and took a step toward her but stopped short. "I'll fetch the doctor," he said and grabbed his heavy coat from the clothes cabinet. Taking one more look at her misery, he rushed outside.

He ran next door to rouse Newton and Jennie, feeling the short distance from Rilla as if it were a separation of miles. When he returned, he found her racked with pain, one leg splayed to the floor. Kneeling beside her he cradled her head in his hands. The heat and dampness of her hair opened a hollow cavern in his gut.

"You got to hang on," he whispered. "My brother has gone for the doctor."

As he lifted her back into the bed, she tightened her grip on him with a strength he had not thought her capable. He pushed away to keep his weight off her swollen belly, but from her fierce hold on his coat lapels, she began to rise with him.

"Let me go wet a towel," he said, but still he had to pry her fingers loose.

Through the backdoor came Newton, his wife Jennie right behind him. Her thick, dark hair—usually pinned up on her head—fell loosely around her shoulders, making her appear almost a stranger. Both began to pull out of their heavy coats as Newton's eyes seemed to ask Wyatt for any news. Not knowing what to say, Wyatt worked the pitcher pump and squeezed the towel of excess water, but Jennie took it from him and hurried into the bedroom.

"The doctor's coming," Newton said quietly and looked around the kitchen, finally nodding at the stove. "I'll bring in some wood. We might need to boil some water." He waited, but when Wyatt said nothing, Newton squeezed his brother's upper arm. "Havin' a baby can be as hard on a man as a woman."

Wyatt shook his head. "It ain't just that," he said hoarsely. "Somethin' bad's wrong."

Newton's dark eyes softened with the same tenderness he had bestowed on Wyatt as a child. "It'll be all right, Wyatt." He waited for Wyatt to accept his counsel, but Wyatt could only stare at the bedroom door. "I'll get the wood," Newton said again and slipped out the door.

When Wyatt returned to the bedroom, Jennie turned, unable to hide the alarm on her face. Rilla was limp and her breathing so shallow, he paused to assure himself she was still alive. When Jennie pressed the towel to her face, Rilla shivered violently about her shoulders.

"I'll get another blanket," Wyatt said, his voice sounding distant even to himself.

"She's burning up with fever, Wyatt," Jennie said. "Wet another towel for her stomach."

When he returned, Jennie lifted Rilla's nightgown, and time seemed to stop as they stared mutely at red blotches scattered across Rilla's skin. Jennie grabbed the towel and covered the spots, but the image had seared into Wyatt's memory.

Only when the doctor arrived did Rilla open her eyes. Wyatt felt his gut tighten when he saw how the bright blue had drained from her irises, leaving them drab and listless. She turned her head to the doctor and pushed a feeble voice through her clamped teeth.

"This baby is killing me!" She hissed the words like an accusation, then slumped back into the bed as if the admission had cost her everything.

Wyatt stood back and watched the doctor administer to Rilla's needs as Jennie fussed with the sheets. When he heard footsteps on the side porch, Wyatt turned to see Newton opening the door for Mrs. Sutherland, her mouth grim and set with purpose, her eyes already sagging with hopelessness. Her head was bare and her hair unkempt in a way Wyatt had never seen. After Newton helped her struggle out of her coat, she tightened the sash of her night robe.

"Is it the baby?" she said, looking at Newton. He turned, deferring to Wyatt.

"She said it was . . . killin' her," Wyatt said quietly.

Her gaze held on Wyatt's face long enough to convey the certainty of a crisis. She pulled him from the door and stood him by the woodstove.

"Don't go in there, Wyatt. She wouldn't want it."

Without another word, she swept into the bedroom and closed the door, leaving Wyatt to stare at the dividing wall between them. He stood stock-still and listened for any sound that might reach him. Right away the door opened, and the doctor's head leaned through the crack.

"Heat some water to a boil, Wyatt!"

Newton hurried to the sideboard and worked the pitcher pump. Wyatt was like a man banished from a dream, watching himself from outside the bubble of a nightmare. The repetitious sound of the pump handle mocked him for his ineptness. If the doctor had not come, he would not have known how to help his wife. Nothing had prepared him for this. He was accustomed to meeting problems head on, providing the action that balanced the need. He felt like a child as he watched Newton space pots of water on the stove top. Wyatt knew he should have already done that. Any fool would know to heat water.

"The doc'll know what to do, Wyatt," Newton said in his kind and gentle way. When Wyatt made no response, Newton picked up a stick of firewood from the pile and hesitated at the door to the stove. "Hey, I had me a good idea. Some of the farmers around the town are planning to vote for Old Man Yard for constable. I know for a fact they'll vote for me if I put my name on the slate. I figure that'll help spread out the vote in your favor."

Wyatt stared at his brother, seeing only the image of Rilla he had carried from the bedroom. She had been sinking . . . away from him. If she died, the part of him he had invested in her—in their life together—would turn against him and break what was left of his ambitions. He was as sure of that as he was of the eventual coming of the dawn. Already he could sense the permanent hole losing her would open up inside him.

Each time Mrs. Sutherland came for the water, her face looked more haggard, her eyes in red-rimmed anguish. "Keep up with the water, Wyatt. We need more towels."

She squeezed his hand, and the feel of her grip sent a chill through his body, as though she were serving as a surrogate to inform him that Rilla might never touch him again. He wanted to say to her that she was wrong, that he should be in there with her at that moment, but his words hardened, as if a piece of ice had lodged in his throat. He turned away lest she see his stricken face, and then, remembering the towels, he grabbed his coat off the chair.

"I'll go, Wyatt," Newton said. "I've got plenty in my back storeroom."

Newton had been gone only a minute when the doctor shuffled from the bedroom, closed the door behind him, and leaned against the jamb. Wyatt could only stare at the man's bloodstained hands.

"The baby was stillborn, Wyatt."

Wyatt stared at the closed door to the bedroom. "What about Aurilla?" he said hoarsely.

The doctor looked down at the floor and shook his head before meeting Wyatt's eyes. "It's more than the baby. She has typhus." His voice dropped to a whisper. "She gave it all for the child. I don't know that I can help her." He hitched his head toward the door. "Go in and see her, son."

Wyatt crossed the floor and quietly pushed open the bedroom door. The first thing he saw was blood, soaked into the linens in a garish pattern, as though a bucket of red paint had been upended on the bed. Jennie looked at him, her eyes brimming with tears. Rilla's mother was slumped on the floor by the bed, her forehead pressed into the mattress and one hand resting on Aurilla's unmoving arm. Still holding the doctor's medical words in his ears, Wyatt stared at his wife lying among the twisted bed sheets. A tiny, lifeless rag of a body lay beside her. It was a boy, tinted red all over as though it had been drowned in blood.

Already he knew he would carry this indelible scene with him through whatever was left of his life. "Rilla . . ." he said, but was not sure to whom he was speaking. The silence that followed was like the still air in an empty house.

Jennie rose and left the room, touching Wyatt's sleeve as she passed. The doctor moved back to the bed and sat. Very gently, he pressed two fingers to Rilla's neck and remained still for a time. Slowly he turned and gave Wyatt the solemn look that could never be recanted.

"She can't hear you, Wyatt. She's gone." The doctor's moist eyes filled with the reflection of the lamplight. "She's with God now."

Rilla's mother began to convulse with racking sobs. Wyatt did not know if he was supposed to go to her or let her be. Until she had touched him in the kitchen he had never had physical contact with her. How could he begin such a thing now? Her wail was like the victorious scream of death itself. Backing away from the wretchedness trapped inside the room, he turned and walked out of the house in his shirtsleeves, moving aimlessly toward the back lot, wondering if his legs would carry him to a place of privacy.

The light from the kitchen window sufficed to guide him to the well, where he stopped and leaned into the mortared stone wall and stared out at the dark scrim of trees beyond. Behind him the kitchen door opened, and he heard Newton quietly call his name.

Without turning, Wyatt raised a hand to halt his brother.

Soon the door pulled shut, and Wyatt was alone again. Closing his eyes he let his head sag, and when he opened his eyes, he peered down into the dark maw of the well. The wind picked up and flapped his blouse, drawing a shiver from the center of him. He could hear the trees swaying gently at the back of the lot, their bare limbs tapping out a message that held no relevance for him.

Rilla, he tried to say, but no sound would issue from his throat.

Daylight was beginning to fan across the eastern sky. There was no color, only gray. The world was a wasteland. And though he could not see it, he felt the curse of that amber moon resurrected, hanging over him like a cruel eye risen from common mud.

CHAPTER 16

Fall, 1870—early spring, 1871: Lamar, Missouri

After the funeral, Wyatt let no one in the house and spent his aimless energy cleaning the bed mattress and scrubbing the floor, just as Rilla would have done. In a stack of brush piled behind the house, he burned the dark-stained sheets along with dozens of bloody rags and towels. He even fed to the flames the crib he had built with the scrap lumber left over from the horse shed.

He set the fire late at night, standing under a vast firmament of stars, soaking up the radiant heat of the flames until there was nothing left but a smoking black scar on the land. The scorch mark that remained was like a monument to his spiritual ruin, and he found himself drawn to it at all times of the day and night, sometimes staring at it from the bedroom window, as though he were standing vigil over a last glimpse of what his life might have become.

Newton was the first to visit. Everyone in the family knew it was he who stood the best chance of reaching Wyatt. He came early on a Sunday, but Wyatt would not see him. Sympathy was not what he needed.

Then Virginia came, with Morg and Warren in tow. The two boys remained in the spring wagon and stared at the house, watching their mother knock on a door that remained closed and locked. Reluctantly, she left a basket of food and a vase of flowers on the porch.

Nicholas had lost a wife, too—Newton's mother. He had always been quick to contribute something on the subject of whipping oneself back into shape and getting on with life, but with Wyatt, he was not prepared to voice his philosophy, and not once did he try.

Although Virgil argued against it, Virginia finally forced him to take a fresh basket to Wyatt. After knocking on the door off and on for ten minutes, Virgil sat in the rocker where Rilla—just weeks ago—had knitted clothes for the baby and confided the names she had chosen. Together they had listened to Wyatt hammer together the crib out in the horse shed, and, in listening to her, Virgil had come to understand that she and Wyatt had found that kind of partnership that made other men feel they had come up short in the world.

A scraping sound brought Virgil out of his reverie. Rilla's bay gelding had worked its head through the lower opening in the fence to nose at a tussock of dried grass. The horse's head retreated and it looked back at him as it chewed. The bay snorted and then ducked through the slats for more. Just beyond, Wyatt's blaze chestnut mare nipped at the withered grass bunched around a fence post. Its mane and tail were crusted with burrs. Virgil pushed up from the chair.

"Wyatt?" he called, pounding the door. He waited again, wondering if he could be heard over the blowing wind. "It's Virge. I come to talk to you." When no sound could be heard from the house, Virgil stuffed his hands into his pockets, widened his stance, and let his head slump. "We're all wanting you to come stay with us. I figure you and I can do some huntin'."

When Wyatt opened the door, Virgil tried not to look shocked at the face so drawn and pale. Wyatt's blond hair hung over his forehead, partially covering his dead eyes. His face was rough with a weed-bed of whiskers around his tawny moustache.

"You won the election," Virgil said, evening his voice. He tried to smile and opened his mouth to speak again but failed on both attempts. When Wyatt stepped outside to stare at the horses, Virgil turned, too, and together they watched the animals nose at the dry grass. The two horses seemed bound by an invisible tether, maintaining an easy proximity as they moved about.

"You got hay in the shed?" Virgil asked. "I could throw some out."

Wyatt made no response. Virgil picked up the basket of food he had brought with him, as though he might formally present it. Instead, he set it down and walked to the shed. When he had tossed the hay over the fence, he started back for the house, but the porch was empty. The basket sat where he had left it.

After climbing into his saddle, Virgil looked back at the horses, thinking he should have saddled Wyatt's horse and coaxed his brother out for a ride. After a minute, he kicked his heels into the flanks of his horse and made for the constable's office. That was where he could help his brother. There was nothing to do at the house. Wyatt needed time.

In two days, Wyatt showed up at the office and found Virgil sitting at the desk, sorting out the active circulars and summonses. They nodded to one another, and Virgil stood, gathered up the papers, and laid them out on the table where the jailor took his meals. Wyatt hung up his coat, sat at the desk, and pulled out the city ledger. He began to enter the school tax figures from the fines he had collected before taking leave of his post, but he found Virgil had already posted the numbers. His brother's scrawling was almost identical to his own.

"Didn' realize how much money passed through this office," Virgil said as he thumbed through papers, his back still to Wyatt. "Do they allow you a percentage like the county does?"

"No," Wyatt said. His voice had no bottom. The word floated about the room, light as a dust mote. It was the first he had spoken since the funeral. "Being constable won't ever help a man to get rich."

Virgil turned at that. "Well, it's better'n a lot o' other work around here." Resting his forearm on the windowsill, he stared absently across the square at the bakery. Virge took in a lot of air, and let it ease out. "Hell, I ain't cut out to be no damned baker."

Wyatt stared at Virge's back. "I'm beholden to you for what you done here."

After a time of silence, Virgil held up a paper and slapped it with the back of his hand. "Jim Cromwell's brother-in-law died. No need to serve his papers. Probate court will take what he owes out of his holdings." Virgil walked to Wyatt, laid the warrant on the desk, took his mackinaw from the coat rack, and slid his arms into the sleeves. "No call to be beholdin', Wyatt. That's what brothers do . . . help each other out." Virge looked down at the top of Wyatt's head as he read the paper. "I could stick around if you want," Virgil suggested.

Wyatt looked up and then turned his gaze to the window. "No need."

Virgil continued to watch his brother. It was as though he had already left, and Wyatt was alone in the room. The only sound was the light rattle of a pane of glass worried by the wind.

"I'll be down at the bakery if you need anything," Virgil offered. He waited for a reply, but none was forthcoming. "Hell, you'd be doin' me a favor if you did."

Wyatt laid down the paper. "What about Rozilla? Can't she take it over and free you up?"

Virgil made the deep, raspy laugh in his chest that served to sum up untenable situations. "She can't hardly make coffee without me showing her how." Virgil turned his head to the holding cell, and the cartilage in his jaw flexed in a steady rhythm like a pulse. When he looked back at Wyatt's taut face, he exhaled heavily. "I ain't so sure I like this married life."

Wyatt sat back in his chair, stood his pen in its perch beside the inkwell, and stared at the ledger. Virgil stepped back to the window and watched the town go about its business. When he spoke, his voice came off the windowglass with the blur of an echo.

"I should'n'a said nothing like that . . . about bein' married." Virgil turned, his face darkened to a shade of embarrassment. "Not with what you just been through." He leaned against the windowsill and lowered his eyes to the floor. "Hell, a big brother is s'posed to know what to say." He took in another long breath and exhaled it slowly. "Hell, I ain't really your big brother no more." He looked back at Wyatt. "We're just brothers."

A gentler silence filled the room, and with it came remembrances of their history before the war. Each brother knew that their bond was somehow tighter with Rilla passing.

Virgil pushed off from the window. "Ma's wantin' you to come out for dinner."

Wyatt opened the drawer at his belly, put away the ledger, and pushed the drawer shut. "I ain't gonna be out at the folks' house any time soon, Virge."

Virgil pursed his lips and began to nod. "Hell, I wouldn' either. I reckon Pa's pious platitudes are hard enough to swallow on a good day." He moved to the door and took a grip on the doorknob. "Let me know if you need me," he said and left.

For the next weeks, Wyatt went about his constable duties with a plodding single-mindedness, patrolling the streets late into the nights, sometimes repeating the routes when the moon was late to rise. He had never told Rilla about Valenzuela Cos and that moon putting its contrived limits on the Mexican girl's life. That experience had held no relevance for Missouri. Now it did. He thought of that cursed orb as his partner in a nightly ritual. Though he could no longer call up the image of Valenzuela Cos's face, her prophecy in that California peach orchard stuck with him like a crimson stain on a bedsheet.

"*La luna de adobe,*" she had said in her beguiling border accent. The memory of that night was now like an exotic tale that had reached him secondhand from a far-off land. Each time the moon floated up over Lamar, he felt its story exhume the sense of loss he had tried to bury with Rilla's coffin. He had become morose, he knew, and the amber glow of the moon had become an unwanted emblem of his temperament.

On the streets he seldom spoke, and it did not take long for his stoic demeanor to wear thin on some of the self-important citizens who warranted they deserved more from a city employee. As these businessmen reasoned, no special allowances were due a man in mourning if he refused to receive their condolences. One of the town's leading merchants quietly petitioned for his dismissal. To convince him to step down, the council became more selective about which of his court duties warranted extra pay.

It galled Wyatt that he was collecting fines for the very people who were shorting him his due. He was now serving like a rich man's puppet, but, worse than that, he was playing the fool. He knew he could tolerate neither practice for long.

His resolve finally broke when a farmer laid down seventy-five dollars to cover a court cost. Wyatt entered the amount in his ledger, but, after the man left, he stared for a long minute at the stack of bills, before taking twenty dollars off the top. He pocketed the money and altered the figure in the book.

"To hell with 'em," he muttered. He would keep a private tally of what he was owed. The practice became a habit that transferred into other areas of his job, even skimming off the taxes he collected for the school fund. It was easy to rationalize the "adjustment," but he knew Rilla would not have approved. He came to understand that she had been his conscience for the past year. Without her now, he didn't care what the city elders thought of his methods. He almost hoped they would challenge him.

When the city clerk discovered the deficit of school funds, word spread from city hall into the general populace, until a few weeks before Christmas everything came to a head. At the Bon Ton Saloon, Gran Brummett and his two brothers cornered Virgil and were getting loud about the misappropriation of funds and the hypocrisy of the elder Earp's moonshining enterprise. Irrationally, the accusations swung in an all-encompassing arc to include some kind of vague culpability for Wyatt in Aurilla's death. Virgil was livid.

When the news reached Wyatt that Virgil was outnumbered, he marched from the office to the saloon and found Newton standing beside Virgil, his face set for a fight. Wyatt stood in the doorway long enough to hear his wife's name thrown out for all to hear.

"Granville!" Wyatt bellowed. Every face turned to him, and the room went suddenly quiet. "Outside!" Wyatt ordered, his authority coming not from his badge but from the iron in his voice. Wyatt walked into the street, pulled his revolver from its holster, and handed it to the first man he met. Without comment the bystander received the weapon and backed away.

Wyatt squared himself in the street and watched the three Brummett boys file out. When Gran was close enough, Wyatt broke his nose. Gran went down on his knees, his hands pressed to his face like a decrepit beggar offering a prayer. The other Brummetts came at him like savage dogs, dragging Wyatt down, their fists pounding at every part of him. Virgil jerked one of them back by his hair and flung him into the edge of the boardwalk. From out of the crowd came the Sutherland brothers, then Newton, and the altercation escalated into a brawl that spread from the walkway to the center of the street.

Neither side fared well. At five-to-three odds against them, the Earp boys were bloodied and their blouses torn. But the Earps kept getting up. They got up so many times, it became evident that quitting was not a part of their makeup. Virgil's lower lip had burst open like an over-ripe plum. Newton's left eye was swollen shut, and he was fighting with one arm.

Wyatt fought without a sound, his face set like stone. His head chimed with the punishment doled out to him, but the latent poison of his grief boiled in his veins, giving him a kind of vindictive energy. He held to the single-minded purpose of fighting as though it were the only reasonable course of action to embrace. He almost welcomed the diversion of physical pain.

Someone led Gran away to a doctor before his nose became irreparable. Then some of the gamier citizens insinuated themselves like a wall between the two factions and yelled for the combatants to go home. But the Earps would not give up their ground until their opponents were escorted away. The Sutherlands and the Brummetts walked backward toward their homes, all of them vociferous and vain and boasting of damage done.

Wyatt retrieved his gun and walked to Newton to check on his damaged hand. A storekeeper gave Virgil a rag soaked in witch hazel, which he pressed to his lip as he walked stiffly to his brothers.

"Those sons of bitches got damned big mouths on 'em," Virgil growled.

Wyatt's face was still hard and unyielding but for a blue vein pulsing at the bridge of his nose. "They know who walked away."

"You'll catch hell for this, Wyatt," Newton said. "Likely throw you off the police force."

Wyatt spat blood into the dirt and looked west down the street. The town of Lamar appeared to him now like a door forever closed. He wiped at the blood on his mouth and spat again.

"Hell, I was gone a month ago."

CHAPTER 17

Late winter, spring, 1871: Fort Gibson and Indian Territory

There was no solace in the openness of the land, just as there was no healing in the isolation he sought in the barren plain of winter-killed grasses. The prairie seemed nothing more than an extension of the boundless emptiness that had opened inside him. Neither his mount nor his packhorse seemed a companion—but victims of his own aimlessness. The voiceless plain only provided a silent space for his demons to follow and murmur in his ear. Rilla's bloodied body shadowed him as vividly as if dragged behind his horse on a travois, scraping a scar across the dry land.

The child was not real. There were no memories attached to a nameless son to haunt him, save the mental picture of that inanimate thing tucked against its dead mother's ribs. The child had seemed more an extension of Rilla's suffering, giving her death a measurable size and shape. Mother and son comprised a common image rendered in scarlet, and the image had been painted on a permanent altar inside Wyatt's mind.

Secondary to that, but nagging, was the compromised way he'd handled things in the constable's office. He had left behind a smear on the Earp name. Without knowing about his docked pay, they would call him a thief . . . a man who had absconded with money collected for a new school. Now that he had so much time, it was difficult to rationalize what he had done, so he simply added the theft to the memory of the funeral pyre behind the house.

He plodded on southwest with no destination, no plan, just moving, sometimes drifting toward a town but usually cutting a wide path around it. The closest he got to any kind of peace of mind was in that flash of a second when he flushed a prairie chicken and raised the breech-loader shotgun, seated the stock against his shoulder, and engaged in the delicate duet of leading and squeezing fluidly at once. The illusion of normality was short-lived. After stuffing the bird in a saddlebag, he was back on his horse with only the blank slate of sky to swallow his thoughts.

Only early morning and twilight offered any redemption. It was the change of light, the feel of the world turning toward something new. Something beyond the monotony of his failed dreams. But those crepuscular transitions were fleeting and, in the end, only teased him. One bled into the bleakness of another day. The other ushered in the darkness waiting for that damning moon.

He crossed into the Indian Territory—the most lawless piece of real estate on the continent. It was probably where he belonged, he thought. In that exiled land, most men were hiding from something. Only the Indians retained any right of dignity, which, by their known scorn of the whites, merely fortified his low opinion of himself.

Well into the territory, in the late afternoon, he made camp near a grove of cottonwoods and chanced to look up from his meal as a rider crested a rise to the east. Wyatt threw a bone into his fire, wiped his fingers on a rag, and reached for the old over-and-under. Standing, he watched the distant silhouette approach, one dark shape against the gray sea of grass until, with only a hundred yards separating them, he recognized Kennedy, the tanner he had jailed in the Sutherland Hotel. The stocky Irishman halted his mule twenty yards out.

"That you, Earp?"

"It's me," Wyatt said flatly, and put away the antiquated weapon.

Kennedy looked around, still not dismounting. "You alone out here?"

"I *was.*"

"I see that you're cooking. Can I share your fire? I've got some whiskey."

"Don't need your whiskey. If you need the fire, there it is."

Kennedy slid off his mule. "This beast ain't much of a ride. I need to find me a horse."

Wyatt sized up the man's animal. It was sound and well-muscled. There was nothing wrong with a mule, he knew, as long as you didn't figure to race it. But he said nothing.

"So Judge Earp ain't with you?"

Wyatt turned his head slowly toward the man and stared, trying to read his face for the unspoken portion of that question. "I reckon he's at his home."

Kennedy's eyes pinched, and he busied himself with unscrewing the cap of his bottle. "No, it's for certain he ain't there," he mumbled, a half smile pulling at his mouth. He sat down near the fire and drank and stared at Wyatt over the up-tilted bottle until he had to come up for air. Kennedy squinted. "You don't know, do you?"

Wyatt kept staring, his patience wearing thin. "Know what?"

Kennedy softened his voice to an irritating whine. "A case was filed agin' you for money that was owed. The city was tryin' to get it out of your family's properties."

"My family?" Wyatt stiffened as if he might kick something. He walked away a few paces and stopped, keeping his back to Kennedy. "Tell me the rest," Wyatt said without turning.

"Well . . . your pa . . . he sold everything off and pulled out before that come about." Kennedy breathed in deeply and capped his bottle. "They're even tryin' to squeeze money out of the feller you sold your house to. I hate to be the one telling you all this. You treated me decent in Lamar."

Hardly hearing the man's voice, Wyatt was back in Lamar, picturing the faces of the councilmen who would direct their discontent toward his father. "Where is my father now?"

"Don't know. Don't know anybody who does."

Wyatt stilled, as if he were listening for something in the distance. After a time he began packing up his cookware, moving with the deliberation of a man who had made a decision.

"You're leavin'?" Kennedy asked.

"Might be some weather come in tonight," Wyatt said. "I'm gonna set up under the trees." He nodded toward the fire. "You can have what's left of that hen."

Kennedy's eyes locked eagerly on the bird roasting on the spit. "Well, I won't let it waste."

In the morning Wyatt rode out of the cottonwoods and found Kennedy sprawled out under a slicker, a light dusting of snow stippled across the contours of his body. The fire was dead. Chewing on a twist of dried venison, Wyatt rode west, stitching a line of tracks in the snow that followed him like a silent wraith.

He wandered into Fort Gibson and, planning to winter over in the small settlement, purchased an axe and bucksaw and put money down on a wagon. Tramping through the frozen woods, he rang his axe against dead timber, supplying firewood to homes and stores, the bite of the axe blade like a private therapy, helping him chew up some of his sadness to spit back at the world. He had pushed the memory of Rilla into the past, where he swore never to revisit it. He came to realize he was not wholly broken by the loss of her, but what was left of him was less than what he had been before her. He had no ambitions. He could not think his way toward a plan that included improving his situation. Physical labor, he came to learn, passed as an anesthetic for a man who wanted to forget how to want anything.

Physically, he was changed. Taller than most men . . . and stronger. There was not a soft part to his body. As a wood-splitter, he had learned something about the economy of applying his strength so as not to waste energy. More than one customer had watched him skid logs behind his team of horses, saw, or split the wood, and they had commented that he made difficult things look easy.

Wyatt had been hacking at timber for only two weeks when a US deputy marshal set up an office in the settlement. Knowing his misdeeds in Lamar could catch up to him, Wyatt, like any man who cannot stand still too long inside his flawed inner terrain, decided to move on. To anywhere. It didn't matter.

Many of the men in town were heading to the summer buffalo grounds north of the Kansas railheads. Wyatt had seen Kennedy, the one-time tanner, ride out of town on his mule with such a "buff'ler" outfit. Apparently anyone could try it, but Wyatt wagered that most would not take to the skinning and would eventually abandon the hard life of sleeping on the rough sod of the prairie for nights on end.

Hunting was something he could do, so he decided to try his hand on the killing fields. Hides were selling at three and a half dollars. He could hire a skinner. He didn't mind the killing, but he didn't care to mire up to his elbows in blood. It was too close to the memory of Lamar.

On a blustery morning in March he set it all into motion, the howl of the wind as good a reason to push on as any other. He sold his wagon, tools, and the old over-and-under and bought a Sharps "big-fifty" and ammunition. He would pick up another wagon somewhere near the Kansas rail lines. With his gear packed, in that first instant when he mounted his horse and looked at his entire belongings strapped onto the packhorse behind him, the bleakness of his future almost undermined his will to go on. But he was packed, and it seemed easier just to move out. Drifting might lead to something.

On the fourth day crossing the prairie, he encountered Kennedy's mule, dead and flyblown, lying beneath a vortex of vultures wheeling about the gray sky. Later that afternoon he spotted an unlikely sight: perched on a rise, a spring wagon sat with its tongue and traces angled down into the earth like an anchor. There were no horses in sight. Two figures hovered close around a campfire, its flame flapping in the wind like a yellow rag. Above the camp, racing off at an angle, a plume of gray smoke climbed into the sky, a shade paler than the clouds. The weather was volatile, and Wyatt wondered if there were people who were ignorant to the possibilities of lightning on the spring prairie. As he rode closer, a stocky man ran out to meet him. It was Kennedy.

"My damn mule died!" he declared and propped his hands on his wide hips as though Wyatt might have something to say on the subject. Wyatt looked at the woman huddled near the fire. She was witch-like, stirring a long-handled spoon in a black pot. Her mouth moved as if she were conversing with the contents of the pot. Kennedy glanced over his shoulder at her.

"I rode in the wagon with that woman and her husband. It was just one old nag a-pulling. But that damn horse will never make it through the Ozarks."

"Where's the horse?"

Kennedy pointed east. "Her husband rode off on it to somewhere. She told him to go and get some horses, so without a word, he up and goes. That woman's crazy, I think . . . and he's not far behind. She wants my saddle as payment for the ride, but I won't part with it."

"Maybe you'd better hoof it back to Fort Gibson."

Kennedy licked his lips and frowned at the ground. "I can't

go back there."

Wyatt let that alone. "Best give the woman your saddle then and take the ride."

Kennedy's eyes took a deliberate bead on Wyatt's packhorse. "I could set my saddle on your gelding there. I can't be walking out here in this devil's land. I'd pay you back."

"Leave me with one animal, and I'm no better off than you before your luck went bad."

"Earp, I need the favor. I'm out here in the goddamn middle o' nowhere."

"It ain't a favor you're askin' for. It's foolishness." Wyatt nodded to the wagon. "You've got a way out of this. You'd best take it."

Kennedy filled his cheeks and let the air spew out noisily. "These people ain't right. I ain't real sure what she's saying mostly. Would you at least talk to her?"

Wyatt looked at the woman again. She was sullen, staring back at him.

"I'll talk to her, but I ain't promisin' you nothin'. You made a bad decision settin' out without a backup mount. You may have to turn back."

"Their name is Shown," Kennedy said hopefully.

Wyatt dismounted and walked just within speaking distance of the woman. She was missing part of an eyebrow, and her skin was splotched. Her concentration on him was fierce.

"Can you give this man transportation to the next town?"

"Cain't *give* 'im nothin'," she snapped. "Fort Gibson's closer." She turned her pale eyes back on the cookpot. Kennedy came up beside Wyatt, and she lifted her chin and stared a hole into the Irishman. "I'll take his saddle for it."

"Where's your husband?" Wyatt said.

"Don't rightly know."

Wyatt studied the sky. "You're in a bad spot, come some

lightning." The woman did not acknowledge the warning. "We'll ease your rig down into the swale for you."

"Already got my fire up here," she said.

Wyatt nodded. "We'll move that, too."

He was not willing to hitch his horses to the tongue, as the offer might suggest something more permanent. They manhandled the wagon to the bottomland with the woman walking alongside, steadying a fry pan filled with hot coals. Kennedy went back up the hill for the cauldron.

When the wheels were chocked and a new fire established out of the wind, the woman resumed her cooking. The first lightning bolt flickered in the west, and ten seconds later the sky grumbled with a deep and sonorous warning. The woman raised her pointed chin to Wyatt.

"You're the one sold firewood at Fort Gibson."

"Name is Earp."

"I don't care 'bout your name," she mumbled. Then she looked sharply to the east. Two horses and one rider approached from the high ground.

"It's Shown!" Kennedy called out.

The rider bounced bareback on a bay as he led a sorrel behind. "Anna!" the man yelled and kicked his heels into his mount. She paid him no attention. The horses pulled up, heavily lathered and snorting strings of mucus. Both were wellmuscled and newly shod.

"Well," Kennedy purred, "those are a sight better'n the one he rode out on."

With his attention fixed on Wyatt, the man named Shown scissored a leg over the bay's mane and dropped to the ground. "Who the hell're you?"

"Helped get your wagon down to low ground. Storm's coming in."

The man looked at his wife, but the gap in their communication remained an eerie constant. He turned as though studying the weather, but his gaze returned to the hill he had just crested.

"You folks going to be able to take Mr. Kennedy to the next town?" Wyatt delivered his question direct, using the same tone of voice he had once regularly employed as a constable.

"For one goddamn saddle," the hag croaked. "Don't nothing come for free!"

The husband walked past Wyatt, jerked the woman by an arm, and pulled her to the back of the wagon where he commenced a freshet of harsh whispers. Kennedy stepped next to Wyatt.

"Daft as a couple of cross-eyed crows," the Irishman murmured.

Wyatt turned up the collar of his coat and secured the button at his neck. The sky was almost black. Another lightning bolt trembled against the clouds, and the air filled with a cracking sound like splitting oak.

"I'm moving on," Wyatt said.

"You're leaving me with 'em?"

"I am."

Raindrops intermittently dolloped in the pot and hissed in the coals. Wyatt mounted, took up his lead rope, and started past the two spent horses tied to the rear of the wagon. On each rump was the clear singe of a Circle K brand. Kennedy followed in Wyatt's wake a few stumbling steps, but he stopped and said no more.

CHAPTER 18

Spring, 1871: Indian Territory to Van Buren, Arkansas, and back
The sky was clear and the morning washed clean from the night's storm. Wyatt was carving a stick down to dry wood for kindling when he heard footsteps crashing through the brush. He laid down both stick and knife and slid the Sharps from its leather case.

"Earp!" Kennedy's voice rasped from the effort of running. "Thank God you're still here!" He appeared like a bear pushing through the wet foliage. "That sonovabitch Shown run off with the horses last night. We're stranded." He approached tentatively, but his desperation had him wound tightly. "I think he must've stole the damned things and panicked."

Wyatt put away the rifle. "He left his wife?"

"Hell, yes, and me with her." Kennedy wiped his brow with his sleeve and sucked in air.

Wyatt looked north, where the land rolled away into the hill country. He cursed, picked up his knife, and sheathed it. Keeping his expression empty, he turned back to Kennedy, knowing the man still thought of him as an officer of the law.

"Tracks go north," Kennedy said hurriedly. "A little west of the way he come in last night. He's done lit out, and she don't seem to give a damn."

Wyatt gave his wet canvas tarpaulin a smart flap, snapping droplets of water into the air, and then he turned his anger on Kennedy. "Go back to her. I'll be over directly."

181

Within the hour, Wyatt's belongings were stowed in the bed of the wagon and his two horses harnessed to the rig. Alone up front in the driver's box, he snapped the reins, speaking to no one. Mute as children who had earned a scolding, the two passengers sat in the bed, as Wyatt could tolerate neither of them in his dark mood. The night's rain had softened the ground, making the tracking easy but the going slow.

They found Shown two days later in a stand of willows at the foot of the Ozarks. Wyatt pulled the wagon up, tied off the reins, and climbed down. Shown started talking so fast, his words ran together in a meaningless chain of babble.

"I had to keep going. I think these horses was stole by some Injuns. There's probably men looking for them. When I—"

Wyatt slapped him hard across the mouth, and Shown stumbled into the rear wheel hub. Anna Shown shrieked something unintelligible and jumped down from the wagon. When Wyatt slapped her husband again, Shown slid off the wheel and dropped onto the seat of his pants, and the woman began flailing at Wyatt with her bony fists.

"Get her off me!" he ordered Kennedy, and the Irishman reluctantly complied.

Setting his face with purpose, Wyatt unharnessed his horses from the wagon tongue and began loading his gear onto his packhorse. Kennedy began hitching the bay and sorrel to the traces. When Wyatt threw his saddle over his mount, Kennedy brought over Wyatt's roll of canvas and stood like a supplicant come to make his offering.

"She must'a thought you were going to kill him. She's calmed down some now."

Wyatt lashed down the canvas, keeping his eyes on his work. "He probably needs killing."

Kennedy took off his hat and shifted his weight from one leg to the other. "You ain't still gonna leave me here, are you?" Wyatt toed into the stirrup and rose and sat his horse. "What's coming up here is the worse leg of it," Kennedy pleaded. "The law don't reach this far. There's white men out here who'll kill a man for his boots. Indians are probably worse. All I got is a single-shot, and it jams sometimes."

"You think about that when you started out?" Wyatt said.

"When I started out, I didn't know my mule would die and leave me with these addle-brained mooncalves."

"If those horses are stolen," Wyatt said, "it's likely Shown stole 'em. You may as well re-steal one and get the hell away from these people. They started with one horse. I don't see as how you're leaving 'em any worse off."

Kennedy looked back at the woman, squatting over her husband and weeping. "I can't be traveling on a stole horse in this country. There's people already looking for me." He put a hand on Wyatt's arm. "You were a lawman, Earp."

"Well, I ain't no more," Wyatt shot back.

"But your family is connected to the law . . . your pa was a judge."

Wyatt's gaze cut to the man's grip on his sleeve, and the Irishman's hand slid deferentially from Wyatt's coat. The image of Nicholas Earp dressed out in his fine dark suit floated into sharp resolution in Wyatt's mind.

"He's already drunk out of his head," Kennedy said, scowling at the couple. "Don't leave me stranded out here, not with the likes of those two."

When Wyatt lifted his reins, Kennedy turned desperate and grabbed the cheek strap on the horse's bridle, but the Irishman stilled as his attention fixed on something out on the prairie. Wyatt turned in his saddle to see six men riding up on their camp, each carrying a repeater rifle balanced behind the pommel. They fanned out into a flank and reined up in a semicircle.

None wore badges, but by the way they took in the harnessed horses and the party before them, Wyatt knew they had come to recover stolen goods.

The man in the center leveled his rifle on Wyatt, eased his horse closer, leaned, and slipped Wyatt's pistol from the scabbard at his belt. "My name is Keys. I need you to climb down off o' there and stand with this'n here." He indicated Kennedy with a jerk of his head, and then, without taking his gaze off Wyatt, he pivoted his head partway toward his party. "You boys keep these two covered, whilst I have a talk with the woman."

"She ain't the one you need to talk to," Wyatt said to Keys's back.

A tall rider in a long white duster walked his horse forward and brought his Henry rifle to bear on Wyatt. "You just let *us* decide who talks to who. Now git on down like Mr. Keys said."

Wyatt dismounted and listened to the Shown woman explain how the men named Earp and Kennedy had got her husband drunk and threatened both their lives.

"She's crazy," Wyatt told the man guarding him.

With his rifle still centered on Wyatt's chest, the man leaned from his horse and spat. "You can tell it to the judge."

Kennedy stepped beside Wyatt and addressed all the riders. "He's telling you the truth. They're both crazy. That man Shown there . . . he's the one rode off and stole these horses." The tall man stared at them with a shut-down expression.

Keys took the reins of Wyatt's horses and led them away to one of his men, who in turn walked the horses to the front of the wagon and began the process of switching off the two pair. Keys stood before Wyatt, addressing him as though he were the leader of this ill-matched crew.

"You know as well as I do those are my horses. They're carrying my brand. I'm taking all of you into Van Buren to the marshal. I want you two to climb up into the back of the wagon.

If I have any trouble with you, understand I will shoot you and save the court time and money. Now get on up there!"

"Her story ain't what happened," Wyatt said and pointed to Shown. "That man was—"

"*He's* the one threatened our lives if we talked!" Anna Shown squawked from the wagon box, her voice now sounding terrified. She thrust a bony finger at Wyatt. "That one . . . Earp!"

Keys ran his tongue across the front of his teeth and stared at the woman. Then he spat and settled a hard look on Wyatt.

Wyatt gritted his teeth. "It ain't like you're thinkin'."

Keys spat again and curled his lip to a scowl. "Git in the wagon, and don't say nothin' more. I don't wanna hear it."

In three days, Wyatt was sharing a foul-smelling Van Buren jail cell with Kennedy and three drunks. Shown was in the adjoining cell, separated from Wyatt's by a plank wall. One room away Anna Shown put her mark to an affidavit that heaped the blame of the horse theft on everyone but herself. All three men were arraigned with bail set at five hundred dollars each, a sum which none could meet.

Two days after the arraignment, the marshal brought Wyatt into the office to serve him another summons. Anna Shown sat at a table staring at her hands, her eyes wavering with the same wild desperation he had seen the morning her husband had run off with the horses. The two deputies who gripped Wyatt's arms pushed him into a chair across from the Shown woman.

"This woman has sworn that you and Kennedy threatened to kill her and her husband if either of them turned state's evidence," the marshal began.

Wyatt stared at Anna Shown, as she bent over the papers before her. "She's lying," Wyatt said evenly. "She was lying when she said they had nothing to do with it, and she's lying now. Everything involving those horses was their doin'."

Anna Shown's eyes teared up. "You ain't gonna lay this on me! It was you . . . and the Irish."

The deputies' hands tightened on Wyatt's shoulders. The marshal pointed at Wyatt.

"You're going to be behind bars a spell, Earp, until we get this settled."

"What about the bail? I'll have the money if I can sell my horses."

The marshal's face closed down. "Bail was before we knew about this threat."

All the apathy that had accumulated in him the months since his wife's death—fogging his clear thinking—burned away with a fury that rose inside him. The two guards pulled him to his feet and widened their stances to hold him in check. The marshal pointed at him again.

"Don't make it harder than it has to be. Put him back in his cell."

Anna Shown stood. "Don't put him in with my husband!" she shrieked. "Earp will kill him!"

Wyatt was led back into his cell and, without returning Kennedy's stare, he crossed the floor, sat on his bunk, and leaned his forearms on his thighs. Glaring at the floor, he listened to the slam of the door and the trip of the tumbler in the lock. When the deputies left, he stood and walked to the wall separating him from Shown and slammed it with the flat of his hands. The men behind him went still. No sound came from the other cell.

"Did you tell 'em you was a lawman back in Missouri?" Kennedy asked.

Wyatt turned quickly to the Irishman. "Don't say nothin' about that, you understand?"

Kennedy made an involuntarily step back and raised both palms. "All right, all right."

For a month Wyatt and his cellmates lived in the stench of close proximity, eating boardinghouse leftovers stirred into an amorphous mush and drinking water from a common cup and bucket. A rusted chamber pot was pushed into one corner, and this they emptied once a day when the jailor marched them outside under the authority of a lever-action shotgun.

Each night Wyatt heard the whispers of the prisoners in the other cell as they pried at a ceiling board above the dividing wall. When the board finally broke free in the dark of an early morning, Wyatt listened as two men crawled through the gap into the garret space. Their voices were hushed and frantic but ecstatic with the taste of freedom. Wyatt climbed to the window in time to see three men scale the wall behind the yard and drop out of sight.

Behind him Kennedy cracked open his side of the ceiling and helped three men up before he pulled himself up to peer into the crawl space. "That goddamned skinny Shown slithered through there like a snake," he growled. "Hell, *I* can't squeeze through that damned crack."

Wyatt put a stranglehold on the window bars as he watched the last man claw his way up and over the wall. "Goddamnit," he hissed. "Shown's lit out."

"Go!" Kennedy said. "Hell, *I* would. There ain't nothing right about this whole goddamn thing. Sure as hell, we'll pay for it."

In the next instant Wyatt was squirming over the rafters in the attic, pushing his coat ahead of him. He dropped to the yard, scrambled over the wall, and made his way to a corral at the end of the alley. No one was in sight. By the faint glow of starlight, Wyatt recognized Rilla's gelding standing in a paddock. Beside it, the chestnut raised its head and nickered.

From the tack room he stole a bridle, halter, and lead rope. After walking the two horses down an alley, he mounted the chestnut bareback and pulled the gelding along behind him. The dawn found him churning up Arkansas soil for points north, this time a fugitive from federal law, no gun, no provisions. One more white man gone bad in the no-man's-land of the Cherokee Nations.

CHAPTER 19

Summer and fall, 1871: Kansas plains to Peoria

Disappearing into the Kansas plains, Wyatt found anonymity in the melting pot of filthy buffalo hunters who wore the rancid scent of their occupation like a creed. It was the rough life again, but he found his need for open land and endless sky reawakened. For a time he hired on with a seasoned outfit as a skinner, as it was the only position available. He stomached the gore of the knife work, staying with the crew primarily for the nightly card games at the base camp.

Most of his gambling earnings were scratched on rough promissory notes to be cashed in when the hides were sold at Buffalo City, the hub of the hunting craze that had swept the midsection of the country. There the hunters carried the bison skins and stacked them into shaggy mountains to be carried off by freight haulers to the nearest railheads, where they were shipped east.

When he had saved enough capital to make new choices, Wyatt decided to put more distance between him and Indian Territory, where his name was sure to be on a wanted list. He rode east to the one place he knew he could disappear in a sea of other nameless faces. Peoria had once seemed to him a wilderness of depravity. Now, as a fugitive, it would be his ally.

The seedy Bunker Hill district appeared unchanged in the three years since Wyatt had seen it. At a little before noon he walked into Vansteel's saloon one block off the waterfront. He remembered the tall bartender, who twisted a towel inside a shot glass. Seeing Wyatt, the man set the glass on a shelf and lumbered over.

"You're an Earp," he said, whipping the towel over a shoulder.

"That's right. I'm lookin' for Vansteel."

The barman glanced briefly at the upper landing, and then gave Wyatt a cryptic slant of his eyes. "He sleeps till about two o'clock," he said and lowered his voice a notch, "but he ain't fit to talk to nobody till around four."

From his vest pocket Wyatt fingered a coin and set it on the bar. "Got any coffee?"

"I need to brew up another pot if you've got time."

"Got plenty of that," he said. "Is Vansteel hiring right now?"

The man frowned and cocked his head. "Enforcer?" When Wyatt nodded, the barman could not suppress a smug smile. "I thought you were one didn' wanna have nothin'a do with all that." When Wyatt made no reply, the man's smile disappeared. He slipped the towel off his shoulder and began folding it into consecutive halves. "He might could use you." When he could fold the towel no smaller, he opened it again. "You boys spreadin' yourselves out on the waterfront?"

"Meaning what?" Wyatt said and watched the man's expression go cautious.

"Nothin'. Just that your brother is down at Haspel's." The bartender looked toward the front door and gestured down the street with a nod of his head.

"Virgil is in Peoria?"

The skin on the barman's forehead furrowed with two lines. "Morgan," he said. When Wyatt made no response, the barman leaned an elbow on the bar. "He was workin' here till about a month ago. I think Haspel offered him more money." The corners of his mouth turned down, and he shook his head.

"Feller we got enforcin' here now ain't as reliable. I reckon Vansteel might be glad to put one o' you boys on the payroll."

"How do I get to Haspel's?"

The bartender pointed. "Down the block, this side o' the rail yards. Red brick two-story."

Wyatt nodded once. " 'Preciate the information. Don't need the coffee." He pushed a coin across the bar and left.

Jane Haspel's brothel looked like it might have once been a clerks' office for one of the shipping companies. The rail tracks behind it ran parallel, six wide through a maze of rust-dappled warehouses all the way to the river. Smoke and cinders of burning coal spewed from the factory chimneys, stinging his throat and casting a dirty veil of black across the sky.

On his third series of knocks, the door cracked a few inches, and a finely etched porcelain face appeared in the opening. After a moment of routine inspection, the girl's eyes flashed with recognition . . . but only for an instant. Sarah Haspel's good looks had been hardened by time, and it was clear from her expression that she had left every trace of her youth behind her.

"Wyatt," she said, straightening as she opened the door. She was taller and more developed, her eyes seeming to gaze out at the world from a more settled place. "Look at you," she said, her smile less a welcome than a practiced tool of her trade. "Come in."

"You grew up," he said, stepping over the threshold.

She gave him a half-lidded glare, as though he had questioned her judgment. "Well, that's what people do. I'm eighteen," she said, as if the number carried some primal significance.

She closed the door and then turned at the sound of footsteps. Down the dimly lighted hallway, Wyatt watched a buxom woman wrapped in a robe and long shawl approach in a slow, measured gait, as though she were walking a narrow beam.

191

Her face was dry and crusty, coated with some kind of cosmetic application. She could have been forty or sixty; he could not tell. Her lips and fingernails were painted the shade of dried blood.

"Mother," Sarah said, moving toward the woman, "this is Morgan's brother . . . Wyatt."

The woman stopped out of arm's reach and crossed the shawl over her chest making an *X* with her arms. With her powdered face, she looked ready to be laid out in a coffin.

"Jane Haspel," she intoned, correcting her daughter's introduction.

Wyatt took off his hat and looked up the stairwell that led to the dark upper story. "I'm lookin' for my brother." When he faced her again, she was studying him, her gaze moving boldly over his chest and shoulders much the way a farmer appraised livestock at an auction.

"He's asleep," Sarah said, "but I know he'll want to see you." She turned and climbed the flight of stairs in a slow, economical glide.

"You're the one was a policeman in Missouri," Jane Haspel said in a lifeless tone.

Wyatt nodded. "Constable."

"Are you here to stay?"

"For a spell, I reckon."

"You intend to work for the police here?"

"No, ma'am, I got no plans to."

Jane Haspel stepped forward, letting the shawl hang down to expose her robe and ample breasts. Without preamble she placed her palms flat against Wyatt's shirt beneath his coat and kneaded the muscles of his chest. Pursing her lips, she then gripped the span of his shoulders and squeezed. His impulse was to back away from her, but he did not want to retreat.

"Are you looking for work?" she said, snapping the proposition like a whip.

Before he could answer, three loud knocks sounded behind Wyatt. He stepped aside while Jane Haspel opened the door. Two stout men stood side by side, both wearing the blue leather-billed caps that marked them as stevedores. The sleeves of their soiled blouses were rolled to their elbows, and their thick forearms were spangled with tattoos.

"Lady, we was here Saturday night, and some money come up missing from my pocket."

Jane Haspel coughed up a wet sound that might have served as a laugh. "How would I know what money you had on you? I doubt you know yourself. As I remember, you were drunk." She started to close the door. "Anyway, we're closed. You want one of the girls, come back at eight."

The man with the grievance pushed the door open wider, forcing the woman back a step. "I ain't leaving without my money. That was five dollars shy of a week's pay."

"Get your goddamned hand off my door," she said, her voice turning effortlessly vicious. "There's no money for you here. I don't know where you lost it, but I don't run the kind of place that would keep customers from coming back for fear of being robbed."

"Well, let me talk to Minnie," he demanded.

"I told you we're closed!" She held out both hands limp from the wrists and flicked the backs of her fingers toward him. "Go! Get off my doorstep!"

He stepped across the threshold into the hallway, looked uncertainly at Wyatt, and spread his feet as though he were rooting to the floor. "Minnie!" he yelled roughly to the upper level, his voice filling the hall and stairwell.

His friend followed him in, crossed his arms against his chest, and leaned a shoulder into the wall as he challenged Wyatt with taunting eyes. "You work in this rat's nest, sport?"

Wyatt let his eyes go flat. "Mister, your business ain't mine, and mine ain't yours."

At the top of the stairs Morgan appeared, his suspenders strapped over the top of his union suit and his bare feet extending from his trousers. "Well, goddamn! If it ain't my favorite brother." He had filled out with the long rangy limbs of a brawler, but the effervescent light in his eye still glimmered with mischief. He tapped lightly down the stairs wearing a sly smile that let Wyatt know he was aware of the situation with the two visitors. Ignoring them, he wrapped Wyatt in a bear hug and then stepped back, giving his brother a telling wink, as if to say: *Watch this!*

"Minnie!" the dockworker called out again, this time in a more insistent tone.

Morgan turned as if he had not noticed the two intruders. "Excuse me, boys. We're havin' a little reunion here. You mind stepping outside?"

The man who had been calling for Minnie turned his head to Morgan and curled his upper lip into a snarl. "*You* go to hell, you damned pimp!"

Morgan hit the man so fast, his head collided with the wall before his friend could uncross his arms. "Both o' you outside," Morgan ordered.

He pushed the dazed man out the doorway ahead of him, and they began to grapple on the sidewalk. The other laborer charged out the door but came to a halt when Wyatt grabbed the back of his collar. The shirt ripped down the length of the man's broad back. Turning, he lunged at Wyatt and was immediately laid out on the front steps.

Wyatt made a quick assessment of Morgan's situation, and when he looked back at his opponent, the man was opening a folding knife and rolling to a seated position. Wyatt kicked the toe of his boot into the side of the man's head. The stevedore dropped to an elbow, and Wyatt came down hard with his boot heel on the hand with the knife, drawing from the man a sharp intake of air through his teeth. Moaning, the laborer curled into a ball and cradled his fingers.

Wyatt picked up the weapon from the sidewalk. When he straightened, an arm draped around his shoulder, and he turned to see Morgan's boyish smile inches from his face.

"Welcome to Peoria, brother." Morgan laughed, shooting a look at the Haspel women in the doorway. "Ladies, how 'bout another Earp on the payroll. Gives a helluva job interview, don't he?"

"Come put your clothes on, Morgan," Sarah said. "You look ridiculous."

When mother and daughter went inside, Morgan nodded down to the man Wyatt had bested. "This one's a big trouble-maker. 'Mick the Mauler' they call him." Morgan patted Wyatt's shoulder. "Only he don't usually go down against just one man."

Mick rolled to his side, gently kneaded the bones in his hand, and glared up at Wyatt. "I thought this wasn't none o' your business."

Wyatt folded the knife and tossed it out into the street. "Got to be my business when you tried to up the odds against my brother."

Mick glanced at the knife where it lay, and then looked from one Earp to the other. "Yeah . . . well . . . what about his money?" He canted his head toward his friend in the gutter.

Morgan squatted on the balls of his feet and got in the man's face. "I hear you tried this over at McClelland's, too. Maybe you boys better come up with a new game."

Mick frowned and turned his glare on Wyatt. "You didn't have to break my goddamn hand."

Morgan clamped his hand under Mick's chin and turned the dockworker's face back to his. "Maybe you shouldn't be playin' with knives, sonny boy." Morgan snorted. "You're just lucky you didn't make my big brother *mad.*" He stood and hitched his head toward the inert body in the gutter. "Now, take your friend outta here. You boys wore out your welcome at Haspel's."

Morgan's gaze lingered on the two horses tethered to the lamp post. Wyatt could see in his brother's expression that he recognized Rilla's gelding, packed with gear and standing patiently next to the blaze. But the sober appraisal was short-lived. With his arm wrapped around Wyatt's shoulder again, Morgan put on the smile that crinkled his eyes.

"Let me get dressed, and we'll go down to Vansteel's. I believe I owe you a drink."

CHAPTER 20

Fall 1871 to spring 1872: Peoria

The bartender brought coffee for Wyatt and set down a foaming mug before Morgan. "Damn, Leland," Morgan said, smiling and frowning at once, "there's more head on this beer than there is hair on a bear's ass in winter. Is Vansteel still mad at me for quittin'?"

Leland cocked his head to one side, putting on a tease. "I figure you can afford to buy more'n one now," he jibed. Morgan grabbed for his apron, but Leland dodged him.

Morgan sipped his beer, set down the mug, and backhanded Wyatt's shoulder. "Well, I'd say we polished off those two jokers from the docks in short order."

Wyatt broke into a half smile; few people amused him the way Morgan did. "Looks like you've learned the trade well enough."

Morgan struck a noble pose and slapped his right hand over his heart. "I owe it all to Warren. Hell, if I didn't have a job beatin' on other people's heads, I'd probably miss him." He drank again and gestured toward Wyatt with the mug. "What the hell've you been up to?"

"Just tryin' to keep my head above water," Wyatt said. He drank from his cup and watched Morgan settle in, waiting for more. Wyatt set down his coffee, and the silence drew out until the space around them took on a private air. "I ran into some trouble with the law."

Morgan leaned in closer. "What'd you do?" he asked with that devilish spark of humor in his eyes. "You hit the wrong man?"

"Got mixed up with some people I shouldn't have in the Nations. Had to break out of an Arkansas jail. I reckon there's a federal warrant out on me."

"For what!" Morgan barked, all his wit suddenly dampened.

"Said I stole some horses. That's why I came here to Peoria."

"Hell," Morgan huffed, "you're prob'ly better hid in these slums than you are out on the prairie." He pointed upstairs. "Only time we see the law around here is when they come to dip their peckers in our goods." Morg laughed. "They get a discount . . . kind o' like a permit tax to keep us legal."

Wyatt checked a movement on the upstairs landing, where two women conversed as they leaned on the balustrade. One with dark hair stared at Wyatt and smoked a thin cigar.

"That Rozilla?" he said.

Morgan turned and waved to her, but she only blew a casual stream of smoke and then looked away. "Yeah, it don't appear Virge's married no more," he said and took a pull on his beer.

"Where is Virge?"

Morgan shook his head as he wiped his mouth with his sleeve. "No idea." When Wyatt looked back at Rozilla, Morgan laughed again. "Virgil's goin' through wives like pairs o' boots. Can't tell if he's wearin' 'em out or they're just a bad fit."

Abruptly Morgan's eyes dulled and he looked down into his beer. "Sorry, Wyatt. I didn' mean . . ."

Wyatt shook his head and, keeping the heel of his hand on the table, lifted his fingers to wave away the comment. "Thought I'd look for some work here."

"Well, hell . . . team up with me at Haspel's," Morgan said, his enthusiasm back in place. "Ain't a bad life, I'm here to tell you. Good money and plenty o' accommodatin' women. *You* saw Sarah." Morgan's smile stretched across his face. "And there's McClelland's. They're looking for another hard-ass. We'll see can we keep the clientele from killing the whores."

Wyatt let his attention drift up to the landing, where the whore with Rozilla made a coquettish laugh. "I reckon I'll try it," he said. "Banging on heads might be just what I need for a while."

The two Earps built a reputation on the Peoria waterfront, providing the owners of three brothels with a show of managerial muscle, drifting from one establishment to the other as the businesses flourished or foundered. The houses of Haspel, Vansteel, and McClelland became Wyatt's unlikely collective home. Doing his best to leave every memory of his previous life behind him, he fell into the routines of a debauched life with mistreated whores, card sharps, and drunken men, who would as soon fight as take their leave from the premises. The days ran together in blurs of arguments in dark hallways and sporadic violence . . . and might have continued that way indefinitely had not Peoria elected a new mayor on a platform of moral reform.

The first time Wyatt and Morgan were arrested during a police raid on Haspel's, they were assumed to be customers and fined accordingly by the judge—twenty dollars each. On the occasion of their second arrest at McClelland's, with their faces now familiar to the court, the fine more than doubled. Unwilling to pay, the Earp brothers spent three nights sleeping on the floor of a filthy, overcrowded cell, until finally two bunks opened up. There were no mattresses, just platforms of rough-sawn pine, which they held claim to for seven more nights.

By the tenth night of their incarceration, Morgan had secured the bunk next to Wyatt's. Wyatt lay stretched out on his back with his coat rolled under his head and one elbow crooked over his eyes. Morgan sat with his back to the brick wall, his arms wrapped around his bent knees as he listened to the snores of the inmates.

"Sounds a little like Pa, don't it?" Morgan whispered.

Wyatt turned his head to see his brother looking around at the sleeping prisoners.

"Shit, I ain't never been cooped up this long," Morg complained. "What about you?"

Wyatt's arm lowered to his face again. "What *about* me?"

Morgan's voice turned as earnest as when he had been a boy asking about the things that turn a boy into a man. "How long were you in jail that time in Arkansas?"

Wyatt laced his fingers across his stomach and stared up at the heavy timber beams that shored up the roof. "Too damned long," he said and turned to his brother.

Morgan studied the walls, the window, and the ceiling. "So how'd you break out?"

Wyatt inhaled deeply and let his breath seep out slowly. "Somebody broke out through the roof. The rest of us just followed." He raised up on an elbow to better look at Morgan. "Don't be thinkin' about breakin' out, you hear? We'll just do our time."

When Morgan said nothing, Wyatt lay back and covered his eyes again. He could feel his brother's questions stacking up—spontaneous and fragile—like a house of cards.

"Why do you reckon these jacklegs ain't figured out you're wanted in Arkansas?"

Wyatt had no answer for that. Concentrating on sleep, he tried to ignore the stench.

"Well, what if they find out about it?" Morg persisted.

Wyatt took in a lot of air and then let it ease out. "Every day I'm in here, the odds of that stack against me."

"Are you worried?"

"When you're wanted by the law, a part of you stays worried."

Something scurried across the floor, but neither of them remarked on it.

"Gettin' arrested and payin' a fine now and then looks like it's gettin' to be part of the job," Morgan said. "But if you got to dodge a federal warrant . . . hell . . . that ain't no way to live, Wyatt. Maybe you ought to get out of this line o' work. Hell, maybe we both should."

Wyatt refolded his coat and stuffed it back under his head. "If I can get out of this place without Arkansas catchin' up to me, that's just what I aim to do."

Wyatt closed his eyes again, but Morgan leaned closer. "Wyatt?" he whispered, "reckon you'll ever get married again?"

Wyatt opened his eyes to the plank ceiling and tried to head off the memory, but the image of Rilla crystallized in his mind. Conjuring up her face in the filth of the cell felt to him like a sacrilege, yet he knew it was a transgression worthy of a man who had chosen this profession.

"I ain't hardly over bein' married the first time, Morg."

The following week on a rainy May mid-afternoon, Wyatt and Morgan stepped into Vansteel's saloon. They took the table nearest the front windows, as the other daytime patrons had preferred to drink in the darker privacy of the back of the room. Leland brought their regular drinks and then lingered to hear Morgan describe the squalor of the jail cell.

"Yeah," Leland said, "they made a raid here, too. This new mayor has got a church steeple stuck up his arse." Leland frowned. "How come you boys didn't shell out the cash and be done with it?"

"It was a helluva lot o' money," Morgan said. He leaned forward and dropped his elbows on the table. "I wish you'd explain to me why they got to have a law against providin' whores. It's a necessary service, ain't it? Men need it. They're willin' to pay. It's supply and demand . . . good income for the girls, too."

Leland shrugged. "I reckon it don't sit well with the Bible thumpers and the married folk."

Morgan snorted. "Hell, half o' our customers are married. Prob'ly go to church, too."

Leland conceded this point with his silence. Wyatt sipped his coffee and looked out the window at the rain turning Water Street to sludge. He recalled a buffalo wallow he had once seen in the Smoky Hill country, where there must have been a hundred swallows gathering mud for their nests. When his outfit had come upon it, the birds rose like a great sparkling net swirling in a vortex of wind. For a time his thoughts remained with the prairie and the endless expanses of grass that stretched toward whatever horizon one chose to face on the plains.

"Did you get hauled in?" Morgan asked Leland.

Leland raised both palms like a man being robbed at gunpoint. "Hey, I'm just a bartender," he said in a mocking singsong voice. His innocent eyes rolled up to the top landing. "I don't know what goes on up there." He dropped his hands and smiled. "By the way," he said, turning, "got something for you."

He walked behind the bar and searched the pockets of a checkered coat hanging on the wall. When he returned, Leland dropped a postmarked letter on the table before Morgan.

"From James," Morg said and squinted at the postmark. "In Montana!" Excited, he looked at Wyatt for a reaction. "What the hell is he still doin' in Montana?"

"I reckon they got saloons in Montana," Wyatt said.

Morgan unfolded the paper and cocked his head slightly for the reading. " 'Brother Morg,' " he began. " 'Virgil wrote and

told me where to find you. If you have tired of life in Peoria,
you should pack up for Montana. We got winters up here that
would snap the hairs off a well-digger's ass, but the weather is
fine now and there are men swarming through here for the gold
fields. I am more than happy to relieve them of their nuggets by
letting them nestle up next to my precious rubies of the night.
Do you know where Wyatt is? You boys ought to come up and
join me here in Deer Lodge. Business is good. If you know
where Ma and Pa are living now, send me an address. A letter I
sent to Lamar was returned. And send me Wyatt's if you have
it. Your brother, James.' "

Morgan studied the letter again, his eyes fixed on a spot
halfway down the page. "Hell," he said and looked up at Wyatt.
"I might wanna go make my fortune up there, too."

"Which way?" Leland chuckled. "The gems in the stream
beds . . . or the brothel beds?"

Morgan's smile broke off, and he squinted at Wyatt. "Is that
what he meant by 'rubies'?"

Leland patted the tawny hair on the top of the younger Earp's
head. "Sounds like he's in the same business as you boys." He
walked back to the bar, retying his apron strings and rolling his
sleeves to his elbows. Wyatt picked up the envelope and read the
return address.

"I might just head up there," Morgan declared. "I could stand
a little gettin' rich." He stacked his forearms side by side, fists
to elbows, and leaned closer. "You ought'a come with me,
Wyatt."

Wyatt finished his coffee. "I was thinking I might get back to
the plains . . . try my hand at hunting buffalo again before the
herds are gone. Head up my own outfit this time."

Morgan's eyebrows came together into a tawny peak. "What
about that warrant?"

Wyatt faced the rain again, thinking. "I reckon most of the

threat will come from the towns. I'll avoid 'em as best I can." He studied the dilapidated buildings across the muddy street, where a boy and a ragged old man huddled under an awning on the sidewalk and scraped food from a can with a stick. "I've had enough of towns to last me for a while," Wyatt said.

CHAPTER 21

Summer, 1872: Peoria

It would take three months for the contract to run out with the man to whom Wyatt had leased his horses. He could not leave Rilla's gelding behind, not in Peoria. Biding his time after Morgan had set out for Montana, Wyatt stayed on as a bartender in a dive closer to the docks.

In the middle of August, John Walton appeared at his bar and slapped down a small felt purse that clinked with heavy coins. The two men with him leaned on the bar and stared at Walton as if awaiting orders.

"Wyatt Earp!" Walton said through a wide smile. "I heard you were on the riverfront."

"John," Wyatt said and extended his hand over the bar.

As they shook, Walton studied Wyatt until finally he remembered the men beside him. "Give us three beers, Wyatt, would you?"

Wyatt served the drinks and lingered when Walton opened the drawstring on the felt bag. The jovial entrepreneur inverted his purse, letting a waterfall of three-dollar gold pieces tumble onto the polished wood. Wyatt picked one up, made change from the till, and held out the coins in his palm, waiting, but Walton only smiled.

"You could be making better money working for me, Wyatt," Walton said and raised his chin at the bottles of whiskey and the glasses lined up on the shelves. "You rate better than this."

Wyatt laid down the coins. "I'm leaving Illinois, John, as soon as I can get my horses back."

"And when is that?"

"I let the fellow at the stable lease 'em out to a wheelwright. He's using 'em to deliver a new wagon to Beardstown next week. After that I'm gone."

Walton pursed his lips, collected his money off the bar, and dropped the coins into his bag. "Can you pick up your horses in Beardstown?"

"Reckon I could. Why?"

Walton jerked a thumb toward the river. "I've got my keelboat docked here. You work for me on the run downriver, and you'll have sixty dollars in your pocket for your trip."

Wyatt gave Walton a questioning look. "For poling?"

John shook his head. "Enforcing. Same as you've been doing at Haspel's. We'll tie up each night near a village, take in customers, stay on the move, and keep ahead of the law."

Wyatt gripped the edge of the bar, leaned on stiffened arms, and stared blindly at the sundry assortment of patrons in the room. "Sixty dollars," he said, as though weighing the words on his tongue. He watched Walton's eyebrows lift with the pending offer. "When do we leave?"

On Saturday night, Wyatt stood on the deck of Walton's floating brothel and took in his last view of Peoria's docks and the dimly lighted streets beyond. The gunboat was moored forty yards out from the river's west bank, where an oarsman delivered customers in a leaky rowboat. The long one-room cabin on board was more depraved than he remembered, stinking of urine and filthy pallets in the cribs along the perimeter of the room. Only two improvements had been made: the once curtained-off cribs were now wooden cubicles with latch-locked doors, and the crude bar selling watered-down whiskey now featured a countertop of varnished wood. Wyatt reasoned that enforcing aboard would be easier than at Haspel's or McClelland's, due to the confined space and to most customers' aversion to swimming ashore if they ran afoul of the rules.

Lighting a cigar, Wyatt watched a boatload of passengers ferry from the pier. The group was loud, the revelers well on their way to a drunken spree. A slurred chanty echoed over the water, and one man stood to lead the song, until the oarsman ordered him down. When the boat came alongside, Wyatt tied the bow and stern lines and stepped back to size up the patrons. Five strapping dock workers, a long-haired gambler, and a bandy-legged street vendor pulled themselves over the rails. The eighth passenger was Sarah Haspel.

"So, you're back at it," she said through her sly smile.

"Just enough to get downriver," Wyatt said, giving her a hand to climb aboard.

Her eyes seemed to flicker with a mischievous flash of light. "And *what's* downriver?"

"My horses," he said.

She stared into Wyatt's eyes before allowing an amused smile to surface on her painted lips. "Your horses," she echoed, mocking his tone. Shaking her head, she walked inside the cabin, leaving the rowdy knot of customers on the deck with Wyatt.

As the ferryman untied the ropes and pushed away, Wyatt gathered the newcomers at the door. "You boys, listen up," he said, getting down to business. "Three things . . . inside, you pay the owner up front for every drink and for every girl. You've got thirty minutes in the crib that's assigned to you. And last, you don't get rough with the girls." He nodded once to show he had concluded his obligations. "Abide by the rules, and we'll all have a good evening."

Wyatt followed the customers inside, taking his seat just inside the door. The banjo player struck up a rhythm of tinny notes, and then the fiddler sawed an upbeat melody that rode atop the lively, plucked tempo. One of the dock workers snatched up a reluctant partner and twirled her on the dance floor. At the bar, Walton laughed at a joke as he kept one arm draped over the small metal box that served as his till. Wyatt sized up each man for a poker game, in case someone finished his business early.

All but one couple had retired to a crib when a heavy bump on the upstream side of the boat brought up Wyatt's head from his game of solitaire. Walton stared at Wyatt for two seconds, before shrugging and returning to his tally of the night's income.

"Prob'ly a log," Walton mumbled, and continued recording numbers in his ledger.

Wyatt listened for a time, hearing only the grunts of the customers and the steady lap of the current as it carved around the hull. He checked the few windows, but the sparsely lighted room had transformed the glass into mirrors. As soon as he had returned to his cards, a shrill, whistle pierced the night outside, and instantly the doors burst open. Uniformed policemen streamed in, spread out through the cabin, and stood like a showroom of mannequins, all of them displaying the same attire. Every officer wielded the same regulation skull-cracker in a tight-fisted grip, and each wore a revolver holstered high on a polished leather belt. The music stopped, and the two dancers stared wide-eyed at the intruders.

Some of the men in the cribs sensed a foil to their evening plans and could be heard mumbling obscenities and scrambling for their clothes. Others, oblivious to the disturbance, continued to slake their passions, contributing damning testimony to the occasion.

A stout officer wearing a captain's insignia strolled past his men and walked the perimeter of the cabin, trying doors until he found one unlocked. He leaned inside and then faced the room.

"All right, everybody listen up!" he announced. "I'm Captain Gill with the city police. Everyone on this vessel is under arrest."

Walton stepped from behind the bar and approached the captain. "Is this about the taxes?"

"I'll ask the questions," Gill interrupted. "Who are you?"

"John Walton, owner of this boat . . . a boat, by the way, which is not within—"

Walton closed his mouth when the police captain rapped his baton on the nearest crib.

"You're running whores on this tub," Gill bellowed. He turned from Walton and came face to face with Wyatt. "Earp, isn't it? You're getting to be a regular at this, aren't you?"

Wyatt said nothing. He rolled down his shirtsleeves and began buttoning the cuffs.

"I don't want any trouble with you, Earp, you understand?"

Wyatt shook his head and spoke evenly. "No trouble."

Holding his grim expression on Wyatt, Gill called out to his men. "O'Connor! Go out on deck and signal our pilot to come alongside. The rest of you men collect all weapons and prepare these people for boarding." He leaned to look Wyatt over. "Where's your weapon?"

Wyatt parted the front of his unbuttoned vest. "Not carryin'."

As the officers went into motion, Wyatt casually walked to the bar and opened the metal cash box. Walton started to speak but closed his mouth when Wyatt looked at him.

"I'm taking what's owed me, John," he said, stuffing the money into his trouser pocket. He picked up his coat and hat from behind the bar. When he stepped abreast of Walton, he spoke quietly. "It's for the court fine. I ain't spending ten nights in that rat's nest of a jail again."

Properly dressed, Sarah reappeared from her crib and walked

directly to Wyatt, where she slipped her arm into his. "This is my husband," she said to the room at large.

"Congratulations," Gill said flatly. "You can line up with him now, but you girls will have your own cell once we get to the station."

At Monday's arraignment, the judge heard each plea with his chin propped in a hand. Two of the brothel's patrons denied knowing the barge was an enterprise of prostitution. But finally, when the gavel went down, everyone paid a fine. Wyatt's penalty was levied at forty-three dollars, fifteen cents.

"Mr. Earp," the judge intoned in a weary voice, "you're a young, able-bodied man with your whole life ahead of you. Don't you think—especially for the sake of your wife's well-being—that you two might consider pursuing some other line of work?"

Wyatt spoke up before Sarah Haspel had a chance to say something he might regret. "Yes, sir. That's just what I aim to do."

CHAPTER 22

Fall, 1872: Peoria to the south Kansas plains

The Atchison, Topeka, and Santa Fe Railroad had run its rails to Buffalo City, and the camp had renamed itself Dodge City. Dodge was still the hunter's Mecca, where a man outfitted, disembarked for his chosen destination, and returned to the middlemen hide brokers to trade his hard-earned goods for cash. Furthering the town's economic prosperity, ranchers from Texas were rounding up the old Spaniards' longhorn cattle that had multiplied during the war years, and they were driving them up the eastern branch of the Chisholm Trail to the new railhead.

When these cattle companies reached Dodge, the town imploded with the vent of young drovers who had slept on the trail for two months. The bawling of cattle, the stench of the holding pens, and the celebratory roar of six-guns became symbols of profit for Dodge City. With the resulting cash flow, the town had become a thriving venue for merchants, a gambler's paradise, and a hotbed of mayhem and wickedness. Dodge was "wide open"—plenty wide enough to hide a wanted man among the nameless plainsmen who moved in and out of its town limits.

On his second night in the boom town, Wyatt sat in on a poker game at the Alhambra Saloon with a rotund German named Deger, two Masterson brothers, a jobless drifter named Jim Elder, and a stocky, round-faced sharp known only as

"Prairie Dog Dave." The Mastersons appeared to be untested in the murky waters of gambling and fell prey to the questionable tactics of Dave. The older Masterson, Ed, knowing he was new to the game, seemed to take his losses in stride. Bat was another story. He was a pot about to boil over. Dave was so busy fleecing them, he paid little attention to Wyatt's unassuming presence at the table.

After two hours of play, the younger Masterson was so hellbent on breaking Dave's run on their money that he parlayed an unlikely bluff, upping the stakes by forty dollars. Deger and Elder folded. The betting went around twice more before Bat called and laid down a trio of eights. Dave's steely eyes showed nothing as he fanned three tens on the table. Wyatt's full house stole everyone's thunder, and as he raked in the pot, Dave gathered what chips remained before him, took his coat and hat from the rack, and left with a mumbled *"adios."*

"You boys want to go another?" Wyatt said.

"Hell, yes," Bat replied. He slapped his forearms to the table and clasped his fingers together. His pale-blue eyes were piercing as they fixed on Wyatt's hands gathering the deck.

Ed Masterson dug a hand into his trouser pocket and combined a smile and a sigh. "Better not, young'un. Let's stop while we can still buy breakfast."

The obese German laughed. "Hell, I buy you breakfast if you boys'll stay in and let me win the rest o' what you not give to Prairie Dog."

Bat's face darkened as he glared at Deger. "What the hell's that supposed to mean?"

When Deger chuckled and busied himself counting his chips, Wyatt tapped the edges of the cards and set down the deck. "What he's saying is that Dave was working you boys."

The skin on Bat's forehead tightened. "You mean the squinty-eyed sonovabitch was cheatin' us?"

Deger's laugh wheezed from deep in his chest. "Not cheat unless get caught."

Ed folded his arms on the table and leaned forward, looking squarely at Wyatt. "Well, mister, if you don't mind educating us . . . exactly how'd he do it?"

Wyatt hesitated, weighing the Masterson brothers' inexperience against the accepted protocol of taboo subjects at the gaming tables. "Can I give you a pointer?" he said.

The younger brother stood and leaned with his knuckles pressing into the tabletop. "Prob'ly easy to give advice when you're holding our money. I reckon we can figure it out for ourselves."

Jim Elder lifted his coat off the back of his chair and squirmed into the sleeves. "I'm out," he announced quietly. "I'm goin' while I still got money enough for a whore." When he stood, Wyatt sized him up with work in mind. Elder was small-boned and reserved, but seemed to pour himself into the task at hand. He might be a tolerable companion.

"Can I have a word outside?" Wyatt said. "I might have a proposition for you."

Elder's lackluster eyes quickly sparked with interest. He nodded and, with a lively step, marched out the door. Wyatt swept his chips into his hat, eased back his chair, and stood. As he faced the hotheaded Masterson, Wyatt one-handedly buttoned the front of his coat.

"No offense intended," he said, but Masterson was too proud to look at Wyatt. Bat dropped back into the chair and busied his hands with the cards. Wyatt stepped to the bar and turned in his chips. After collecting his money, he slid two coins across the counter to the bartender. "Give a couple a beers to the boys at the table with Deger. My compliments."

The saloon man looked at the coins. "Deger, too?"

Wyatt turned and studied the three remaining at the table.

Deger and Ed were deep in conversation. Bat practiced his deal, making the cards flash in a steady rhythm. Wyatt turned back to the bartender, nodded, and pushed another coin across the bar.

The bartender leaned in and muttered, "My mother'll be out here huntin' buffalo next."

Wyatt looked back at the Mastersons. "Everybody starts somewhere," he said. "They'll do fine."

With Jim Elder as his skinner, Wyatt hunted the territory around the Salt Fork of the Arkansas.

Elder went about his work with an uncomplaining demeanor. He was a typical range hand, who preferred wages to being in charge, but he grew to like Wyatt's ethic of a semi-partnership. Wyatt did the shooting and then helped with the skinning by looping a line over the pommel of his saddle to supply the pull, while Elder sliced with his knife. They staked the hides as a team, but from there it was Elder's job to scrape off the gore and to powder the skin with arsenic to keep off the flies. Together they processed far fewer hides than the bigger outfits, but there was adequate profit when divided between two, rather than half a dozen men.

The buffalo herds could not last forever, Wyatt knew, and once the slaughter was complete, his options would be limited. If US marshals carried papers on him, he could undertake no enterprise that might draw attention to himself. How long that would be, he did not know, but one thing was clear to him now: by running from the Van Buren jail, he had traded one prison for another.

One moonless night over the campfire, he told Elder the whole story about the Showns and Kennedy. It was not a cathartic exercise but a pragmatic one. Elder was loyal, and Wyatt needed the man's eyes and ears to pick up information whenever he went into a town for supplies. If Wyatt's likeness was posted in a courtroom, police station, or post office in a town on the plains, he needed to know.

"Well," Elder replied, "you keep growin' that moustache, and I'll always be the one to go in for supplies. It's a big country, Wyatt. A man can stay lost in it, if need be." Elder poked at the fire with a stick and wrinkled his brow. "Whyn't you just change your name, Wyatt?"

The cartilage in Wyatt's jaw flexed. "Won't be doin' that," he said. Wyatt's eyes hardened and reflected the flames, and Elder never raised the subject again.

Three days later when the little skinner was overdue for his return with supplies, Wyatt rode out for Medicine Lodge to check on his partner's welfare. A mile from town he met Elder with the packhorse loaded. Elder's usually somber face beamed as he stopped abreast of Wyatt.

"Got some news," he said. "Met a big Irish tub named Kennedy looking to sign on with a buff'ler crew. Said he was cleared of charges for horse theft in Fort Smith. I poked at it a little. Said the whole affair was dropped for him and the other two men with him."

"What about the jailbreak?"

"I thought about that, so I went to the federal marshal's office to say I might'a seen a man named Shown down near the Otoe agency and wanted to know if there was a reward. He never heard of 'im. So I asked about anybody named Earp. Same reply."

As Wyatt listened to Jim Elder, the last year in Peoria and on the buffalo fields flashed through his mind like a deck of cards flipped so fast that the numbers were of no value. He looked down the trail toward the town and imagined the gates of humanity opened for him.

"I been wantin' my picture took," Elder announced. "Might like one with my business partner to send back to my sister.

Will the camp hold for a spell?"

Wyatt considered the leap of faith and wondered how wide those gates of freedom really were. "I left the wagon and horses with Tom Nixon's outfit. They'll keep another day."

Elder's face softened to a child's wonderment. "I say we dig into some boardin' house cookin'," he said. "Somethin' besides buff'ler hump. And then a piece o' sour cherry pie. Then maybe a bath and a woman, if I can find one who'll bed a stinkin' skinner."

With a new bounce in the saddle, Elder led the way. He talked more than he had the entire season—about his sister, the sod home he had built in Kansas, and the other outfits for which he had skinned. Wyatt barely listened as he sorted through the information about Kennedy and the warrants, letting the news sink into him like a slow baptism of waters washing him clean.

They visited the photographer's studio first and then walked the main street to take in the business establishments. Elder followed as Wyatt stepped from the harsh summer sun into the twilight of the Nations Saloon—a single room of spare adornment with a short bar tucked against the west wall. It was busy for early afternoon. In the rear of the room, six men sat around a table shrouded in a haze of cigar smoke, each man concentrating on a hand of cards cupped before his chest. Spectators stood around the table, and two whores lounged in a corner.

Bellied up to the countertop, Elder drank for both of them as Wyatt stood with his back to the bar, watching the poker players, reading the game by their facial expressions. One of the gamblers was young Masterson, now aged some, the youthful color of his cheeks replaced by the burn of sun and wind. Seasoned inside as well as out, his gray-blue eyes were settled and alert.

When Elder had fortified himself sufficiently to proposition a whore, he straightened from the bar and neatened the tuck of his blouse into his trousers. "I ain't so sure these women here would have me. Think I'll go down the street a ways. How do I look?"

Wyatt gave him a one-eyed squint. "It ain't me you got to look good for. I reckon if you got the money and the right equipment, you'll do all right."

With his head cocked to one side, Elder marched out of the Nations—a man on a mission—and Wyatt joined the onlookers circled around the table, where he stood behind Masterson. A whore with flaming red hair and freckles dusted across her cheeks attached herself to Wyatt's arm and watched the game with him. After a few minutes, she pressed her bosom into his upper arm.

"You're a tall one, aren't you? You wanna buy me a drink and see what that leads to?"

Wyatt looked down into her face. "Might wanna skip that drink and get to the other." He nodded toward the table. "Let me watch this hand play out."

Masterson flattened his cards against his chest, turned, and looked Wyatt squarely in the eyes. "You mind?"

It was a standard request with an obligatory response. Wyatt nodded and pushed away from the wall. The game resumed without issue, as the whore pulled Wyatt toward a back doorway.

"Looks like he don't want you breathin' down his back," she said and gave him a crooked grin. "But you can breathe down mine, honey."

In an hour Wyatt was out front checking the tie-downs on the packhorse as he waited for Jim Elder for the trip back to their camp. Counting a handful of coins, young Masterson pushed out through the doors into the broil of the sun and leaned against the awning post. When he looked up and saw Wyatt, he pocketed the money.

"No offense in there, mister. I don't know who's working with who in that crowd."

Wyatt nodded. "Better to be smart with your money than courteous with some shill."

Elder came up the boardwalk at a fast walk, all his attention on the photographer's images he held in his hands. "Hey, Wyatt . . . look'a here." He handed over a tintype. Wyatt studied the portrait only briefly and tried to hand the plate back. "That'n is yours," Elder said. "Hey . . . how 'bout I join up with you tomorrow back at camp?" He jerked a thumb over his shoulder in the direction from which he had come. "It appears this little yeller-haired girl back there ain't done with me." He smiled, spat in his hand, and tried to flatten the wave of hair that rose atop his head.

Wyatt swung into the saddle and watched Elder hurry down the street as he ran his fingers through his long locks. Wyatt crossed his wrists over the pommel and looked at Masterson.

"Name's Earp. We met in Dodge when I tried to give you a speech about playin' poker."

"Appears I should have listened." Bat nodded toward the saloon. "They cheatin' in there?"

Wyatt buttoned his shirt pocket over the tintype portrait. "Any man'll cheat when he thinks he can get away with it. Part o' the game."

Masterson frowned. "One o' them in there is a deputy sheriff."

Wyatt looked into the dark interior of the saloon. "Don't matter. Gamblin's got its own rules on what's right and wrong. Different from everything else." Masterson frowned and tumbled the coins in his pocket. "Tell you what," Wyatt suggested, "next time you got a winning hand, close up your cards and tap the edges on the table."

Masterson's frown deepened, and his eyes went hard. "What the hell for?"

"That's what you done every time you held a poor hand. It'll likely throw 'em."

Masterson tried for a look of indignation, but the doubt on his face would not yield to it.

"Every time you're holding high cards," Wyatt continued, "you're closing 'em with two hands and holdin' 'em like they'll break. There's two fellows in there reading you like a book."

Bat's eyebrows lowered, and his upper lip curled to his nose. "Well, hell . . ."

Wyatt touched his hat brim and leaned as he reined his horse around. "Good luck."

The next morning Wyatt looked up from his pan of sizzling pork to see a lone rider approaching—someone too straight in the saddle to be Jim Elder. Masterson reined up short of stirring up dust into Wyatt's breakfast. Setting down the fry pan, Wyatt stood and raised his cup as an invitation.

"Coffee?" he asked.

"No, sir. I come over to thank you."

Wyatt sipped coffee and watched the boy over the rim of the cup. "How'd you come out?"

Masterson smiled. "Walked out two hundred dollars better'n I walked in."

Wyatt laughed deep in his chest, the sound reminding him of Virgil. It was the first time he could remember laughing since he'd left Missouri.

"Mr. Nixon says you're a damned hard worker. You're out here alone?"

"I got help." Wyatt pointed with the cup. "He's in town throwing his money at a whore."

Masterson looked off that way and nodded slowly. In the

silence that followed, he surveyed Wyatt's camp, letting his eyes linger on the stack of hides loaded in the wagon and then on the five horses picketed just beyond.

"That's some handsome horses you got." The young gambler looked to Wyatt for some response, but Wyatt just sipped his coffee. "I got to get back. I just come over to thank you."

The boy looked down at his horse's mane and fingered a strand of coarse hairs from one side to the other. Still looking down, he nodded as if assuring himself of some private thought. When he looked up, he eased his horse forward then leaned from the saddle to offer his hand.

"Name's Bat. Just call me Bat." Their hands clasped and pumped once.

"Wyatt Earp."

Bat nodded. "Mr. Nixon told me your name, Mr. Earp. I like that game too much to quit. I appreciate what you told me."

Wyatt smiled. "You tried faro yet?"

Bat shifted in his saddle and hardened his face to cover his lack of experience. "I reckon not. I'm still trying to figure out this poker business."

Wyatt recognized the fire in the boy's blue-gray eyes. "We all learn it one way or the other," he said. "Keep your hands idle when you gamble. You already got the face for it."

When Masterson rode off toward Nixon's camp, Wyatt watched as the boy dipped into a swale and then moved smoothly up the rise on the other side. His grip had been firm but not testing. His back was strong measured against the horse's gallop, but he knew how to break and give with the rhythm of the stride. Out of earshot, man and horse crested the swell in the land and appeared for a moment to float above the grass before the dark silhouette sank into the land.

Something in the boy's youth had left Wyatt open to a remembrance from his past. Something about options and the freedom to pursue them. The feeling came to Wyatt like a forgotten note from a song plucked right out of the air. He let his gaze extend to the horizon, and he felt that same elevated perspective he had sometimes gained from the old blackjack oak back in Iowa. That one step up onto the root had meant the difference between "what was" and "what could be."

Time was running out on this mad killing spree with the buffalo. And the waste was horrendous. In truth, nothing about the shaggy animals appealed to Wyatt. In size and solidarity perhaps they were regal, but in the sights of his Sharps rifle, they were big stupid beasts with a price tag. Now their rotting carcasses and sun-bleached ribs jutted up from the landscape like gravestones scattered along the plains. But for the skinning and scraping, it was all too easy. There was a tacit shame in the occupation that, as long as it was bringing in money, no one was willing to put into words. A few remnants of the great herds might last another season or two, but as a business venture, Wyatt knew, the books were closing. It was time to open a new book.

At the end of the season he paid Jim Elder, sold off his rig and three of the horses to Tom Nixon, and then rode north through Kansas with no destination in mind. Now with the federal warrant a thing of the past, he simply wanted to be shed of the hunter's life.

Without his brothers to partner with in the saloon business, he began to consider cattle. Buying up livestock and making a fortune off selling beef might bring a certain respectability, the kind gambling alone might not afford. The cattle trade had become the rock upon which many of the railroad towns were now flourishing. Cattle, it seemed, were here to stay. After all, the buffalo grass would be here. Something had to eat it.

CHAPTER 23

Summer, 1873: Ellsworth, Kansas

The cattle business suffered that dry summer of '73 on the plains. Those Texas drovers who did push their stock north to Kansas eventually gravitated to the Smoky Hill country, where an anomalous but merciful pattern of weather had kept the grama grass green on the flats. There the force-marched longhorns were fattened up to boost their selling price in the town of Ellsworth. By the time Wyatt crossed the bridge over the Smoky Hill River into the new cattle-shipping center, most of the Texas drovers had blown off their steam and pointed their ponies south for home. The best Wyatt could hope for in Ellsworth was to engage any lingering cattlemen in a high-stakes card game.

After securing a boardinghouse room, he crossed the tracks in the main plaza to Brennan's Saloon. The room was spare with mismatched chairs. For decoration a longhorn skull hung on the east wall, a buffalo skull on the west. The symbolism of the face-off was not lost on Wyatt.

The gaming tables were empty. Behind the bar a stoop-shouldered man in a clean white apron leaned over a news-paper, a mug of coffee steaming by his elbow. At the sound of Wyatt's boots, the man's head came up.

"Come on in and enjoy a little quiet. It's a welcome commodity these days."

Wyatt stepped to the bar. "What time does your gambling

crowd come in?"

The man straightened and squinted at the empty back table. "Depends on where our damned police force is. If they set up in here I ain't likely to see a Texas boy all night."

When the man asked his pleasure, Wyatt nodded to his coffee. "Any more of that?"

The old man walked into the backroom and out a backdoor. Returning with a black kettle swinging from a wire handle, he took down a ceramic mug from a shelf and blew into it.

"Where'd you come in from? You're not a drover, are you?"

Wyatt shook his head and waited while the man poured. "Problem with your officers?"

The man set the pot on the floor and spewed air from his lips. "Ain't a one of 'em worth spit. Crookeder'n snakes, all but the sheriff. Our marshal and his deputies . . . if they run a losing streak at the tables . . . they trump up charges against the winners—if they're from Texas, that is—and haul 'em off to court and take their share of any collected fines. Hell . . . 'bout the only difference between the law and the hell-raisers is the badge, which lets 'em carry their pistols."

Wyatt sipped his coffee and studied the room. "Who runs the biggest cattle outfit . . . if a man wanted to talk some business?"

The bartender laughed a single humorless note and went back to his paper. "Any man with enough sense to do that's already gone back to Texas. Only ones left are the troublemakers."

"How's the gambling?" Wyatt said.

The bartender pointed toward the back of the room. "You want high stakes, find you a game at that table in the corner back there. Them that play there . . . their pockets ain't empty yet."

Wyatt dug into his pocket for a coin, but the man waved a hand before him. "No charge. Coffee's on me. Come back tonight and buy a drink. That'll square us."

Wyatt sorted out the proper change and set it on the bar. "Then I'll pay for yours," he said and nodded toward the old man's cup. "Now we're square."

Wyatt cleaned up in his room and slept the afternoon. After dark when the August heat was beginning to lift from the day, he donned a new linen shirt, brushed the dust from his hat, and returned to Brennan's. By ten o'clock he was one of six players at the back table. It was the only game in the room. No chips were on the table, only cash.

In his company were a local cattle buyer, a railroad clerk, and two brothers—the latter being Englishmen, who were vocal to a fault about their adopted home of central Texas. The older, Ben Thompson, was a stout, round-faced man with bushy moustaches and confident eyes. Wyatt sized him up as the kingpin of what remained of the Texas crowd. Thompson was a man accustomed to having his way—that domination backed up by the ring of loiterers who hovered around him. The more he drank, the more his acquired Texas twang gave in to the clipped manner of his native tongue. As a gambler he was all business.

The younger Thompson—Billy—was a dedicated drunk, and in that condition he was volatile and loose with insults toward any man he chose. His youthful face knew only two expressions: outrage and sulk. Despite the disagreeable nature of Bill's personality, Wyatt recognized in Ben the same loyalty that bound Wyatt to his brothers, only in Ben's case, the effort had to be considerable.

As the game progressed into morning, Wyatt bided his time, placing small bets and letting the averages work for him, but for the one time when the stakes were low enough that he could afford to lose the hand. He pushed the pot to thirty-five dollars with only a pair of jacks to show for it. Billy Thompson beat it with three nines. It was a tactical sacrifice.

Three hands later, Ben raised the pot by fifty dollars, trying to bluff the nickel-and-dimers. When Wyatt's turn came, he met the bet and upped it fifty again. The others assumed the newcomer had finally come into a winning hand, and they bowed out—all but Ben and, of course, Billy, who never folded.

When it came time for Ben to call the play, he stared at Wyatt a long time. "Looks like the cards are favoring you this time." Thompson's gaze held steady. When he smiled, his eyes squeezed to half their size. " 'Course, could be you're a fancy gun with no cartridges."

Wyatt's face was unreadable. "Could be."

Thompson stared at him for a quarter minute, then let the smile drop from his face. "Son, you either got ice in your veins or you're dumber'n hell."

Billy slouched back in his chair and glared at Wyatt. "He ain't got nothing. Raise his ass again and watch him go pale. He'll have shit in his breeches, is what he'll have."

Ben Thompson paid no attention to his brother. "Here's eighty more," Thompson barked, holding the coins at eye level. The older gambler posed like this with the little shining tower of silver stacked between his thumb and index finger.

Wyatt breathed in heavily through his nose and let it out slowly, staring at the coins as though they threatened to tip the scales away from his favor. It was as far as he was willing to go with the subtle theatrics that figured into moments like this.

"I don't care to break you, Mr. Thompson."

Thompson laughed and slapped the stack of coins at the edge of the pot. "My pockets are a helluva lot deeper than this, son."

Billy flung an arm on the table and gawked at his brother. "How the hell am I gonna meet that?" he whined.

Ben snorted. "What the hell does it matter, Bill, if it all stays in the family?"

Wyatt pulled reserves from his money belt. "I'll see yours and go another fifty."

Billy tossed his cards into the scatter of deadwood and cursed. Ben held his smile, sat back, and smoothed the front of his shirt. "Rest of my money's over at the hotel."

"Your note is good with me," Wyatt said.

Thompson thought about his decision for a time and then privately fanned open his cards to study them again. He tapped the fingertips of one hand across his moustaches.

"What about an English-made shotgun?" he offered.

"If it's a part of the bet," Wyatt said, "I'd like to take a look at it."

Billy leaned so close to Wyatt that his breath violated Wyatt's space. "It's as goddamned good a gun as you'll ever fuckin' hope to see."

Wyatt kept his eyes on Ben. "That about right?"

Ben pushed Billy back into his chair. "Gibbs, twelve gauge. Precision made. Well took care of." His voice was earnest, connected to that pragmatism common to men who knew guns.

Wyatt, not dismissive of the man's loyalty to a prized tool, closed his cards and nodded once. "Let's call it then."

Thompson's moustaches lifted as he spread out three queens and two aces. Wyatt laid down his cards. He had the fourth queen . . . and next to her were four tens.

Thompson flung his cards down. "Shit!" He chewed on his defeat as his brother carped about a foolhardy play. Finally he scraped back his chair. "I'll have to walk over to the hotel to get the scattergun."

"No hurry," Wyatt offered. "We can settle later. I'm overdue on some sleep."

Ben Thompson settled back into his chair and studied Wyatt's face. "You've played this game some before." Wyatt stacked the paper money on the table, folded it, and tucked it into his money belt. Then he started on the coins. Billy splashed more whiskey into a glass and downed it with a spastic toss of his head. Ben stuck his thumbs in the armholes of his vest. "I like your manner. No bluster. Just get the job done. But I might like a chance to win back that shotgun tomorrow, if you're of a mind. You be around?"

As Wyatt looked across the table, he was already considering the new tactics he would need to employ with Thompson come another night. "I'll be around."

Wyatt slept until mid-afternoon, paid the boardinghouse keeper for another night, and then ate a meal in the dining room of the Grand Central Hotel. Afterward he stepped outside into the oppressive heat of the broad plaza and walked across the sun-baked thoroughfare over the railroad tracks to Brennan's, where the bar was already lined with customers.

He was surprised to see the Thompsons at the back table. They wore the same wrinkled clothes from the night before. The man in Wyatt's chair had his sleeves rolled up past thick, hairy wrists, and his shoulders hunched around a thick neck. In the dim light of the room, a silver badge glinted on the breast of his shirt.

A shorter man with greasy, coal-black hair sat with his back to the door and turned to look at Wyatt. He also wore a badge— his metal pinned to a flashy, crimson shirt. His olive skin suggested mixed blood, and the whites of his eyes shone brightly against his swarthy face. Sucking on a tooth he spat something on the floor with a light popping sound from his lips and turned back to the game. Wyatt stepped to the bar and ordered coffee.

"Well, I'll be goddamned. And here I thought I was rid of my tight-ass kinfolk."

Wyatt turned to the shorter man at his left. His face was bordered in whiskers, and his scalp shone where his hair had receded from the temples. But the eyes were Earp. James was thicker in the face and around the middle. The two brothers grasped hands and squeezed nine years of separation into their grip.

"What are you doing in Kansas?" Wyatt asked. "You give up on Montana?"

"Morg and me did all right up there. Did you know he was on the police force there?" Wyatt nodded his approval, and James slapped his brother's upper arm. "You look lean as a prairie wolf. What the hell have you been doing since Peoria?" James grinned. "I heard all about that from Morg."

"Tryin' to make a dollar." Wyatt received his coffee from the bartender and then nodded to his brother's inert left arm. "How's the shoulder?"

James assumed a solemn expression and bumped his good fist against his backside. "Hurts all the way down here." He winked. "It's a pain in the ass." He pulled a cigar from his coat, clamped it in his teeth, and smiled around it.

A chair scraped loudly on the wood floor at the gamblers' table. "What kind of horse shit is this!" Billy Thompson screeched. Still seated, he threw his cards facedown on the table. Everyone at the bar quieted and turned to the disruption. "What do you mean you ain't payin'?" The drunken slur of Billy's words was gone. His eyes snapped with anger. "You goddamned son of a whore!" But his threat passed as quickly as it had flared. Billy folded his arms against his chest and slumped back into his chair to sulk.

Ben leaned across the table and said something low and grumbling to the big deputy, and the two stared at each other. A wiry man sporting a goatee laughed too hard for the deputy's liking, and the policeman backhanded the man in the face, knocking him half out of his chair.

"Here we go," James muttered out of the side of his mouth.

He lit his cigar and settled against the bar to watch things develop.

The deputy struck the man again and immediately winced and snapped his hand in the air, whip-like, shaking out a pain. Billy came out of his drunken stupor enough to enjoy a yammering, high-pitched laugh. The bearded man righted his chair and glared at the deputy. His lip bled, but he said nothing. He just stared at the gun holstered to the deputy's belt. Even when Billy finally quieted, the tension at the table continued to hum in the silence of the saloon.

The deputy in the blood-red shirt casually lowered his hand to his lap. The bartender set down a bottle and took a slow step to his left until a floorboard groaned. Then the big deputy laughed and began stuffing coins into his trouser pockets. Billy looked to his brother, but Ben only glared at the policeman. The other Texans present were either hungover or half-asleep.

Now indifferent to the drama that had seemingly played out, James turned back to Wyatt. "So what in hell are you doing here in Ellsworth?"

Wyatt slowly rotated his coffee cup on the bar. "Mostly passing through to a place I ain't decided on yet."

"Hell, come over to Wichita. You can work with me." James smiled broadly. "If you're the shit-kicker you were in Peoria, I can use you." He nodded toward the back of the room where a full-chested woman squirmed and laughed in the lap of the drover whispering into her ear. "See that prairie flower with the big floaters? She's comin' back with me soon's we settle on terms. I run the best goddamn line o' whores in Kansas. Got a good arrangement with the city police."

Wyatt sipped his coffee and set his cup thoughtfully on the bar. "Might be I'll buy some cattle. See can I work into the middle of this meat market somewhere."

James hitched his head and gave his brother a crooked smile.

"Wyatt, I swear. You're like a goddamn rattlesnake wantin' to learn to play a banjo."

Before Wyatt could reply, Billy exploded with another outburst of profanity, and Ben had to hold him in his chair by his collar. Their brotherly confab deteriorated into a yelling match, and Wyatt leaned closer to James.

"I'll be next door at the general store. Come on down there when you finish your business here." Wyatt set down money and walked from the saloon.

CHAPTER 24

Summer, 1873: Ellsworth, Kansas

Now that he might gamble his way through the frontier towns, Wyatt felt the need for a handgun to replace the one he had abandoned in Arkansas. When he stepped into Beebe's General Store, the storekeeper looked up from a catalogue and made a quick, flat-eyed appraisal of Wyatt's clothes before returning to his reading.

"Help you?" he said in a dry, singsong voice, keeping his eyes on the catalogue. The open page showed a dozen different designs of women's private wear.

"Like to take a look at your new revolvers."

The merchant moved to a modest array of guns behind a glass display case. Wyatt stepped in front of the glass, and right away the storekeeper read the disappointment in his face.

"Bet you're looking for one of these," he said, opening a drawer. "Colt's Army forty-four. Self-contained cartridges. Only got this show model." Setting the hammer at half cock, he opened the gate and let the cartridges slide out one by one into his hand as he rotated the cylinder. Then he lowered the hammer, pocketed the bullets, and tapped the gun down onto the countertop. "Bought this'n off a drunk soldier out of Fort Hayes who'd got up to his ears in gambling debts."

Wyatt took the offered revolver and weighed it in the flat of his palm. He opened the loading gate to satisfy himself the chambers were empty and listened to the crisp clicks that defined the gun's workmanship. The storekeeper leaned on the counter and watched.

"Ticks like a clock, don't it?" the man said. "Army's got first call on 'em. I should be gettin' some in, say, 'round October."

Wyatt closed the gate and completed the pull of the hammer, the moving parts integrating with a pleasing glissando of clicks as the cylinder locked into place. He lowered the gun by his leg and smoothly raised it, extending the arm out to his side, looking down the barrel. He felt in the weapon the same silent authority he had always appreciated in a well-made gun. He lowered the hammer and cocked it again, this time quickly.

"Can I snap it?" Wyatt said.

The storekeeper shrugged. "If you need to. But I can tell you it's a smooth pull."

Wyatt snugged his finger against the trigger, the same feathery touch he used with a loaded weapon. He let the gun extend before him as if he intended not to disturb its weightless slumber. The quick strike of metal on metal delivered a sharp crack in the still air of the room. Wyatt nodded to the weapon as though it had spoken to him.

Before he could voice his approval, deep angry voices carried through the walls from Brennan's, reaching the store in muffled, watery sounds. Wyatt laid the gun on the counter and watched the storekeeper stare at the wall as though he could see through it. Heavy boots thudded and scuffed out onto the boardwalk, where the yelling rose to a higher pitch, the words clearer now without the barrier of the wall.

"You goddamn sonzabitches! We'll be back!" It was Billy Thompson's petulant screech. Beebe's door opened and two men in suits hurried in and gathered at the front window. Following them, James strolled in smoking his cigar, his face showing mild amusement.

"You won't have to wait long!" This challenge came from out

in the plaza where Ben Thompson stood by the railroad tracks. A gun exploded in the next room, and Wyatt heard the bullet slap into the sun-bleached billboard of the hotel across the plaza. Billy Thompson cackled at the missed shot. Wyatt walked to the front window in time to see Billy staggering backward across the street, his arm and finger outstretched toward Brennan's.

"You sonzabitches! You can't kill me!" His shrill voice filled the plaza. Citizens along the shaded boardwalks disappeared into doorways. "You'd *better* run!" Billy yelled. "You goddamn Kansas sonzabitches!" He stumbled into the hotel ahead of Ben.

Bystanders returned to the boardwalk, but no one ventured into the open plaza, which had now become an empty stage waiting for the actors to return. Wyatt took note of the idle cast iron wood heater to his left, judging it to be ample shelter should a pitched battle erupt outside. James joined him, and together they watched a man emerge from the front entrance of the hotel. He wore a dark-blue shirt and gold vest and stood on the toes of ankle-high shoes to examine the damage to his building. He marched toward Brennan's but stopped just past the rail tracks.

"You deputies in there! You're not hired to shoot up my hotel!" With the shouting inside Brennan's, his complaint fell flat.

"That's Larkin, the hotel manager." James laughed. "He's sittin' in the piss pot now."

"What happened?" Wyatt asked.

James just shook his head and blew a swirl of smoke through his tight smile.

"I wouldn't care if they all just kill each other," said Beebe, the storekeeper. "Damned Morco and Sterling . . . they ain't a lick better'n them drunken Texans." He peered out the window and snorted. "Now look at this, would you?" Beebe scowled and shook his head. "Shit."

A hatless, pockmark faced man in a striped shirt strode diagonally across the plaza. Another man hurried to stay abreast of him so as to keep up a running monologue. On the leading man's blouse, Wyatt could make out a town marshal's shield. He carried a pistol in a holster worn in front of his hip.

"Brocky Jack's come to restore the peace," Beebe quipped. "And our mayor's come to talk 'em to death." He hissed a laugh through his teeth. "Last time Brocky Jack arrested the Thompsons, him and Morco kicked 'em like dogs all the way to the courthouse. Thompsons ain't gone stand for it again, I can tell you that." He shook his head again. "Our law ain't worth piss."

"Why the hell doesn't the mayor get rid of 'em?" James said.

Beebe laughed outright. "Miller's the one hired 'em. 'Fight fire with fire,' he says. Hell, it's so out o' control now . . . he figures without Brocky Jack and his damned pack, the Texans would own this town. But there ain't nobody gonna run the Thompsons out."

A six-gun roared from inside Brennan's, followed by two rifle shots outside. Heavy footfalls marked a hasty retreat by several men out the back of the saloon. On the street, Ben Thompson stood his ground wielding a Henry rifle. Behind him Billy stumbled down from the boardwalk carrying a long, double-barreled shotgun. Ben lowered the Henry and tugged his brother by the arm down the street to Wyatt's right. Two louder shots flashed from the doorway of Brennan's. Two feet from Wyatt's head, the door casing splintered, the pieces fracturing like dry kindling.

"Goddamnit, stop your shooting, Morco!" the marshal yelled to Brennan's.

Wyatt turned at the click of a cylinder and watched Beebe

slide cartridges back into the new Colt's pistol. The men, who had moments before taken cover in the store, shuffled to the rear wall. One of them screwed up his face with a question and stared at Beebe.

"What the hell're you fixing to do?"

"Kill the first one o' them who walks through that door with a gun. Ain't nobody gonna shoot up my store, by God."

The backdoor flew open, and Miller—the mayor—hurried in, tugging down the bottom of his vest to cover the gap at his bulging waist. Sweat dripped from his nose as his eyes darted around the room. He marched to the window and made bird-like movements with his head, checking the street up, then down.

"What happened out there, Mayor?" someone asked.

Miller answered without turning. "Sterling and Morco were sitting in on a card game with the Thompsons, if you can believe that. Sterling slapped Bill Thompson." Miller shook his head. "The goddamn idiot! So the deputies pull guns, the table is on its side, money all over the floor, the Thompsons run out. Morco, I think, shot at—"

"Come out and fight, you sonzabitches!" Billy Thompson screamed from the street. Red-faced, he struggled to steady the shotgun.

Ben stepped beside him and bellowed his own challenge. "Get out here and make your fight, Sterling. You too, Morco. You damned yellow curs!" Ben held the Henry angled down from his shoulder, his head erect, like a man expecting to flush a bird. Four men dressed in Texas garb fanned out behind the Thompsons, their pistols showing at their hips. Together they moved toward the hotel again, taunting the officers with their Texas bravado. One of these—a powerfully built man—sidled up to Billy to help him walk. He was a broad-shouldered man who moved like the prizewinners from the boxing and wrestling bouts in the railroad camps. A pale scar underscored his left eye like a flattened gray worm. Each time this man's lips moved, Ben Thompson nodded.

Wyatt mumbled into the windowpane. "What the hell is he doin' here?"

"Who?" James said.

"That big Texan . . . Peshaur . . . I know him. He's trouble."

James laughed. "I'd say most everybody out there is trouble."

"For God's sake, somebody go get Sheriff Whitney," Miller said to the room at large.

"Never mind that," Beebe said. "He's already out there."

As though he might step outside, Miller took the doorknob but then thought better of it. "He'll quiet 'em down," he mumbled more to himself than to the others in the room.

Whitney stood unarmed in his shirtsleeves in front of the Texans, his back to Brennan's. Both his forearms were leveled before him, the palms down and pumping the air in a lowering gesture as he parleyed with the Thompsons. One white shirttail hung out over the back of his trousers, as though he had dressed in haste.

Wyatt watched the mayor open the door and again hesitate. The hotel manager marched out from his awning and joined the sheriff, and both men worked together to appease the Texans, who now numbered seven. Wyatt heard the sheriff offer to buy drinks all around. When the Texans balked, the sheriff took a few steps toward Brennan's and cupped a hand to his mouth.

"This is Sheriff Whitney! You men on the city force in there . . . holster your guns and stand where we can see you! We're coming inside to talk this out!"

As the Texans moved in a slow rippling wave in the hard light of the plaza, Wyatt caught a movement, a flash of color to his left. At the far corner of Brennan's, the greasy-haired deputy in the bright-red shirt appeared, a revolver in each hand, both pointed at the approaching crowd. Ben Thompson's rifle barked twice, the ratcheting of the lever almost lost between shots. As the deputy jumped back for cover, Billy Thompson's shotgun boomed like a cannon, both barrels firing simultaneously. Sheriff Whitney pitched forward into the dust, his white shirt blossoming into liquid roses.

Ben Thompson took a quick glance at Whitney as his Henry rifle turreted like a living thing with a mind of its own, seeking a target. "What the hell have you done, Billy?"

The Texans spread out, back-stepping, their hands on their gun butts. Peshaur began pulling Billy toward the hotel.

"Shoot anybody wearing a badge," Billy screamed. "I don't care if it's Jesus Christ hisself."

The hotel manager was first to get to the sheriff. Then the bartender from Brennan's. Neither man seemed to know what to do. Their eyes were ringed with white as they looked from the downed sheriff to the Texans. Larkin crouched but stood ready to run.

"Damn it!" Miller grunted from the safety of the room. "I think they've killed Whitney."

More Texans gathered in front of the hotel. They grew louder and now brandished pistols in their hands. While the bartender and Larkin dragged the sheriff onto the shade of the boardwalk at Brennan's, someone led a ready mount into the Texas crowd. Ben and Peshaur hoisted the drunken Billy into the saddle and fitted the stirrups over his boots. Ben handed up the Henry, took the shotgun, and jabbed his finger at his brother as he barked commands. Billy emptied a pocketful of shotgun shells onto the dusty street and then took up the slack on the reins. With a slap on its rump, the horse bucked into a quick gallop, and two men had to run alongside to keep the rider upright.

James crushed out his cigar on the wood heater. "I've seen

enough of this town." He pulled Wyatt toward the backdoor, but both hesitated when someone rushed in through the front.

"Is the doctor in here?" It was Larkin, his skin as pale as chalk.

"The doc's over in Junction City," someone offered.

Mayor Miller stepped from the crowd and stood at the window. "How bad is it for Whitney?"

"I don't see how he can survive it. They're taking him down to his house."

Miller covered his eyes and squeezed his temples with a thumb and finger. After taking in a deep breath, he spewed out his frustration. He faced the front door, bared his teeth for a moment, and then marched outside. Larkin ran after him calling for him to wait, but Miller was already yelling into the plaza.

"I'm James H. Miller! I'm the mayor of this town!"

Standing beside Thompson, Peshaur laughed. "We don't care if you're Ulysses H. Grant. You'd best stay on your side of the street. You too, Larkin." The hotel manager bumped into Miller's back when the mayor stopped. "You ain't our friend, and we sure as hell ain't yours."

Both townsmen stood speechless until Miller turned toward Brennan's and yelled so hard that his voice cracked. "The police force is fired! Every last one of you! Norton, Sterling, Morco!" He turned back to the Texans and lifted his arms away from his sides as if he had just exhausted every possibility open to him.

"If they ain't policemen no more, you want us to kill 'em for you?" Peshaur offered.

"I don't care what you call 'em," Ben Thompson said evenly, "I'm shooting the first one o' those sonzabitches I see. They're the ones opened this ball."

Larkin stepped abreast of the mayor. "Mr. Thompson, I—"

"Git out o' my sight!" Ben interrupted. "You ain't our friend neither."

Larkin backed toward the boardwalk, pulling Miller with him. When they re-entered Beebe's store, both men were shaking.

"What about the deputy sheriff . . . Hogue?" Miller asked. "Where the hell is he?"

Beebe snorted. "Hell, Thompson hates him more'n the others."

"Somebody's gone to find him," one man said in a rush.

"We need someone who knows Thompson," Miller said. "Someone who can talk some sense to him."

Larkin's eyes took on a fierce glow as he raised his arm and pointed at Wyatt. "*He* knows him. Ben Thompson asked about him this morning." Every man looked at Wyatt.

"I played poker with him," Wyatt said. "Can't say I know 'im."

"Thompson was looking for him in the hotel to give him his shotgun." Larkin spat this out like a damning piece of evidence. "Thompson called him by name . . . Earp."

Wyatt said nothing.

"Young man," Miller said, "if you know him well enough to talk to him . . ."

"Anybody can talk to him. I don't know why he would listen any better to me."

"Why is he giving you his shotgun?"

"Won it off 'im in poker."

Miller levitated his arms from his sides and looked bewildered. "Well, hell. This would be a good time to collect on it. We've got a powder keg about to blow out there."

Wyatt stared at Miller for three heartbeats. "This ain't *my* powder keg. The way I see it, you used poor judgment in your selection of officers. That shotgun is not important to me."

Mayor Miller flung out his hands. "Forget the shotgun! Will you at least talk to him?" Miller stepped forward and ushered

Wyatt aside with a clammy grip on his elbow. As they moved, the mayor's words began pouring out in a whispery rush. "Tell him we've got to put a good face on this for everybody. Tell him if he'll just give up his gun, we'll wash the slate clean. We've got to get this under control. Judge Osborne will go along with me on this. For Ben, we can call it disturbing the peace. I'll pay the fine myself. It was his brother did the killing. No charges like that will be brought up against Ben."

Wyatt stared at the man for a time. When he spoke, everyone in the room heard him.

"And what about your sheriff? How do you square that?"

Not hearing the censure in Wyatt's words, Miller moved in close again, trying to establish some confidentiality. "We'll take that up with Billy, if and when he's brought up on charges."

In Lamar, Wyatt had known city councilmen like this, and he had never learned how to talk to them. Their words rattled down like dirty water rushing off a rusted roof, wearing a man down by the drone of their voices. Miller narrowed his eyes, and his breath caught.

"Wait . . . do you mean you might like to be sheriff?" The mayor's tongue flicked across his lips. "I can't promise you anything on the county level, but I *can* appoint you the post of city marshal." He searched Wyatt's eyes. "Is that what you mean?" He put a fingertip on Wyatt's chest and tapped lightly. "Soon as I find Norton, I'll get that badge and pin it there myself."

Wyatt took Miller's wrist and moved it aside. Wiping his palm against his trouser leg, Wyatt said, "This ain't my problem." He brushed past the mayor, heading for the back door, and James followed him.

The sound of the Earp brothers' boots on the plank floor dominated the large room of Beebe's store. When the Texans in the street let go with a chorus of rebel yells, Wyatt's hand paused on the doorknob, a sense of unease rising inside him. Stumbling at his heels, James stopped.

"Wyatt?"

For a time, Wyatt stared at the backdoor of the store just as he would a man who had insulted him. In that frozen moment, he realized, a boundary had materialized at the door's threshold, just as clearly as if someone had chalked a line in front of his boots. In his mind he went back to Lamar. That was where he had begun the backslide that had buried him in the slums of Peoria and dogged him to this Kansas town.

When Rilla died, he had allowed himself to believe he could bend the rules. He had taken money that wasn't his . . . and he had run. He had tried to believe the horse theft charge in the Cherokee Nations had been his penance, but it had changed nothing. It had simply been a bad hand dealt to him. He had run then, too, broken out of jail, and fled the territory.

At just twenty-five years old, he had been arrested four times. He had built nothing, not even a house of mud. When he closed his eyes, he saw Valenzuela Cos's dark eyes mock him for the failures he had accrued. He tried to bring up the visage of Rilla to supplant the insult of the Mexican girl's face, but the image would not come.

"Wyatt?" James said again.

Wyatt turned and looked past his brother, past the men crowded at the window. The light in the plaza streamed beyond the boardwalk awning like a bright blade—a clean cut, severing the past from present . . . and laying a fresh start on the future. On the hardpan of the plaza, a precise line of shadow marked his way. The intensity in Wyatt's eyes caused James's face to lose its indifference.

"Wyatt, what the hell are you 'bout to do?"

Wyatt looked at the men in the room, bound together by a common tension, no man rising above it to take control. Some shift of perspective, like light bending through water, set him to one side of this picture, and he saw himself standing before a path of his own choosing. He could bury every ill-taken step of his past, bury it like the corpse of his wife and son. He could do that now. What he would be . . . had meant to be . . . hinged upon his next step.

"Wyatt," James whispered, "let's get the hell out of here!"

"I ain't goin' out the backdoor," Wyatt said and stepped to the front. The crowd of men opened a space for him, just as Peshaur's booming voice filled the plaza.

"There ain't none o' you in this goddamn town got anythin' hangin' down 'tween your legs!"

The line in the street was there, well defined and waiting. Wyatt could see it through the windowglass—the sharp edge of shadow hard against the sun-baked road. Beyond that line lay a second chance. In the few seconds it took to make up his mind, he understood one certainty: that it was better to walk out into that plaza than to carry his sullied history with him out the back. Even if it meant dying. Rilla's face hovered clearly before him now, and he felt himself go cold and resolute. Impenetrable. It didn't matter if he died. Every man died sometime.

Beebe was watching him. "Better take this," he said, offering up the new model Colt's. Wyatt took the gun, checked the loads, and slipped the revolver into his waistband.

James stepped in front of him. "Wyatt?"

Wyatt's face was set like stone. "Someone's got to stop this foolishness," he murmured.

James looked out the door, shook his head, and exhaled heavily. "Well, goddamnit," he said and took off his coat. "Put this on and cover that gun, or you might not make it past the boardwalk." James pulled a short-barreled Remington from the scabbard now exposed under his ruined shoulder. "I'll be right here in the doorway. Just keep yourself out of my goddamn line of fire. We'll burn down the whole damned lot of 'em if we need to."

Wyatt donned the coat and pushed a button through its hole. Without another word he opened the front door and walked out. He strode across the planks of the boardwalk and stepped down into the street. When he crossed the line of the shadow into the light of the plaza, everything dark fell behind him.

A wave of heat radiated off the hardpan. Stepping into it was like walking through flames. Wyatt moved toward the Texans slowly, deliberately, knowing at his core that he was made for a moment like this: to walk through fire . . . to set straight something gone askew.

Though he didn't fear Thompson, he was wary of him. It was the showboater, Peshaur, who could be the more pressing problem. Utterly unpredictable, the big Texan carried the bluster of a reputation—something he would have to protect. Wyatt focused on both men as he crossed the open ground, letting his peripheral vision include the others.

"What do *you* want?" Thompson yelled.

"I'm delivering a message," Wyatt answered flatly. Halfway to the rail tracks he added, "To you."

"Well, deliver it from there!" Peshaur called out. It was only then that the muscular Texan seemed to recognize Wyatt, and a broad smile sliced across his face. "I'll be damned." He laughed, but then just as quickly he frowned, and his eyes tightened. "Stop right there, California boy!"

Wyatt maintained his steady pace. "My message is for Ben Thompson . . . nobody else."

Thompson pointed the shotgun loosely at the ground in Wyatt's path. "You heeled, son?"

In midstride Wyatt opened his coat and let the material fall back to expose the new Colt's jammed into the waistband of his trousers.

Thompson's eyes sharpened. "You need a gun to deliver a message?"

Wyatt kept walking. "Not to you, I reckon. These others I ain't so sure about." Wyatt let his arms swing their natural rhythm, showing no indication that he intended to use the gun. "I'll deliver the message, Mr. Thompson. What you do then is your decision."

"Why're you doing this, son? Are you standin' with these Kansas bastards?"

"A man's dying right now. Might be more to die unless you see this out legal."

"How do you mean?"

Ten feet from Thompson, Wyatt stopped and spread his boots, his arms hanging relaxed at his sides. He angled his eyes toward Peshaur, and the quiet in the plaza became absolute. Peshaur began to sidestep in a careful rocking motion away from Thompson, his boots barely scuffing the dust in the dry street.

In a quiet voice, meant only for Thompson's ears, Wyatt spelled out the mayor's offer. He displayed no emotion, no inflection of distaste, no air of authority. He said the message in his own words, not the mayor's, but the gist was the same. By the time he had finished talking, his plan was clear as to the order of the men he would shoot, if shooting commenced.

"The mayor is trying to give you a way out of all this," Wyatt said. "So make up your mind right now which way it's gonna go."

"They're tryin' to candy-coat it, Ben!" Peshaur crowed. "So it reads right in the papers. They're scared."

Thompson chewed on that for a time. "That about right?" he said to Wyatt.

Wyatt said nothing. He noted the position of the revolver in Peshaur's hand—the barrel pointing at the ground, hammer not cocked, the thumb wrapped around the butt of the pistol. Wyatt felt the borrowed Colt's press against his belly, the gun butt positioned just so.

"What if I agree?" Thompson said. "How do we go about it?"

"*Agree!*" Peshaur jerked his head around to the Texas leader. "Hell, Ben, what're—"

"Shut up, Peshaur! I'm the one's got his brother's head stickin' in a noose. I might can work somethin' out." He looked at Wyatt. "You think that's about right, son?"

Wyatt hitched his head back toward Beebe's store. "That mayor back there might deny knowing his mother if he thought you'd agree to this."

Thompson's hands remained relaxed on the shotgun. "So, what do we do here?"

"You surrender up your guns. Make it official. I reckon you've got enough friends here with guns to make you feel comfortable about doin' that."

Thompson shifted his weight left, then right. "I don't like giving up my guns." He nodded toward Brennan's. "Those damned yellow law dogs are prob'ly waitin' to get off a shot at me."

Wyatt looked squarely at Peshaur. "Go over to Brennan's," he said. "Take a look. I think you'll find they've hightailed it out the back a half hour ago."

Something changed in Peshaur's eyes, a nervous shimmer of light that could not find its way out. The Texan frowned and looked across the street to the saloon. The challenge had been tacit but clear: Wyatt had crossed over on his own; now it was Peshaur's turn.

The muscular man attempted a bray of a laugh. "How'd I know it ain't a set-up?" When Wyatt did not answer, Peshaur scowled at Brennan's. "That damned Morco is a back-shooter."

"I'll walk in with you," Wyatt said, "if that's what you need."

"Hell," Peshaur scoffed, "*you* might be a back-shooter, too."

For five seconds Wyatt looked at the Texan with dead eyes, and then he turned back to Ben Thompson. "Guess he ain't going."

Ben Thompson narrowed his eyes at Wyatt. "But why'd you get involved? I don't see how you've got any stake in this."

"Wasn't no one else to do it," Wyatt said.

Thompson cocked his head to one side, the question on his face creasing the skin around the corners of his eyes like the spokes of a broken wheel. "I give the word . . . and you'll be lyin' here in the street like the sheriff."

Wyatt stared at Thompson, letting his eyes go to ice. "Won't be just me."

No one moved or spoke. The sunlight bore down mercilessly all around them, as though burning a tintype of every detail of the plaza, each man standing inside the fragile scene as if it could be his last chance at life.

"He's bluffin'," Peshaur growled, but his voice sounded empty.

"No," Thompson said, a calm now smoothing the lines of his face as he studied Wyatt. "He ain't." The Texas leader looked toward Brennan's and began shaking his head. The shotgun sagged in his arms. "Hell, I know there ain't none o' those bastards over there no more. Those boys are halfway to Salina. They're yellow. And now they ain't got no badge to take up the difference."

"That's the way I figure it," Wyatt said.

"So who do I give my guns to? You?"

"I'm not an officer. Just the one delivering the message. I can call the mayor out here."

Thompson thought about it. "Yeah, get his sorry ass out here, 'n case the ball opens."

Wyatt half twisted at the waist and called over his shoulder. When Miller came out, a short man in a straight-brimmed, gray hat walked beside him. This man wore a sheriff's deputy badge and a holstered gun strapped to his waist. His arms hovered well clear of his body to show he had no intention of using his weapon. His face was ashen, and his bulging eyes shone like wet creek stones.

"This is Deputy Hogue, Ben," Miller announced. "All right? So let's all just go down to Judge Osborne's and get this thing settled. How does that sound to you?"

"I know who the hell the little runt is. You stay over there where you are, Hogue."

Hogue stopped and eased a hand forward, palm up. "If I could just have your guns, Ben."

Thompson, seeming suddenly irritated, threw the shotgun toward him into the street. Hogue jumped at the clatter, and Peshaur laughed. Ben unbuckled his pistol belt and spoke to Miller. "This one you can have for a while." He dropped the holstered pistol in the dirt. "But the shotgun . . . that belongs to him." He canted his head toward Wyatt.

With head bowed, Hogue shuffled in front of Miller, bent, and retrieved both guns. "I'll have to carry these down to the courtroom," he explained to no one in particular.

It was a charade of police work. The mayor and the deputy followed Thompson while the rest of the Texans—still armed—trailed behind . . . all but Peshaur, who holstered his gun and stood glaring at Wyatt, his ugly gray scar shining under his eye like a mark of insolence.

"So, now the California boy is runnin' errands in Kansas," Peshaur drawled, his words impudent and taunting. He sneered and turned to join the parade headed for the courtroom.

"Need me to walk with you?" Wyatt said in the flat tone of insult.

Peshaur hesitated and lowered his eyes to the Colt's tucked into Wyatt's waistband.

"It's just you and me now, Texas," Wyatt said.

Peshaur's lips parted, but he only forced a smile as he hooked both thumbs into his cartridge belt.

"Nobody here to watch you strut now 'cept me," Wyatt said, "and I ain't impressed."

Now James appeared, stepping beside Wyatt, his hand on the revolver holstered under his arm. Peshaur managed an amused snort, turned, and ambled down the street where his friends had gone. He didn't look back, but Wyatt could feel the thread of animosity stretch taut between them.

"Little brother, you damn sure know how to poke your nose in a hornets' nest."

Wyatt turned to see Beebe and the others approaching excitedly from the boardwalk. They were like children let out from school.

"This town's wearing thin on me," Wyatt said quietly.

When the group circled around the Earp brothers, Wyatt held out the Colt's to Beebe, who took the gun, smiled broadly, and pumped his hand up and down as if he were trying to draw water from a dry well.

"Son, the goddamn governor could'n'a handled that better'n you," Beebe said.

James laughed. "Ain't politics a goddamn wonder?" He pulled a fresh cigar from the pocket of the coat that Wyatt still wore, and then he pointed it toward Brennan's. "Guess I'll go see if my new dove's acquired any bullet holes." He hesitated as he watched the party of townspeople move off down the street toward the courthouse and their contrived version of justice. "What about you, Wyatt? You goin' down to watch the sham?"

Wyatt shook his head. "Think I'll go wash this town off my skin."

CHAPTER 25

August, 1873: Last night in Ellsworth, Kansas

At the boardinghouse Wyatt washed his face and torso from a small porcelain basin of fresh water. The bar of lye soap was scented with sage, reminding him of the prairie just after a rain. He had heard that Indians used sage to cleanse not only the skin but the soul, and he wondered if he were doing something like that now in the privacy of his room.

As he dried his hands with a towel, the image of Sheriff Whitney would not leave his mind. The sheriff had lain sprawled out in the street, his white shirt glistening bright red in the hard light of the plaza. The shotgun blast had come without warning, changing everything in an instant. Every plan and ambition the sheriff might have laid claim to had drained out of him into the street. Wyatt's thoughts began to run to Rilla and crimson sheets when a knock rattled his door.

"Mr. Earp? It's Larkin, manager over at the Grand Central."

Still holding the towel, Wyatt opened the door to find the hotel man smiling and rubbing his palms together in the hallway.

"Well, it's all settled. They've fined him. And the city police are all out."

"What did the judge say?" Wyatt asked.

"Oh, that," Larkin said, pushing a hand at the air. "Twenty-five dollars, just like the mayor said . . . disturbing the peace." He flashed a sneer as if someone had cracked a lame joke.

Wyatt turned and carried the towel to the washstand. Larkin

followed him into the room and partially closed the door as he watched Wyatt button up a shirt.

" 'Disturbing the peace,' " Wyatt muttered. He stopped buttoning, pivoted his head to the window, and stared for a time at the fading light beyond the windowglass. When he turned back to Larkin, the hotelier seemed to be appraising the room.

"Mr. Earp, I hope you'll consider letting me put you up at the hotel. I would say that our amenities are several cuts above what you have here. I can give you a good rate for an extended stay. Now that you'll be—"

"What about the sheriff?" Wyatt said.

Larkin appeared surprised at the change in the conversation's direction, but he quickly adjusted, frowning to show his concern. "He's at home. Very weak. Not much hope for him, I expect." Pressing his lips into a thin line, he shook his head. "It's a shame. He was a good family man . . . an Indian fighter, you know . . . fought at Beecher's Island." Larkin tried for a remorseful smile but dropped it when Wyatt said nothing. "Mr. Earp, we'd like you to join us in the hotel dining room for supper. It'll be the mayor and a few of the council. We've invited your brother, too. The mayor would like to make the appointment official tonight. And the newspaper editor wants to interview you. They're all convening at the hotel at seven."

Larkin was just a messenger, he knew, but Wyatt made no effort to keep the coldness out of his voice. "Where's my brother now?"

Larkin frowned at Wyatt's gear laid out on the bed. The blanket and slicker were tightly rolled and lashed, the saddlebags stuffed full and cinched tight.

"I can have my boy come over to transfer your belongings, if you like."

Wyatt shook his head. "My brother?"

"Oh," Larkin said, "he's already at the hotel dining room,

having drinks with the mayor. I've opened up our bar gratis for the occasion . . . for your party, I mean."

Wyatt lifted the dark frock coat he had draped over a chair back. "When you head back there, would you give this to my brother?"

Again the hotel man surveyed the gear packed on the bed. His eyes narrowed with a question that he seemed incapable of asking.

"Of course, I'll give it to him," he managed and cleared his phlegmy throat.

Wyatt gathered his travel gear off the bed. Larkin started to speak, but when Wyatt hoisted his bags to his shoulders and started his way, the hotelier stepped aside to let Wyatt pass.

"Mr. Earp, you are coming to dinner, aren't you?"

Wyatt stopped in the hallway and turned. Judging by the man's expression, Wyatt figured the hotel manager spent most of his life in a bewildered state.

"No."

"But . . . what about your appointment?"

"Don't figure on working where a man's life is valued at twenty-five dollars."

Larkin swallowed and then took a step forward quickly. "But . . . what should I tell the mayor?"

"Same thing I just told you."

With James's coat draped over one arm, Larkin raised the other arm away from his side and let it fall to slap against his body. "But they all think you are going to accept the city marshal position."

"Easy to think something," Wyatt said.

As Larkin frowned and licked his lips, Wyatt waited, but he was tiring of the man. Larkin looked down at the coat as if it might have some bearing on the conversation.

"Well . . ."

"There'll always be men willing to take a job on your police force," Wyatt said. "The trick will be knowing which kind you want." When the puzzled expression returned to Larkin's face, Wyatt turned and descended the stairs.

Outside the night showed little promise of cooling. The street was dark along the business district, except across the plaza, where the lights from Brennan's spilled out onto the rutted dirt thoroughfare, pushing a yellow halo halfway to the rail tracks. Wyatt stopped and listened for a time. Judging by the quiet, he deemed the saloon to be empty.

He walked west to the livery, roused the stable hand, and retrieved his Sharps rifle and gear from the tack room. He paid the boy with two of the coins he had won off of Ben Thompson, and with one more he purchased a sack of grain to compensate for the dearth of good grass along the trail.

He had loaded the packhorse, saddled the chestnut, and just tamped the Sharps into its leather boot when James appeared in the livery entrance, the lantern light illuminating him like an actor making his appearance on a stage. Despite the heat, James wore the frock coat. When he walked toward Wyatt, there was something in the movement that showed James's shoulder wound trespassed into every corner of his life.

"Sort o' figured you weren't gonna sit down to a social event with that oily-tongued mayor and his crowd." James laughed. "But damned if I'll pass up their liquor." He put a hand on the chestnut's rump and swung around the animal to face Wyatt. "Now where're you off to?"

Wyatt nodded toward the open entrance of the barn. "Away from here," he said. When he took up the reins and lead rope and walked the two horses into the street, James fingered a cigar from his breast pocket and followed.

The night had darkened enough to release a horde of stars. They spread across the sky like a flurry of sparks captured in a tintype. There was no moon yet, but Wyatt knew its rising time. It was why he had allowed for leaving town this late.

James scraped a matchstick across a horseshoe nailed to the front wall of the livery. His face bloomed with the flare of light as he sucked at the flame through his cigar. His skin appeared pasty and bloated. Wyatt tried to recall his brother's farm-hardened appearance before he went off to the war, but the image was irretrievable. James offered a cigar, but Wyatt shook his head.

"I guess you know they're waitin' for you over at the hotel," James said around the cigar. "They want to swear you in as the new town marshal."

Wyatt circled the packhorse, checking the tie-downs. "Yeah, I know."

They both looked up at the stars for a time. The quiet of the town seemed unnatural, as if a curfew had been imposed on the citizens.

"What about the sheriff?" Wyatt said.

James curled his mouth into a sneer. "They've sent for the doctor over in Junction City, but a man can't survive a wound like that." He shook his head. "Saw it too many times in the war." He shook his head again and allowed a cynical smile. "Did you hear how much Thompson paid the judge to settle for his brother shootin' the sheriff?"

Wyatt nodded. "I heard."

They stood again without words, and the two horses matched their stillness. The only movement in the heat of the night was the smoke rising from James's cigar.

"So, where *are* you headed?" James finally said.

"Fort Larned. See if I can make some money off the cards there."

"Soldiers?" James laughed. "That how you plan to get rich? Fleecin' soldiers? They hardly make enough wages to spit on."

"Maybe so, but there's a lot of 'em that come into town. What else have they got to spend their money on?"

James laughed sharply and bent at the waist, making a small, theatrical bow. "Now we're talkin' my line o' work."

Wyatt gripped the pommel and tested the play of his saddle. "Under the right circumstances, a fellow can make a lot of money in one night on the green cloth. Once I make a stake, I'll see can I work my way into this cattle market."

James gave Wyatt a doubtful glance. "Thing is . . . with this drought . . . and it being late in the season . . . how're you gonna find your way into owning some livestock? Assuming, that is, you get a hold o' that kind of money."

Wyatt nodded south toward the bridge. "I can ride to Texas if I need to."

"Wyatt, why don't you think about coming to Wichita? Work with me for a while. You could travel with me and my new prairie flower when we pull out." James lifted his eyebrows and bared his teeth around the cigar. "What do you say?"

Wyatt leaned an arm into the bow of the saddle and gave the question some thought. "I'd like to do something with more promise to it. Something that can last me a lifetime."

James's eyes crinkled just like Morgan's. "Hell, if there's anything for certain about the future, it's that men are always gonna want to poke their prods into a beguiling woman." He shrugged. " 'Course . . . if you want the truth," he said wistfully, "it's clear enough what you're cut out for."

Wyatt studied the profile of his brother's face. "What might that be?"

James smiled toward the plaza. "Why d'you reckon things are so quiet here tonight?" He turned his head to show off his devilish smile. "Hell, even those Texas boys ain't showed their faces." James tapped Wyatt's shoulder with the back of his fist. "You handled things out there today, son. Don't get me wrong, I

thought you were crazy as a cross-eyed preacher at a shootin'
match, but by God, nobody doubted you meant business."

"Somebody had to do something," Wyatt said.

James's eyes angled to Wyatt. "You mean, *you* had to do
something."

Wyatt stood quietly, exhuming the picture of Sheriff
Whitney's bloodied shirt. "You can't let men like that run it
over on a town. That's why we got laws."

James stared, half amused. "Yeah, but you didn't have to go
at it like you were planning your suicide. What was it . . . eight
to one? What if they'd opened up on you?"

In his mind Wyatt returned to that moment on the street
when he had determined which Texans he would shoot. "There
were at least two of 'em would'a died with me . . . that big 'un,
Peshaur . . . and Thompson."

James narrowed his eyes. "So you'd'a died for *them*?"

Wyatt shook his head. "Not for them. For what they done."

James frowned. "Ain't that the same thing?"

Wyatt shook his head. "No, it ain't."

One of the horses in the livery nickered, and Wyatt's mount
began to snort and shift its weight. He led the packhorse behind
the chestnut, and then he swung up into the saddle. James
backed away, chewed on the cigar, and thrust both hands into
his trouser pockets.

"When you get tired of countin' your pennies at Larned,
come over to Wichita, Wyatt. Maybe you were cut out to wear a
badge, but workin' as an enforcer at a brothel you'll make a
helluva lot more money. It's the same kind o' work, when you
think about it."

Wyatt chose not to argue the point. "What about you?"

"Oh, my new dove and I will pull out tomorrow for Wichita."
James's smile widened. "Tonight I'll see how much free whiskey
I can drink."

Wyatt gathered the reins and took a grip on the lead rope of the packhorse. "Take care of yourself, James," he said and prodded the horses forward to clatter across the railroad ties.

"Wyatt!" James called.

Wyatt reined up and watched his brother move in his peculiar gait out into the street. James stepped close and looked up at Wyatt with an unexpected luminescence on his face, as though he were about to recite a poem.

"I reckon there ain't nobody said it . . . so I guess I will." James lowered his eyes and shrugged. "Regardless to how goddamn crazy it was . . . that was a helluva thing you done out there today. There'd'a probably been more killin' if you hadn't done what you did."

Wyatt waited. He could see there was more his brother would say.

"But you need to understand something," James continued. "Back in Beebe's store . . . all those men huddled in there, hidin' like children . . . they might have something you think you want, but not one of 'em could'a done what you done." He shook his head, as if agreeing with his own assessment. "Every man has got some gift, Wyatt . . . or at least he's got some inclination. The trick is to figure out what it is. Then you act on it." James edged closer, looked up at his brother, and softened his voice. "You don't want to hear this, but you got something of Pa in you, son. You know how to handle people. But instead of doin' it by makin' 'em hate you, you got another way." He jerked a thumb toward Brennan's. "Hell, I even heard Ben Thompson say he respected you."

Wyatt sat his horse without moving, his back straight, his chin up, as though he were listening for the murmur of the river. "You're tellin' me it's wrong for a man to want more'n what he's got?"

James stepped back, sucked on the cigar, and shook his head

again as he exhaled a stream of smoke. "Hell, we all want more. We just got to know what it is we oughta be askin' for." He managed the smile of an older brother. "Listen, Wyatt, if it's really cattle you want . . . the Texans have had enough of Ellsworth. Everybody's sayin' Wichita will be the main shipping center next season. Think about getting into the business there. That way, if it don't work out, you got something to fall back on." James nodded his encouragement. "Enforcin' at a brothel ain't so bad."

Wyatt nodded once. "I'll keep it in mind."

James raised his good arm, and the two Earps shook hands. After crossing the bridge, Wyatt could still feel the strength of his brother's grip. It was good to have family out here on the frontier. Like money in the bank. If he could get a toehold in the cattle business, maybe James would partner with him. Then the two of them could draw in Virgil . . . and maybe Morg. The Earps could build a dynasty as legitimate businessmen.

A mile into the journey, he felt the solitude of the dark trail envelop him like a ragged set of clothes. All the words he had spoken to James . . . they were just that—words. They might as well be pebbles rattling around inside a tin can.

When the rusty-hewed slice of moon rose in the east, its pale light served to remind him that by traveling toward Fort Larned, he was little more than a seed blowing in the wind. But he kept on. It was some kind of plan. And it might lead to something.

Now and again he heard a coyote howling to the night, and as it always did, the sound conjured the memory of a San Bernardino peach orchard and the young Mexican girl who had spoken to him of omens and prophecies. A moon made of mud. She had tried to teach him that life was about settling for less than one's ambitions. He had argued then. If Valenzuela Cos were here now, he wondered what argument he might mount against her claims. He had little to show for the years that had passed—a string of fights in railroad camps, a dead wife and child, an arrest record that had included a federal warrant, and the extended company of whores in his longest stints of employment.

There was still time, he knew. As long as he was hungry enough to want for more, sooner or later a winning hand would be dealt him, and, when that happened, he was determined to play his cards smart. It was all about timing. And acting upon decisions. Going about it direct. The same way he had stepped across that line into the street with Ben Thompson. He'd simply made up his mind, and then he'd done it. It shouldn't be much more complicated than that to make a fortune.

BIBLIOGRAPHY

Wyatt Earp, The Life Behind the Legend by Casey Tefertiller: John Wiley & Sons, Inc., 1997

Doc Holliday, The Life and the Legend by Gary Roberts: John Wiley & Sons, Inc., 2006

Wyatt Earp, A Biography of the Legend by Lee Silva: Graphic Publishers, 2002

Wyatt Earp, The Biography by Timothy Fattig: Talei Publishers, Inc., 2002

Wyatt Earp, Frontier Marshal, Stuart Lake: Houghton Mifflin Co., 1931

Wyatt Earp, The Untold Story, 1848–1880 by Ed Bartholomew: Frontier Book Co., 1963

Dodge City by Frederic Young: Boot Hill Museum, Inc., 1972

The Illustrated Life and Times of Wyatt Earp by Bob Boze Bell: Boze Books, 1993

The Buffalo Hunters by Charles Robinson III: State House Press, 1995

The Clantons of Tombstone by Ben Traywick: Red Marie's Bookstore, 1996

Inventing Wyatt Earp, His Life and Many Legends by Allen Barra: Carroll & Graf Publishers, Inc., 1998

Bat Masterson, The Man and the Legend by Robert DeArment: University of Oklahoma Press, 1979

Wyatt Earp, A Biography of a Western Lawman by Steve Gatto: San Simon Publishing Co., 1997

Bibliography

Wyatt Earp Speaks by John Stevens: Fern Canyon Press, 1998

Wyatt Earp's Lost Year by Roger Jay; *Wild West* magazine, June, 2006

The Earp Papers, In a Brother's Image by Don Chaput: Affiliated Writers of America, Inc., 1994

The Truth About Wyatt Earp by Richard Erwin: The O.K. Press, 1993

The Earps Talk by Al Turner: Creative Publishing Co., 1980

Virgil Earp, Western Peace Officer by Don Chaput: Affiliated Writers of America, Inc., 1994

ACKNOWLEDGMENTS

With gratitude

*To friends and fellow researchers who have dug so diligently
for the truth:*

Peter Brand, (the late) Jack Burrows, (the late) Carl Chafin, Anne Collier, (the late) Paul Cool, (the late) Mark Dworkin, Bill Evans, Tim Fattig, Tom Gaumer, Paul Andrew Hutton, (the late) Roger Jay, Billy "B.J." Johnson, Paul Johnson, Bob McCubbin, (the late) Carol Mitchell, Jeff Morey, Bob Palmquist, Pam Potter, Cindy Reidhead, Gary Roberts, (the late) Lee Silva, Jean and Chuck Smith, Casey Tefertiller, Ben Traywick, Vickie Wilcox, and Roy Young.

Thanks to Angela Halifax for that rusty-hued moon.

ABOUT THE AUTHOR

Mark Warren is a teacher of Native American survival skills in the Appalachian Mountains of north Georgia, where he lives with his wife Susan. His study of Wyatt Earp's life spans sixty years. Through his travels he has interviewed the storied writers of the Earp saga and trekked with them to sites where the actual events in Earp's life took place.

Adobe Moon is the opening volume of his Earp trilogy, *Wyatt Earp: An American Odyssey*. His book *Two Winters in a Tipi* (Lyons Press, 2012) chronicles the years he spent living in the primitive abode of the Plains Indians. *Secrets of the Forest* (Waldenhouse Publishers, Inc., 2016) is a comprehensive guide to primitive survival skills and plant lore.

The employees of Five Star Publishing hope you have enjoyed this book.

Our Five Star novels explore little-known chapters from America's history, stories told from unique perspectives that will entertain a broad range of readers.

Other Five Star books are available at your local library, bookstore, all major book distributors, and directly from Five Star/Gale.

Connect with Five Star Publishing

Visit us on Facebook:
    https://www.facebook.com/FiveStarCengage

Email:
    FiveStar@cengage.com

For information about titles and placing orders:
    (800) 223-1244
    gale.orders@cengage.com

To share your comments, write to us:
    Five Star Publishing
    Attn: Publisher
    10 Water St., Suite 310
    Waterville, ME 04901